BLOODY MARKO

J. Madison Davis

Walker and Company
New York

The writing of this novel was partially supported by a grant from the Pennsylvania Council of the Arts.

First published in the United States of America in 1991 by Walker Publishing Company, Inc.

Published simultaneously in Canada by Thomas Allen & Son Canada, Limited, Markham, Ontario.

Library of Congress Cataloging-in-Publication Data
Davis, J. Madison.
Bloody Marko / J. Madison Davis.
p.   cm.
ISBN 0-8027-1149-9
I. Title.
PS3554.A934636B46   1991
813'.54—dc20   90-22155
CIP

Printed in the United States of America

2   4   6   8   10   9   7   5   3   1

for Simonne
my best friend for many years

Author's Note

Transliterating from Serbo-Croatian can be difficult. Not only does Yugoslavia use several alphabets (Cyrillic and Latin), but certain sounds do not have orthographic equivalents in English. Where there is a common English equivalent for a word I have used it: Belgrade for Beograd, Serbia for Srbija, Danube for Dunav, Georgevich for Djordjević. The sounds represented by č, ć, ž, and š have been replaced by ch, ch, zh, and sh respectively. Thus Nedić becomes Nedich, for example.

Do not fear, Kraljevich Marko; being a brave adventurous warrior you had a dream befitting your nature. Dreams are just idle lies, and God is the only truth on this earth.

from a medieval Serbian ballad
(trans. Nada Ćurčija-Prodanović)

There is no sight more touching than a boy who intends to conquer the world, though there is that within himself which means he is more likely to be its slave.

Rebecca West, *The New Meaning of Treason*

Esma Smilovich, Magistrate

◆

(Belgrade, February 13–19, 1990)

She rises celestially, thought Zeljko.

Silently, steadily rising off the blue sheets even bluer in the moment when the sun hangs between night and day, Esma opened the slatted shutters and stood naked in the dawn. Zeljko kept his arm across his face, watching her under the angle in his elbow, but she neither glanced at him nor gave any other indication she cared whether he was awake or not. She rested one hand against the glass, staring into the mists oozing over the trees and between the buildings surrounding the Tashmajdan park. Zeljko held his breath as if he might learn some holy secret about her and through it finally possess her in the way he ached to: completely.

Could she be praying? That would be amusing. The Party, such as it was anymore, would not like that very much. If she were praying, her lips were still. She owned a prayer rug, a beautiful piece of thirteenth-century Levant handiwork passed through her family, but it hung under glass in her living room in Nish. Then, too, she should be prostrate if praying, and, as sublime as that would be with her spine arching from the sharp bones in her shoulder to her smooth hips, Zeljko did not think Allah approved of nakedness, especially from women, especially at dawn prayer. The Moslems had never understood what was truly divine.

Perhaps Esma interpreted the Koran in her own way. In court, she could contort the law to say whatever she wished it to. He had seen her so befuddle judges and opposing attorneys that they sputtered helplessly, red-faced, their mouths gaping, their hands seining the air in a vain attempt to catch the words that could make their crumbling cases seem reasonable. She was slippery as an old Turkish merchant, and everyone prepared for that, but it never did them any good. She was also a tigress. She smelled weakness and she went after it relentlessly. She seemed to know what they were thinking before they thought it. They could hear her claws coming closer, closer, and most simply threw themselves to the ground.

She was sly, yes, and cruel, in a sense, but most of the other stereotypes about Moslems which Zeljko had been taught growing up Catholic in Zagreb did not apply to her. She showed no inclination to live up to Islam's notion of womanhood. Religion was a liability to her ambition, and she was too intelligent, too controlled to let it interfere. Perhaps, despite her rational exterior, she had inherited a residue of the Oriental spiritual impulse and conceded the dawn to it. He closed his eyes in languid amusement. You could sleep with her, love her, beg her to marry you, but you were a fool to think you could know her. There was always a secret core. It was why she was such an incredible lover. It was why as a prosecutor she was so deadly.

When he opened his eyes again, she was lighting a cigarette, a Gauloise from the pack given her by the reporter from *Paris Match*. She puffed at it quickly, then took one long draw. The hand holding it covered her face momentarily as she rubbed the corner of her eye with her thumb, then dropped to rest on the sharp jut of her hip. She continued to stare as the sky shifted to pink and gray. The hues made her skin even more delicious—silvery moist, like damp pavement. "Come back to bed," he said abruptly.

She glanced at him, as if she had forgotten he was there, but also as if it did not much matter. She calmly drew again on her cigarette and shook her head.

"You are beautiful, darling. Come back to bed." It sounded false. He was awkward at compliments, a weakness in an attorney. "Come back to bed," he quickly repeated.

"No." She unlatched the French doors and flicked the

cigarette straight out over the balcony rail. A breeze rippled the curtain. She shivered but did not close the door.

"Come back to bed."

"Not this morning."

"I will put you in the mood."

"Not this morning."

"It will refresh you."

She ignored him.

"Then come back anyway. Rest. It is early. Suppose someone sees you? Suppose there is some German down there with a camera?" The dining room had been nearly filled with Germans last evening. Most Yugoslavs could never afford this hotel, but Esma had insisted and the government had decided it would look better for the foreign press to see their star prosecutor living well.

"Everyone is sleeping."

"Still, something like that in the British papers and poof! to your big chance."

"Marko Renovich is just another defendant. There is no reason to think it is my 'big chance.' Things are happening. If the Russians cannot hold their republics together, why should this trial help maintain Yugoslavian unity? Tito is dead and the memory of the common enemy has faded. Shooting Renovich will not change the fact that the Slovenians are angry with the Serbs and the Serbs with the Albanians and so on and so on. Endless squabbling—it is in the soil." She drifted back from the window and stretched out on the chaise longue in the corner. She put her hands behind her head, raising her breasts, and crossed her thin legs.

"Once we begin you will not care whether there are political motives to this trial or not. You are like a cheetah pretending indifference to the antelope, but Zeljko knows." He snapped his fingers. "You'll have your jaws in his throat before he knows it. You are lean, you are hungry, and you smell blood."

She stretched her legs.

"Zeljko knows," he continued. "Zeljko keeps his ears open. Once you get 'Bloody Marko' shot, maybe you are off to Belgrade. You are headed for the Central Committee. Maybe for a presidency some day. You are perfect for it. You know it."

She studied her toes. "I am not thinking about that. Communism is dissolving like an aspirin and perhaps the Central Committee with it. In any case, I am too young. They just want someone who looks good for the international press."

"It does not matter. They also want to show they are warm to their Moslems. Tell me I am wrong. The next time someone accuses the government of mistreating the Moslems, they will say, 'Look at Esma Smilovich. Is she mistreated? Look how we brought her to Belgrade to prosecute a Serb.'"

"So you've said. But when they ask the old men in my family what they think of a woman in that position, they'll say, 'What kind of Moslem woman goes into the law? Look how the Serbs corrupt our faith.' The past never dies, Zeljko. It just wears different clothes."

"Beside your nationality, beside your brain, darling, your sex is your greatest asset. It gives them even more reason to want you. A beautiful woman, a Moslem. It is certain: as soon as Bloody Marko is dead, your career will skyrocket. They will give you a medal first. That is the rumor. Then, after that—zoom!"

She lowered her hand and absentmindedly scratched the inside of her thigh, just below her shaven pubis. "Why not take a pistol today and put a bullet in his head? That will save the state the cost of this charade and I will still be a hero."

He had been staring at her long fingers so near the soft folds of her crotch—the Moslem women's custom of shaving the genitals had always aroused him (the cleanliness?)—but the tone in her voice startled him. He had never seen her anything but tense about a case—tight, crouched, ready to spring. He was moved. She seemed to be revealing something of herself to him, something no one else might ever know. All her self-assurance covered doubt. Was that it? Did it mean she trusted him? He climbed out of bed and knelt beside her, resting his hand on her hip and turning her chin toward him. "You cannot convince me you do not relish such an internationally famous trial. I know you."

She twisted her head toward the window and her eyes almost shouted her thoughts: *You* do not *know me. Do not presume to think it.*

Her condescension rattled him and the next question was

much less self-assured, though Zeljko intoned it like a father talking to a child. "You cannot dislike the case."

"It is a foregone conclusion. He is eighty-two."

He laughed. "You've lost your taste for a gift. When is it not a foregone conclusion?"

She turned away.

"You really resent all the attention over something so easy? Bloody Marko Renovich is finished and you take offense at it?"

"The case bores me," she finally said.

"Come, come, do you doubt he deserves death? Can you doubt he deserves worse than death? Are you afraid something will go wrong with most of the world looking on? You infuriate me."

"It was more than forty years ago, Zeljko. He refuses to speak for himself, even when some Americans said he should not be extradited to us."

"He was a traitor! Your father was a partisan. Didn't you say Bloody Marko had hunted your father? How can you even hesitate? Shall I tell you how my grandfather died? My grandmother?"

"I am not hesitating. Bloody Marko deserves it. But are we certain this Mark Renault is Bloody Marko? Why all this publicity? There is nothing of real interest here. He will continue to deny he is Bloody Marko, or failing that, he may say he had no choice, the defense you see over and over in war crimes cases. The plea has never helped anyone and it will do him no good either. And what purpose is served by shooting a man who might have only weeks to live anyway? It will provoke sympathy he does not deserve."

"Some eighty-year-olds live to be a hundred. Are you not giving him more sympathy than he deserves? You have never fretted about who was pathetic in the past. All criminals are pathetic. You just cannot accept good things coming to you without your taking them, without your ripping out the heart. You cannot fool me. Zeljko knows you, darling. With all that audience, you want a chance to show your skill. You want a stage on which to astound the world. Do you remember Heillermann, the thief? I fell in love watching you. He was hard as

[5]

granite and you had him blubbering in twenty minutes. It was—how can I say?—astounding. I wanted to applaud."

"But after the interrogatories I could see through Heillermann. I could take him apart because I understood him. I knew why he was as he was. He was revenging himself on his stepfather with every robbery. Once that was grasped it was easy to make him confess, make him see himself. I want not just the conviction of a criminal, I want each one to know the enormity of his crime. Anything less is like losing."

Zeljko suddenly understood he had been told something that Esma herself might not have recognized before. It had never occurred to him that there might be a goal beyond the conviction. Why? That he did not understand. He stared at her with a kind of angry despair. Somehow it was why she was the chief prosecutor and he the assistant, but he did not understand it. If he did not understand it, he could never be her equal. "So, do you think you are some kind of psychiatrist? You are not in court to understand them."

"Criminals are the result of economic inequality. Have you forgotten your schooling? When we understand we may be able to eliminate crime in the socialist state."

He knew this old Party dogma was justification and nothing more. This may have been her rational reason for breaking a criminal but it was not the emotional cause. "So what makes you think you will not tear out Bloody Marko's heart for study? You've never even seen him."

She had no answer and she tossed her head sharply, angry she had no counter. "I feel uneasy about the case. I have read through the files. The facts are there, but where is the man? They do not need me to recite facts. We have documents, a photograph, many records. Fragments of a life, but I get no sense of the whole. Who is he? Our witnesses are like the blind men caressing the elephant. One feels the trunk and concludes the elephant is a serpent; another feels the leg and concludes it is a tree. All they know is what they want to know. After forty years many witnesses would identify anyone, just so they could go to their graves thinking they had gotten vengeance. If this man *is* Bloody Marko—"

"You know he is."

"Assuming he is—how am I to understand him? How am

I to know how I will go at him? This is not a question of simply convicting him. I want to know I have beaten him. You seem to think I go to court only to show off."

He said nothing. She had never talked so much about her feelings, but his failure to grasp what she was saying did not so much confuse him as make her more deliciously intriguing. It was like feeling her from the inside—transcendently beautiful, but ephemeral, shapeless, incomprehensible. He gave up trying to fathom it and began drawing circles on her thigh.

She shifted and reached for another cigarette. She had smoked them too quickly. The package was empty. Tossing it over her shoulder, she shrugged and crossed her arms. "I will finish him. It is what I do."

"It will be different when you face him. And the nation will be grateful, Esma."

"If the nation continues to exist."

"And you will know you have done right and done well. And my woman will be rewarded." He saw that her moment of mental nakedness was ended. He kissed her knee. It twitched as if dismissing a fly.

She diverted her eyes and he knew that "my" had been the wrong thing to say. Every time he tried to join their destinies, she distanced herself. The futility depressed him.

They were silent for several seconds: she staring at the sun, which had now breached the horizon and was burning out a gloriously clear sky. He stroked the satin of her thighs, then lowered his head to kiss again the bony part of her knee. She did not resist, so he stretched his fingers to reach between her legs. She shoved him away and stood.

"I need a shower," she said.

He heard the latch on the bathroom door and settled back on the carpet with a sigh. He ached for her. What a fool he was! Suppose she won her case and was offered a prominent position in Belgrade as expected. What would he do about that? Follow her? The talentless pet following his brilliant mistress. He slapped the chaise longue. *Suppose* she won? It was a certainty. If anyone could pull together the scattered fragments of Bloody Marko's life, she could. She would find his secret weakness. She always did. The tiles would become a mosaic under her long fingers and then she would be satisfied in a way he did not understand.

How long before she tired of faithful Zeljko? How long before she was embarrassed by his mere adequacy? He clasped his knees with his arms. She was a tormenting itch and he hated himself for not being able to get rid of her. He did not care whether she humiliated him or not. He just wanted her as long as he could. Why resist it? Maybe she would feel elation after the trial. He could ignore her warning not to bring up marriage again. Why not? How could she make him more miserable? If she rejected him again, maybe he could get angry enough to reject *her*. He could get on with his life, find a nice Croatian girl and delight his mother by marrying a good Catholic. He could have children, dozens of them parading off to Mass—boys and girls, tall and strong.

"Idiot!" he said.

Sliding back to sit against the bed he felt Esma's slipper under his thigh. He lifted it, held it close to his face, and sniffed it. He pressed it against his cheek and leaned against the mattress, listening to the shower run and the rising tide of traffic on the Boulevard of the Revolution. He threw the slipper against the glass door. "Zeljko," he said to himself, "you are such a fool."

Such an incredible fool.

The room they used for the pretrial interrogatories was larger than usual. The furniture looked new and there was a weak paintlike smell which more likely came off the heavy plastic varnish on the tables than from the dull green walls. Perhaps Esma had specified all this—Zeljko did not know. In proper Socialist fashion, he noted, she had too many assistants: four, besides him, each representing a republic in which Bloody Marko had committed crimes. She had, however, specifically limited the number of her assistants' assistants, which irritated the Montenegrin Boris Georgevich. She further irritated him by the imperious way she had instructed all of them in the conducting of the interrogatories. He had plainly intended to get some credit for the kill and he suspected "the bitch," as he once called her at the urinal, was stealing it all.

The defendant was to be called to the room at nine and

seated at the table. His attorney would be seated slightly behind him so that he would have to turn to speak to him. Esma also would allow his American attorney and a translator to attend, something the Slovenian assistant, Zeljko, and, of course, Georgevich thought inadvisable, but Esma was determined. She also specified that the court reporter would arrive five minutes after the defendant was seated: "They always restlessly fiddle with their machine, their ink, their paper," she remarked. Ten minutes later the assistants were to enter with an enormous pile of files about which they would whisper to each other, as if talking about the defendant. After all of the assistants had trailed in and carried on like this for fifteen minutes, Zeljko would come in. Finally, after another ten minutes, Esma herself would follow. All this was part of the hunt, Zeljko thought. The old man would be somewhat tired by the wait. He might begin to feel the case getting bigger and bigger against him. By the time Esma entered he might already feel he had no choice but to beg mercy. And if he recognized it was a charade? Well, it would anger him, and Zeljko knew how Esma had often turned defendants' anger back on them. For a few days, maybe a couple of weeks, jet lag was on Esma's side, too.

Zeljko had seen the man on television and in the papers, but he seemed tiny, his knotty fingers laced on the table in front of him, his head nodding forward from sleepiness. He was gaunt, his full head of white hair typical of many older Serbs. His oystery red eyes rolled toward Zeljko. He sneered contemptuously then closed them. Zeljko noticed that the strong light hanging on its cord over Marko glared off the glossy table into the man's textured face. Perhaps Esma had arranged this, too. The old man's attorneys were chatting with each other in English as if unconcerned. Perhaps they were playing games, too.

Esma entered several minutes later. She paused in the open door, scrutinized the defendant, then said, "Good morning." She paused. "I am Magistrate Esma Smilovich."

"Good morning," said Marko's attorney. "I am Milan Semich. I wish you to know that I intend to file a protest with the court. The evidence against my client is purely circumstantial. He is a victim of mistaken identity. This is purely a witch hunt."

Esma smiled. "I expect you to be even more creative than that, Mr. Semich."

"We did not receive justice in American courts, so we appeal for justice here. An organization well known to regularly supply war criminals year after year, in order to keep the memory of World War II alive, scoured the records of anyone receiving American passports in 1949. Mr. Renault was then singled out as having an unusual background and evidence was fabricated to make him appear to be the infamous Bloody Marko, who was likely killed in 1945. This is not a case in which my client was walking down the street and someone saw him and knew him to be Bloody Marko, the witnesses were all gathered *after* it had been decided he was Bloody Marko."

"Nonetheless, there are witnesses. This is not the place to begin your defense, sir. It is the five judges who are obligated to listen to your conspiracy theories.

"Furthermore, Mr. Richard Crittenden, who as you know represented Mr. Renault in the proceedings in the United States, wishes to make clear his objection to the interrogatories. He finds it a violation of the defendant's rights to be questioned in this manner before the trial. If your evidence is strong, he wishes to know, why is it necessary to subject his client to this?"

She spoke directly to the translator, a slim blackhaired woman, as if Crittenden were not there. "This is not New York. We operate according to our laws here. Despite what Americans may think, the law of the United States is not the standard by which we measure the laws of other countries."

"Duly noted," said Semich. "Our client has nothing to hide and insists upon cooperating. In America his silence was his right, but here he would not allow his silence to be taken as an admission of any guilt whatsoever." The American spoke to his translator. Semich nodded. "Mr. Crittenden and I also inquire whether you would support releasing Mr. Renault on bail. Jail is a hardship on a man of Mr. Renault's age and health. His blood pressure has been difficult to control since the beginnings of these legal actions nearly five years ago. He has deteriorated drastically."

"I do not think it would look very proper to put a notorious criminal in a hotel. We have had this discussion before and I do not wish to pursue it." Her voice was calm, almost diffident.

"For humanitarian reasons . . ." said Semich. "His son Carlos is flying in from America in two days. Where could my client go?"

"He was responsible for the deaths of thousands. Shall we send him on an Adriatic holiday? Jail is where he belongs. Shall we cease wasting time and begin?"

Semich settled into his chair, shrugging at Crittenden.

The defendant looked up. His eyes twinkled. "I am not such an idiot as my attorneys," he said. He cleared his throat. "I know how much justice and decency one can expect in the worker's paradise." His eyes locked with Esma's. He was amused. Semich touched his shoulder, but Marko jerked away from the hand. Esma stared at him for several seconds, then took one of the files from Zeljko, who noticed her cologne was very strong. Another trick?

"Your name is Marko Renovich, is that correct? You never met my father, but perhaps you remember him. You once hunted him and his friends Milo Vukadich and Meso."

"Who? Me?" He glanced around. "You must be mistaken. Your father told you many fairy tales, I'm sure. I am Mark Renault. I am an American citizen."

"Your Serbo-Croatian is impeccable. Is that the Shumadian accent?"

"My mother would have been very offended. She never thought there was such a thing as language in Croatia." He glanced at the assistants to see if anyone was insulted. Georgevich glanced at Zeljko who ignored it. "But she taught me *Serbian*, of course, as I was growing up in São Paulo."

"Your mother taught you the Serbian dialect of Serbo-Croatian, then, but not as a child in Brazil. You learned it in the village of Krushka, in the Shumadia."

"You know, this is the silly story that was presented to the courts in the United States. I hate to say it, but my own people have terrible judges. They believe any sort of fairy tale. Rather like you, I think."

"Come, come, Bloody Marko, would not it be easier to stop lying? It would certainly be easier for you. What are you ashamed of? You are near the end of your life."

"I will get no younger before the day is out. My father used to say that. He hired my mother to cook for him—right off the docks of Rio. He was an American, you know. He tried to make a fortune in cattle, but he failed and switched to rubber. They fell in love. It is an extraordinarily touching story. It would make a good Hollywood motion picture. Because he was an American, I am an American."

"If this is so touching, it must be a story. Why did the American courts say all this is a lie, that you fabricated it all to conceal yourself in the United States? Why did they send you back here?"

"Back? I've never been here in my life. I look around and it is so dirty and depressing. There are parts of Baltimore like this whole country, but there we call them 'slums.' Why would I come here? My mother fled for a reason."

"Curious, then, that evidence was submitted in your deportation hearing that you dared travel into Yugoslavia as part of a tour in 1978, a dozen years ago. Returning to the scenes of your crimes? You left the tour abruptly in Belgrade. Perhaps you were afraid of being recognized as Bloody Marko? You knew you had not killed everyone who knew you, though you certainly tried."

"Afraid? Of what?" He cleared his throat. "If I were Bloody Marko, I would have to be quite a coward to think you people could ever catch me. If I believed you could catch me, why would I enter the country at all?"

She had gotten a little rise out of him, thought Zeljko. He did not like to be called a coward. Zeljko make a note of it.

"But you _were_ caught," she said coolly.

"A gaggle of lunatic Jews and Gypsies have mistaken me for someone else. They caught me, not you. And they made a mistake. So much for the intellect of the Jews! So much for the cleverness of the Gypsies! I am here only because American judges are afraid to offend the Zionists."

As the translator finished the sentence, Crittenden reached up to Marko and touched his arm. Marko pulled away angrily. "You see? I am not supposed to mention the Jews." He put a finger to his lips and shushed.

"Why do you pretend, Marko Renovich? You, or someone else, forged your documents. You never had an American father who conveniently died in Brazil. I am not going to debate this. The American courts have already shown it was a fabrication. We do not know whether you managed the false identity on your own or with the help of the CIA or the Nazis. Perhaps you and Dr. Mengele were travelling companions? If you did it on your own, you are an extremely clever man, I must say."

The flattery gambit, thought Zeljko. Marko grinned for a moment as if he might snatch the bait, as simple as it was, then he turned toward Zeljko. "Would you explain to this woman how absurd this is? How could I deceive the U.S. immigration on my own? She fails to understand that things *work* in America. It is not like deceiving some Macedonian border guard."

Crittenden crossed his arms and stared at the floor. He had probably told Marko to keep his mouth shut, but the old man was too cocky.

"Then the Nazis helped you deceive them?" ventured Zeljko.

Marko laughed. "Adolf Hitler and I won the samba contest at Carnival in 1955. Boom-chicky-boom. He looks good in a dress." He puckered his lips. "Just beautiful, mmmmmm."

Zeljko glanced at Esma. She did not seem angry he had jumped in, though she had instructed all her assistants to remain silent. Her eyes were alert, sharp. He remembered the sheen of dawn on her body and suddenly craved her. He pretended to be taking more notes.

"A French reporter told me that a Washington newspaper had suggested you were involved with the CIA, like Klaus Barbie."

"Klaus Barbie was a bad man," said Marko. "Do I look like a bad man?"

Semich stood. "My client utterly denies having been involved with the CIA. The CIA utterly denies he has ever been in their employ in any capacity. Is accusing him of being a war criminal not enough?"

"You are interrupting," snorted Georgevich.

[13]

"Yes," said Marko coolly. "Why deny it? I am really the Man from U.N.C.L.E. Yes! I confess Let me explain who U.N.C.L.E. is—"

Esma slapped the table. "We know about television. And we know about you. Do not try to play innocent with me!" She leaned into the old man's face. "You are Marko Renovich, 'Bloody Marko,' you worked for the Germans even before they entered the country. After you saved several of their lives from a rightful retaliation, you were their darling. Under your direction they banished four villages to the death camps. You yourself tortured patriots until they were insane with agony, then you took great pleasure in shooting them. And you did this again and again for nearly two years. You made war against your own people."

The old man crossed his bony arms and stared at her. "They were never my people," he said. "Never."

He sat back in his chair. "My father was an American: Louis Philip Renault. He was married to my mother before I was born. This makes me an American. My arrogant son Carlos is an American because he is my son. His mother was Guatemalan, and was naturalized twenty-five years ago. If the American courts really believe I am this Renovich person, then why do they not take away my son's citizenship? Eh? No, I was selected to be persecuted because I bear some superficial resemblance to this man who disappeared in Italy forty-five years ago."

"You were selected? Why? The American courts have well cited the irregularities in your 'citizenship.' "

"Who knows why? The Zionist conspiracy. Some so-called investigators rooted around in government records looking for anyone who received recognition of their U.S. citizenship in the late forties. Or maybe I bought too many Maryland lottery tickets and I won a prize they are silent about in public. Who knows?"

"We shall speak of resemblance, then." Esma paced to the end of the table and reached into a blue file held by her Slovenian assistant, a fat little man with a rat-like nose. "This is one of several photographs we have of Bloody Marko. Of you." She stretched it out to him. He neither took it nor looked at it.

[14]

"Sorry," he said. "Eyes, you know. But I was much handsomer than this man. It is not me."

"I thought you said your eyes are weak."

"You said it is Bloody Marko. If it is Bloody Marko, then it cannot be me." He smiled. "I am not Bloody Marko."

She dropped the photograph on the table. It was sepia from age. A young man in a Royal Yugoslav uniform stripped of all insignia stood on the left side; a haggard German officer was on the right. Between them a man hung limp by his arms from a pole, his legs buckled under him. There were half a dozen bullet holes in his chest.

Semich stood. "This is hardly acceptable evidence against my client. This photograph has been widely published as a picture of Bloody Marko, yet there is no indication that this man is indeed he. The photograph is fuzzy. You cannot identify the officer or the victim—"

"The German's name was Helmut Grauer, as well you know."

"Grauer denied it until his death."

"No, he refused to talk to the German authorities. That is quite a different matter."

"And was Herr Grauer charged with war crimes?"

"The evidence against him was too weak—or so say the German authorities."

"Ah, then, this photograph proves nothing."

"It is but one piece of the mosaic."

"In fact, out of the entire German army which Bloody Marko supposedly assisted so assiduously, you can produce only one soldier who has mistakenly identified my client as this Marko Renovich, and he, conveniently, is too ill to travel—or so you say—too ill to confront the man he abuses." This argument had come up before. Semich sat down, pursing his lips in satisfaction.

Esma was undaunted. "They are likely afraid to be associated with their heinous crimes. Do they want their children and grandchildren to know they bayoneted babies, raped grandmothers, castrated little boys? It's understandable."

"Excuse me," interrupted Renovich, "but are you not confusing the Germans with the Russians, the Wehrmacht with your own Partisans?"

She did not react to the insult against her father, Zeljko noticed.

"The Germans committed no atrocities? Tell me about it."

"The Wehrmacht was very disciplined."

"Yes?"

Everyone other than Marko was holding their breath. Semich had turned pale. It could never be this easy, thought Zeljko. Not this easy.

"I saw a television program about them. Oh, yes, they were much more disciplined than even the Americans."

"You know this from television," said Esma dryly. "You are a great believer in television?"

"Only the Discovery channel," said Marko, eyes sparkling. "The others are only interested in selling hamburgers."

Semich visibly sagged. The American studied the roof. Georgevich, veins pulsing in his forehead, stared at Marko. Fed up with the fencing, he wanted to shake the truth out of him. He was controlling himself by twisting a pen in his thick hands. Zeljko watched Esma. She kept her penetrating gaze on Marko and showed no feeling. With the same placid look she had first accepted Zeljko's suggestion they go to bed, but her passion always burned hot in her. She was a furnace with a thick, tight door which she opened only when she wished.

"I suggest, Mr. Renovich, that you know more about the German army than you give yourself credit. . . . I suggest, Mr. Renovich, that you were first an agent for the Germans—probably a spy—then an active collaborator with General Nedich and his staff after the invasion."

"Excuse me?" He cleared his throat and turned to one side, then the other.

"Is it not true that on the date of the invasion you had been imprisoned for being a member of Prince Paul's faction, the Fascist, pro-Hitler faction? Is it not true papers were being prepared to charge you with treason?"

The old man turned from side to side again. "Well, answer her, Renovich. Which of you is Renovich? Is it you, Mr. Crittenden? You shock me."

Georgevich slapped the table hard. His red face contorted. "You shall not think it funny when the firing squad is—"

Marko laughed. The outburst was a small victory for him. Esma glared at her assistant who twisted in his chair and crossed his arms.

"I understand," said Marko to Esma. "The ox is the 'bad cop' and you are the 'good cop.' I learned that from cop shows: *Cagney and Lacey, Starsky and Hutch.* You probably did, too." He chuckled. "It will not work on me, *chiquita.* I am the wrong man."

Zeljko gestured at Esma, whose stare was locked with Marko's. They were like two cats with their backs arched, waiting for the other to blink. Zeljko stood and Esma put her ear close to his mouth. "Let's break for a while," he whispered.

She looked at him as if he were crazy.

"Ten minutes. Talk strategy," he whispered.

"*I'll* decide when we break," she whispered sharply.

Now Zeljko was angry, too, but he did not want to give her the satisfaction. He raised his eyebrows as if to say, "As you wish," then sat and went back to taking notes.

She took out another file, flipped three sheets, and began again. "So, we are all mistaken. You are not Bloody Marko. You were not born in Krushka. Your father was an American. Well, then, we are wasting our time."

"That's what I said."

"It would be a great service to us, then, if you would clear up all these falsehoods, if you could explain why you have been identified as Bloody Marko. Could you do that for us?"

"I am totally cooperative," he said.

"We have three photographs of Bloody Marko. One we have shown you. This is our second. It comes from an identity card issued in 1942. He was a handsome man, very virile. You will notice the strong resemblance . . ."

"A fraud!" growled Marko.

The interrogatories went on until well past the normal time for lunch, and then again afterwards. Esma probed all of Marko's vanities, his pride, his arrogance, his manhood, and likely several facets of his personality that Zeljko missed as the questioning began to weary him. After the outburst, Georgevich seemed subdued, as if he felt he would not waste any more energy on such a pointless exercise. Marko, who had begun the day obviously tired, seemed to grow stronger as it

[17]

continued. At one point, for about thirty minutes, Zeljko thought he was weakening. His words began to slur, he got confused, forgot the Serbo-Croatian word for "scapegoat," and mumbled in what sounded like Spanish. Semich began to interrupt and harass Esma about badgering an old man. Esma kept picking at Marko, however, and then suddenly, as if given a new life, Marko revived. As sharp as he had been all morning, he teased her, said things which terrified his lawyers, as if he were about to give in, then twisted them into jokes. Often, he pretended not to hear. Often he dozed off, or pretended to. At the end of the day, when he rose unsteadily from the hard chair, his eyes were twinkling. Inside that eighty-year-old body was a man who was laughing at them.

Even in the hardest criminal Zeljko had proceeded against, there had been a germ of fear, a need to be punished, and part of the wicked pleasure of prosecuting was the knowledge that you could induce fear in people who would otherwise assume their superiority to you. Perhaps fear was in Marko, but Zeljko had not seen it. Nothing could be done to him which he feared. Ironically, Zeljko thought, the oldest men and women he had prosecuted were the ones who valued life the most, and would cut any deal to gain the slightest possibility of escaping death. Any humiliation was a small price. Marko, though, laughed. He was amused at their attacks. He knew they knew who he was. He knew what he had done. He would be a fool to think he could win, so what was it? Stubbornness? Was he a kind of Satan yelling "Kiss my ass!" as God indifferently brushed him into hell?

A chill went through Zeljko as the possibility they were indeed prosecuting the wrong man crept up on him. No, no, no. The evidence was all there: half a century old, some of it dubious, but on the whole undoubtable. Esma would break him down. The old man may not have been behaving like a guilty man, but he was not behaving like an innocent victim, either.

The assistants all left quietly, saying little more than "good evening" to each other. Zeljko studied Esma. As soon as the others left the room her face sagged. She was exhausted. There were lines under her eyes. She leaned on the table with both hands and arched her back. She had never lost her control, as usual, but she paid a price for it. She looked weaker than the old man.

"What do you think?" said Zeljko.

"I still do not know who he is," she said. "I am always on the verge of knowing and then he eludes me."

"Could it be he's not Bloody Marko?"

"Oh, please!" she said.

"All the evidence says he is, I know, but I cannot explain how he acts. Confronted with the enormities of treason, of murder, regardless of his character, almost anyone would try to justify it." The Croatian war criminal Andrija Artukovich had truculently defended his actions, Zeljko remembered.

"It is a matter of time. When I know him, then I will play him like a violin." She yawned as if what she'd said was nothing. "I want to walk. I am going to walk back to the hotel. It will relax me."

"You've paced ten miles on this floor today."

She shrugged.

"It is cold. We will hire a taxi." He reached for her waist. "I will give you a bath and a good massage."

"No," she said, peeling his arm away. "We will meet for breakfast."

"What about dinner?"

"I am not hungry." She pecked him on the forehead. "Until tomorrow then."

She left quickly. He stared into the void she had left for several seconds, then struck the table with his fist. He wanted to understand—she was tired, she was frustrated, love was the last thing on her mind—but he still felt dismissed. He ought to go to her room, throw her on the bed, and—"Shit!" he said. He settled into the chair and waited until he thought the press would be gone. Then he went into a grocery, bought a loaf of bread, hard sausage, and a bottle of vodka. He fell asleep in his room, holding the bottle under his arm like a warm little child.

By the third day of the interrogatories, Georgevich was insisting that they should simply take the man to trial. "How long must this go on?" All the evidence had been thrown in Marko's face, and though he seemed to weaken somewhat at times, he gave no appearance of breaking. Zeljko heard a rumor that Georgevich was angling to get Esma replaced—by himself of course. And with the Slovenian Communist party walking away from the national party, there was speculation that the Slovenian assistant wanted to be off the case because there was less evidence of Marko's committing murder in that republic. The tide of change in Eastern Europe, thought Zeljko, was rolling into Yugoslavia and no one knew where it would end. The rehashing of some old World War II atrocities had turned irrelevant. Why recapture history when history was all around you? Perhaps Esma was right: the "big chance" had evaporated. Still it was too late to forget it—they had gone to much trouble to get Marko out of the United States. Furthermore, the old-line higher-ups were all certain that this reminder of the patriotic struggle would nurture what national unity might remain.

And, of course, Esma would never willingly give up. She had become, as Zeljko saw it, obsessed with the man, fascinated with him. She tried to draw him out on things that were not really germane to the evidence. She spent nearly two hours in the afternoon of the second day asking Marko about what his mother had told him about her life in the Shumadia before she emigrated.

She listened intently as Marko described the "dirty, barbaric ignorance" which his mother had lived among, and it was obvious that Esma, exploiting the fiction of his mother's emigration, had gotten him to talk about his own life. But he never actually gave up the line that this was what his mother had told him, nothing more. He talked sentimentally about the cakes and "delicious *pasulj*" (bean soup) his mother made and about how her family was famous for their deeds against the Turks. He claimed to be distantly and illegitimately—but proudly—related to the Milosh Obrenovich, Prince of Serbia.

None of the others in the room saw the slightest point in all this and Semich grew quite restless, afraid probably that Esma was on to something that he had missed, that somehow Marko was loading his executioners' rifles. Zeljko tried to look as if he were pleased with the way it was going, just to increase Semich's discomfort, but he had no more idea what she was up to than did his attorneys.

Esma had said she needed to understand the man. Very well. He was willing to allow her whatever she liked. Bombarding him with the evidence had not worked. She had thrown the extinct village of Tasadrava at him. According to the three survivors, now in state retirement homes, Bloody Marko had been insulted by one of the village elders and then told the Germans that the partisans who had been sniping at them in the valley were being harbored there. When they did not yield up the partisans—they never had them—everyone was machine-gunned. These three had survived because adults had fallen over them. Esma played a tape of the witnesses trying to explain between sobs what had happened more than forty-five years ago. She also darkened the room, as if to leave Marko with his conscience, and showed grisly slides of the bodies as a group of Macedonian partisans had found them a day later, mutilated by stray dogs. Marko was unmoved, saying only, "War is a terrible thing. So I've heard."

She read him the account of a Wehrmacht private, now a Green Party organizer in Hamburg. He had seen Bloody Marko, emerging from a barn sometime in 1942, his gory hands cradling a bloody hammer. He asked another soldier what was going on. The soldier told him, "Our Serb has been getting answers." Later, several officers appeared. They wanted to use the barn to sleep in that night and several soldiers were sent in to toss out the dozen bodies. It looked like Marko had used the hammer to smash their fingers and toes one by one on an anvil. Some of the men had smashed genitalia. The German was not certain how they had died. Maybe they bled to death or died from the pain. One had had his skull caved in. The private got extra guard duty for not being able to get the blood off his sleeve. That was what was clearest in his memory. By that point in the war, extra duty was more significant than deaths.

The barn incident was known throughout the partisan groups. Tito himself had once referred to it in a speech. It was in the folklore of the revolution. It had earned Marko Renovich his nickname and a price on his head, but there was only the one actual witness surviving and he would not come to Yugoslavia, saying he was too busy with organizing the Greens for the reunification of the Germanys. Esma had no photographs, only the deposition, but somehow this was even more horrible. Semich stared at the floor while she read it; Crittenden studied

[21]

his pencil. Later, he pointed out—as he had in the American courts—that the private's account was almost all hearsay, that there were no witnesses to what had happened inside the barn. At the end Marko simply said, "Just like a coward to blame everything on someone convenient. You perhaps suggested the idea to this crazy old German? Would you do that to get my old hide? I think so."

Each of the eleven living witnesses to the seven specific crimes of violence had identified Marko from photographs, Esma then stated, but Semich interrupted angrily. None of the witnesses had really known Marko Renovich. They had seen him once nearly half a century ago. Furthermore, Semich said, the defense had an expert who pointed out that in presenting the portfolio of pictures the questioner had implied that one of them was definitely Bloody Marko and that Renault's picture had been slightly larger on the sheet. These irregularities tended to prejudice identifications. Esma and he exchanged words, then she terminated the argument by saying he could bring his expert to court for all the man was worth. None of this seemed to make the slightest impression on Marko. "Your witnesses must be bribed," he said. "In the old Slavic tradition."

She had documents from the German army indicating Marko's role. She had a Wehrmacht request to Berlin to give Marko Renovich a medal. She had passages from memoirs of German officers referring to the help they had gotten from Marko Renovich in their long, successful retreat through the Balkans. Marko merely waved his hand and said, "Lies! Forgeries! With the crimes Communists have done, what's a little forgery?" Shortly after this, Marko's head dropped to one side and he began to snore. Georgevich reached across the table and poked him, nearly upsetting his chair. His attorneys yelled, "Don't touch him!" and Semich and Georgevich had a shoving match. In the middle of this chaos, Zeljko noticed the old man grinning. Marko's and Esma's eyes were fixed on each other's, like a pair of lovers communicating wordlessly.

"I like you," said Marko. His quiet voice silenced the room. "You are just like me. Younger, but just like me."

Everyone looked at each other expecting an explanation,

but Esma did not move. The room was as humid as a Turkish bath.

Zeljko suggested the session end early. He lingered behind Esma when the reporters from France, Italy, and the state network crowded around. She said her usual: "We are proceeding with the interrogation of the prisoner and expect to bring him to trial soon." They asked her about a woman named Joan Macklin who had told the American courts that her sister-in-law, one Florence Quinn, had said just before she died in 1986 that Mark Renault was not Bloody Marko, but a concentration camp survivor.

"You must remember," Esma answered, "there are many counter-revolutionaries who disseminate ridiculous lies to confuse the people."

She walked away when Semich and Crittenden began to accuse the prosecutors of needlessly tormenting a guiltless old man. Zeljko would not let her get away today, though. He hurried up beside her and grabbed her elbow at a crosswalk.

"Esma, please," he said, "this is getting out of hand. Let's take him to trial and get it over with."

"Are you siding with Georgevich?"

"I am siding with no one. Something has come over you. Why must you break him? He is a vicious killer, an animal. How can you break a creature like that? The only thing to do with a mad dog is kill him." A man in a hurry knocked them apart. "Idiot!" Zeljko shouted. He hurried to catch up with her.

"Zeljko, I need to walk alone to clear my head. Please go."

"You cannot clear you head. You look like you have been awake since the interrogatories began. If you are not careful you may get relieved. After what happened in there—"

"We shall remove Georgevich from the room."

They scurried around a young man selling jewelry. "That is not the issue. Something is wrong with you. You look calm in there but I can tell you are about to explode."

"Explode? Have you ever seen me explode? Who do you think you are? Just because you have amused me at times, do not presume—"

" 'Amused'? 'Amused'? What do you think I am? Some lap dog? I love you. I want to marry you. How can you—?"

She had walked on. Several old women were watching him

and grinning. He nearly ran into a student on a bicycle. When he caught up to her, he roughly took her arms and pressed her against the wall.

"Very well," he said. "You do not love me. You do not want to marry me. I am tried of asking. Do I need you to live? But for God's sake do not muddy up this business because you think you are the only person in the world who can break Bloody Marko. He is a man who lied to the Germans, then watched them exterminate an entire village. He beat people to death. He looked men and women in the eyes and blew off the tops of their heads. Our only goal is to make him pay. Why do you want more?"

She struggled some, then looked as if she were going to cry. Zeljko released his grasp in astonishment. "What is it?" he said. "What is it?"

She raised her head. "I cannot say." She thought for a moment. "We will end tomorrow. I want to try one more thing. You are right." The final sentence sounded empty.

"If you will just tell me . . ."

"I do not know," she said. "Something is just beyond my grasp." She looked at the tattered awning above her and the dirt that had come off the wall. She turned as if she were going to look at the fabrics in the store window to her left, then sighed.

"Come on," he said. "I will buy you a dinner: a three weeks' salary dinner. In the Skadarlija. Baklava, wine, brandy, old songs."

"You will want to make love afterwards."

"Of course." He took her arm tenderly. "But I will not beg." He touched her chin. "Eh?"

She smiled weakly. "I am sorry." She touched his ear. "You remind me of my father sometimes when you get angry. Did you know that? I was unkind to him sometimes, too. But he taught me not to enter a conflict I do not expect to win."

"You will win this case without breaking him."

"Breaking him is winning. The conviction is expected."

"And what will you do?"

"There is something about when he talks about his mother's village. Perhaps I will see it tonight. If not, I have a gamble I will play."

"We will talk it out. We'll find it."

"No, I want you to leave me alone, again. Do you understand?"

Zeljko stiffened and backed away. His eyes flashed. He tried to speak but anger choked the words. He stalked away. "Zeljko?" Esma called. "Zeljko!" A taxi driver yelled at a pedestrian. He did not hear her after that. His impulse was to drink himself asleep again or find a whore and get revenge, but four blocks later his anger had shifted to sadness. He hired a cab and went back to the justice ministry to get his notes.

Esma found him asleep on his papers the next morning, a half-eaten hamburger he had bought from a street vendor staining his blotter. He blinked at her, uncertain where he was.

"What time is it?" he asked.

"Time," she said. "You can clean up in the washroom. We've got thirty minutes or so."

"I cannot—" he expelled a long sigh. "There is nothing that I can see. I do not even understand what it is you are looking for."

"Nor do I. At least I slept. I have nothing left but the gamble. If that fails, we will simply take him to trial and scrape him off our shoes like dog shit."

"What is the gamble?"

"Neda."

"I do not understand. She is one of the weakest witnesses."

"I have a feeling. Maybe what we need will float up. Do you think we should keep Georgevich out of the chamber?"

"Threaten him, but keep him," he said. "It will keep them on edge that he might lose control again."

She smiled. "Very good." She pointed at the hamburger. "How can you eat those things? Surely you have noticed there are no cats and dogs within five blocks of a Belgrade vendor?"

It was an old joke. The sleep had helped her. He shrugged. "And do you think the street vendors are worse than the state sausage factories? At least the street vendors are cheaper than that American place downtown."

"McDonald's," she said.

"Do you know everything?" he asked pleasantly.

"I know you have twenty-two minutes to clean up."

Esma had viciously threatened Georgevich in her private office, but when the fourth session of the interrogatories began with Semich objecting to the presence of the big Montenegrin, Esma coyly trivialized Semich's protesting the "manhandling" of his client. She insisted upon Georgevich's right to be there and ultimately ordered Semich to sit down. Marko dozed through much of this, raising his head twice to complain of a headache. No one knew whether it was another of his jokes, but the second time he demanded Semich gave him an aspirin. Esma inspected the tablets before she allowed Marko to have them. The questioning was wearing him down physically. He was ashen except for the extraordinary pink in his pockmarked cheeks. Both hands quivered when he moved them. He might have gained another twenty years since they had started. Still, as ancient as he was, perhaps he knew when to conserve his energy by dozing and stalling. He remained mildly amused to be the center of all the intensity around him.

For an hour and a half, Esma probed at Marko along the same lines she had pursued on the previous four days. This further exasperated his attorneys and Georgevich, judging from the way he glanced at the other assistants. Marko appeared totally undisturbed. He and Esma were partners perfectly in step with each other: two ballet dancers pretending to be sword fighting, the Rat King and the Nutcracker. She led him into talking about his father again, then his mother.

"And you say you came back in 1978 to see what your mother had told you about, her life before she emigrated?"

"Yes, I was getting old. I wanted to take a trip." His eyes twinkled. "It was just as she described it. Poor, ignorant, dirty."

"You say that Yugoslavia today is like the Yugoslavia your mother fled? When did she leave again?"

"During the Balkan Wars, 1913."

"There was no Yugoslavia then."

His chuckle brought on a coughing spell. He leaned forward and pinched the bridge of his nose. He was still wrestling the headache. "There is no Yugoslavia now."

"You have a remarkable penchant for ignoring reality, Bloody Marko."

"It is you who speak of Yugoslavia, you virtually alone. If

[26]

you listen to the people you call Yugoslavian, you will not hear this word. You will hear Dalmatia, Slovenia, Macedonia, Serbia. There are termites in the roof beams. You are already ankle deep in the sawdust. Yugoslavia!" He said the name with a sneer. He glanced back. His lawyer had closed his eyes as if he had a headache. Zeljko felt uncomfortable and could see that everyone in the room felt uncomfortable. What Marko had said was always in the back of any Yugoslavian nationalist's mind. It was the thought you did not wish to think, the fear you dared not face.

"Mr. Crittenden asks if we could please stay on the subject of the charges," interrupted the translator. "Mark Renault's political opinions have no bearing on the case, especially since he has been in Yugoslavia only twice in his life."

Esma suddenly stopped pacing. Zeljko thought she was going to instruct Mr. Crittenden to keep quiet as he had no legal standing there. She was thinking. She abruptly leaned forward and put her hands on the table. Everyone stared for several seconds. She said with a quiet, almost amazed, triumphant tone, "You hate your country. It is as simple as that, is it not? You hate it. You spent the war trying to make it a corner of Germany, because for some reason, you hate it. You hate me. You hate Semich there and all of us."

Marko looked into her eyes. "Hate my country? My country is America."

"No," said Esma. "No. I do not know why it is. But I have known criminals who have killed women because every woman represents their mother, or who attack any authority to revenge themselves on their fathers. You, I think, are like these men. You deny your real father exists. You deny our country exists. Your hate is behind these crimes. Is that not true? Well? What makes you hate, Bloody Marko? Why?"

Marko hardly moved. Someone rattled keys in the hallway. Marko leaned toward Esma. "Do not," he hissed, "project your own feelings onto me. I am just a simple American."

"My feelings?"

"Yes. You are what you wish me to be. The smells, the tastes, the primitive squabbling, the barbarity—you can drive five minutes outside the city and see it. You can walk up the Knez Mihailova, up the nice plaza there with all the stores and see that all this supposed modernness is a facade. Cheap goods in the stores. Plastic shoes, wine that tastes like swill. You know it. You are an intelligent woman. Yugoslavia is the Wild West of Europe, nothing more than a reservation for the leftover Slavic tribes. Its only comfort is comparing itself to Albania and Rumania and pretending Italy doesn't exist."

Esma seemed like she had been struck in the face. Zeljko had never seen anything like it.

"My attorney here warns me against you. You are called the Tiger. They think you must be descended from the Janissaries. Esma Smilovich, the descendant of Ismail, a Moslem. *Your* father was a Partisan, was he not? Was he treated well? Did he get all he deserved? Do you suspect his Moslem background interfered with his social life in any way? Is it the Orthodox or the Catholics who have insulted you more often? And now they insult you by using you to prove they have no dislike for Moslems."

"Whatever are you babbling about?" she said uncertainly.

"And then, how do you feel about them? When your people came here they were civilized and the Christians were not. Now they talk about you as if you were Huns. Is that why you are such a Janissary in court? Each infidel you behead is another speck of revenge." Marko laughed.

Esma said nothing. Zeljko knew that this had become very different from the way it had started. Her insight had been twisted by Marko against her. Pieces of things flashed into his mind. Once in bed he had asked her about her father, and she had said he might have been the President of the Bosnia-Herzegovina were it not for his being Moslem. How when the smallpox epidemics broke out in the 1950s, the Christians would blame the Moslems and the Gypsies. Zeljko also remembered telling her that when he was a child everyone had always said Moslems were filthy and spread disease. At the time she had mentioned these and other things, she had seemed almost to be laughing at the foolishness of it, but now with Bloody Marko throwing it in her face, she was stunned, maybe even damaged. He tried to think what to do.

Georgevich broke the long silence. "You will see how united our country is when we all dance on your grave." Everyone seemed embarrassed he had spoken.

Esma straightened. She seemed about to formulate a question, but could not formulate it.

"Shall I call for the witness?" asked Zeljko.

Esma paused, as if trying to understand him, then nodded. He gestured to the policeman at the door.

"Witness?" asked Semich.

"Yes."

The assistants looked at each other. She had not told them and they were clearly offended.

The translator raised her hand. "Mr. Crittenden asks whether this is highly irregular at this point."

"Perhaps," said Esma woodenly, "but it will be a reunion of old friends. She knew Marko as a child. Long ago."

Zeljko studied her. She was going ahead with her gamble purely on instinct, though her heart no longer seemed in it. This was not the diffidence of a tigress who breaks off her charge by pretending she is no longer interested in her prey. Marko had struck deep. Zeljko was not certain why. It was not as if she did not already know the attitudes of Christians to Moslems, Serbs and Croats to the descendants of the Turks. It had to be something she had suspected in herself, something she now had been forced to confront.

"Give me another aspirin," Marko snapped at his lawyer. Semich looked at Esma, who gestured impatiently with her hand. The Slovenian poured Marko a glass of water. "They must be Yugoslavian aspirins," growled Marko. "They do not work."

While they waited, Esma walked to the back of the room and faced the back wall. She was putting her mind back on track, thought Zeljko, gathering what forces she had left. There was a tapping. The policeman opened the door crisply and a policewoman led a frail, timid woman by her withered arm. Neda's hair was back in a tight bun, untidy wisps of gray frizzing out over her ears. Her eyes twitched from side to side behind her spectacles as everyone other than Marko watched her enter. Marko was pinching the bridge of his nose again, his eyes closed.

"Come in, Neda," said Esma. "Would you like to sit?"

The woman looked around as if she were expecting them to pounce on her. "No," she said.

"I am Esma Smilovich."

The woman smiled weakly. "Yes," she said. "Esma Smilovich, the magistrate."

"Yes. How are you feeling today?"

"My hip has been bothering me, but not as bad as yesterday."

"Are you sure you would not prefer to sit?"

"Will we be long?"

"I cannot say."

"I will stand for now." Again she fearfully scanned the others in the room.

"Very well, said Esma. "You tell me when you would like a chair."

Zeljko watched Marko, who had raised his head indifferently. He cleared the phlegm in his throat and began picking at a nick in the table top.

"Who is this woman?" said Semich.

"Neda," said Esma. "For many years she did not have a last name. Eventually the doctors at the hospital gave her the name Broz in honor of her service to the partisans. They helped her appearance with plastic surgery. As her true identity came back to her bit by bit, as she recalled the names she had lived under, she decided to retain the name Neda Broz. She had no home to go back to, no family."

"And you propose to use an amnesiac to identify my client?" said Semich. "Ha! You are desperate, aren't you?"

"You will be quiet, Mr. Semich."

"Well, then, why is she here and why cannot she speak for herself?"

"She is frightened. She tries to stay away from groups of people. They confuse her—Is that correct, Neda?"

"Yes."

"You have brought this woman here only so that she can become familiar with Mr. Renault's face and later identify my client in court. The judges shall be informed of this brazen irregularity."

"Mr. Semich will please be quiet and sit down. Neda is incapable, thanks to your client, of identifying anyone."

"Excuse me?" asked Semich. He leaned forward as if trying to see the woman's eyes.

"Sit down," said Zeljko firmly. Semich whispered to the translator.

"Will this take long?" Neda asked.

"Now, Neda, do you remember two weeks ago when I first located you at the retirement home?"

"Yes. Esma Smilovich came to see me. That is you, is it not?"

"Yes. And I brought a book of photographs."

"Yes."

"And did you recognize anyone in the photographs?"

She lowered her eyes, ashamed. "No."

"If I told you that among them was a photograph of the man known as Bloody Marko, would you have been able to pick it out?"

"No."

"Would you want to be able to pick it out?"

"Oh, yes!" She bit her lower lip. "But I cannot."

Semich looked at Crittenden. The translator had hesitated and then caught up. Georgevich spun around in his chair and stared up at Esma as if she were crazy.

"But you knew this man called Bloody Marko very well, did you not? You saw him many times?"

"Many times."

"But you cannot, say, pick him out from among the people in this room?"

The woman never raised her head. "It was long ago," she answered.

"But you cannot."

"No."

"If he speaks?"

"Possibly. I do not think I could forget his voice."

Semich leaned forward again and studied the woman. "She is blind?"

"The questioner is Mr. Semich," said Esma to her. "No, she is not blind. Please do not interrupt."

Neda lifted her head enough to glance at Semich. She noticed Marko. Their eyes met but he shrugged and looked away. Her eyes, however, widened. She seemed to shiver, then lowered her head again.

"What is it?" asked Esma.

"I do not know. I felt a sudden chill, sorrow—I do not know."

"Did you recognize him?"

"Who?"

"Bloody Marko Renovich. Who once lived in your village. Who left you for dead."

"I cannot recognize anyone."

"Not so that you can name them, but the doctors have told me that it is not unusual for some part of the brain to provoke what they call an autonomic emotional response to a face with great meaning. Do not be frightened. You are safe here." She caressed Neda's clenched hands.

The translator raised her hand. "Excuse me. Mr. Crittenden says he is rather confused. The woman cannot identify Bloody Marko from a photograph, nor here, yet she is not blind. She saw him many times but she can only possibly recognize his voice."

"That is a fair summary."

"And after all of that, you expect us to accept a voice identification after more than four decades?"

"It is what the court accepts that matters. All will be made clear. Are you comfortable, Neda?"

She nodded.

"You see, Neda was injured during the war. Very seriously. On both sides of the brain. Besides the stiffness in her upper shoulder, she is the victim of a rare brain disorder called prosopagnosia. It leaves her unable to recognize faces, or to learn a new one. Her memory is excellent, she has no problem functioning in the world, with this single exception. She cannot recognize a face. Let me show you something." Esma reached into her own valise and lifted out a portrait of herself. She showed it to Semich and Marko.

"Very pretty, darling," said Marko.

She handed the photograph to Neda. "Who is this woman?" Neda shook her head. "Who is it? Don't be embarrassed."

Neda stared at the portrait of Esma, then at Esma, then back at the portrait. She squinted. "This is—I do not know."

"Would you guess?"

"That American actress? The one who married the short man?"

"This is ridiculous," snorted Semich. "What is the point of this game?"

"My head hurts," sighed Marko.

Neda blinked as if she were going to cry.

"Silence!" said Esma. She touched Neda on the shoulder. "Pay no attention to him. That was Mr. Semich. Suppose I were to tell you that this photograph is of someone in this room?"

Neda scanned the room, lingering on each woman: the policewoman, the Serbian assistant, the translator. She settled on Esma. "It is you," she said.

"Very good," said Esma. "And you were guessing, is that not correct?"

"No. Your filigree earrings."

Startled, Esma reached up to her ears. "Oh, yes! Very good, Neda. Very observant."

Zeljko glanced at Georgevich, who was as bewildered as everyone else. He then noticed that Marko had raised his head and begun to stare at Neda, almost straining as he squinted.

"Neda has a hard life," said Esma. "She lives in a world of strangers. No matter how many times she sees the grocer, she cannot recognize him. If someone approaches her, she does not know if he is a stranger or a friend. As a result, she wants no friends, she lives alone. She tries to watch television but loses track of the story because she cannot recognize the people. She reads mostly and when her arthritis is not too painful, she does embroidery, lovely embroidery. It was Bloody Marko who gave her this life."

Marko continued to stare, blinking. He craned his neck as if trying to see the woman.

"It was November 15, 1944, in a small valley near Valjevo—"

Marko began rising from his chair, slowly, as if entranced.

"A German patrol guided by Bloody Marko stumbled across partisans educating the peasants in harassing the Fascists in their retreat."

Marko's arm went up. He pointed. Semich reached for Marko.

"Among them was Neda—"

"Jelena," whispered Marko. "Jelena!"

Neda brought her hands up to her chest and clutched it, as if she were trying to hold herself together.

"You are dead," he said.

"Marko?!" She shivered as if she were going to drop. Esma took her by the shoulders, but Neda looked at her blankly, then pushed her away. Everyone in the room was now standing. Neda turned her head from side to side for several seconds, then moved forward. Her voice quivered, "You are Marko? Marko Renovich?"

His hands were claws squeezing his head. His eyes were wild. "Jelena is dead. Do you think I am a fool? Jelena is dead! Dead!"

She choked on her words. "Yes. Yes . . . and you killed her twice." Her hands reached out imploringly, as if she were going to take his cheeks and hold them. "You child," she said, "you poor child . . ."

His eyes bulged, and Zeljko knew he knew her. Suddenly Marko rocked back as if hit. He did not so much cry out as expel a sharp wheeze. He reeled to his side and fell back, grazing the chair arm and collapsing to the floor. The American shouted in English, the policewoman charged forward, and Semich rushed from the room yelling. Georgevich and the other assistants were gesturing helplessly, babbling directions to each other. The woman called Neda was on her knees, fists over her eyes, crossing herself, praying maniacally. Where is Esma? Zeljko thought, and then he saw her, limp in a chair in the dark corner, her head back. She did not have the look of triumph with which she normally ended a case. The victory was Pyrrhic. If there were a trial, Zeljko instantly knew, she could not prosecute it.

Zeljko hustled Esma out of the building and left the reporters to Georgevich. She said nearly nothing for two days. He gave her large glasses of wine spiked with slivovitz, answered the phone for her, and lit her cigarettes. He tried to get her to eat. He did not try to make her talk because he did not know what to say. She perked up somewhat whenever he called for Marko's condition. The old man made noises but it was not speech. The stroke had also paralyzed half of his body. The doctors said Bloody Marko would die by summer if not next week, though sometimes a younger patient might vegetate for years after the episode. Georgevich argued that the proceedings should go forward regardless of the defendant's health, but no one was interested anymore. Too much else was happening; there had been more shooting in Kossovo between ethnic Albanians and Serbs. Croatians were speaking of independence. Legal action against Bloody Marko was suspended until he was fit to stand trial. Everyone knew that would be never. After fifty years, World War II had finally ended in the collapse of Communism. Only the future mattered. It seemed enough that Bloody Marko would die in jail.

Zeljko himself had lost all interest. It was Esma who worried him. What had happened in the interrogatories? What? He refused to think she had a nervous breakdown and might need a doctor, though the fear kept nudging him. On the second day after Marko's stroke, the sun had begun to drop and the room was turning orange. Her voice startled him. "I am dirty. Draw me a bath, will you?"

"It will help you sleep," he said.

She soaked for a long time. He sat on the floor between the commode and the bath.

"I will marry you, Zeljko."

"What?"

"I will marry you."

"We will talk of it tomorrow." He got up on his knees. "I'll scrub your back."

"You have changed your mind about marrying me."

He dropped the sponge into the tub and watched the splashed water drain off her breasts. "I do not know. I think I love you. No, I know I love you. I have held you, but I've never touched you. Maybe I am frightened. It used to intrigue me—you were exotic, what you hid was what attracted me. Now I am confused. Maybe what you hide inside is not something I want to know." He picked up the sponge. "What I am saying may be stupidity. I am exhausted. Lean forward."

She lowered her eyes. She did not seem angry or disappointed.

"Do you remember once I asked you why early in your career you moved from Sarajevo to Nish, away from all your family? You abandoned one republic for another and set your legal career back by two years at least."

"I made up the difference."

"Because you are brilliant. But there are other things brilliance cannot make up. I will not let you marry me," he said, "in order to escape. I intended to marry an important magistrate. I would never let you hide in my kitchen." He no sooner got it out than he felt as if he were throwing his life away. "You *could* not hide in my kitchen because you would still have your tiger's heart." He thought of Marko Renovich. "No one escapes himself for very long, no matter how far he runs."

She lit a cigarette. "So much for the trial," she muttered. "So much for my career on the Central Committee."

"By tomorrow there may not be a Central Committee. Communism is finished even in Russia. But your career will still be a great one. I know you. I believe this."

She faced him and thought. "You are kind."

"I do not say it out of kindness."

"You *are* kind. You have a faithful soul."

"Like a pet dog."

"No," she said, "do not say that. Like a man who loves too much."

He rinsed her back with the hand shower. "I was worried about you."

"Bloody Marko." she said quietly.

He straightened. "What did Neda Broz mean when she said he killed her twice? Something in their village? We could ask her."

"She has suffered enough. Maybe she will never have to speak of it again."

He caressed Esma's wet knee. She did not respond.

"For a moment—God, it seemed like an eternity—there in the chamber, he was open to me," she said. "Wide open. Like an animal splayed upon a dissecting table. I understood him. Not so I could explain it. It terrified me. Like seeing yourself as others might see you. Somehow I was part of him. And he of me. I saw the monster in all of us. It was like watching an autopsy of yourself." She sank lower in the water, propping her feet on the spigots. "I am talking nonsense."

"You tore out his heart. Then you ate it like a cannibal. It is the union of the killer and the victim."

She peered at him, her hair floating out on the water like long dark seaweed. Like all simple explanations, thought Zeljko, it was catchy and too simple to be entire. She might not have heard; her ears were under water.

"And what does he think now?" she said. "Can he think? Can he feel? Can he suffer as he ought to suffer for the people he killed? Can he remember?"

"No one can know that."

"He stares at the wall, the truth of his life locked in his brain or erased. Either way lost forever. We will never know who he is, who he was. We see fragments, others share their fragments, and we try to make sense. What composes a man? Any man? My father used to say, 'First your parents betray you, then your lovers betray you, then your own body betrays you. This is man's lot.' "

"I would never betray you."

"One man suffers and is serene; another hates. At the center of him is there a tiny piece of something we could identify as Evil? And if so, do we each have it?"

"Is there any adequate explanation for evil? You and I have never massacred a village, have we?"

She said nothing.

"You are becoming a reactionary capitalist theologian," he joked.

She thought for some time then lifted her head out of the water. He turned to reach for a towel but she took his arm. "I think you need a bath," she said. "There is room." She coyly hooked her index finger under the button of Zeljko's shirt and pulled his face to hers. For the moment, she was in charge again. Joy cracked like an egg in him and oozed through his body. He yielded and they threw off time. There was no past, no future, no memory, no longing, no sorrows or regrets, no wishes or hopes. Only the present. Only the ecstasy of life, the infant's cry against the nothingness of being.

Florence Quinn, née Floritza Hurban, the Tourist

◆

(Venice to Belgrade, May 20–26, 1978)

After St. Mark's they returned to the station. Florence was counting lira when Brewster lowered his head and winked over the top of his bifocals at his wife Joan. "Hey, Flo," he said, "Where's your boyfriend?"

"You just stop that," she said, but Brewster laughed that har-har-haar of his so loud it echoed off the marble walls. He was getting on her nerves and she looked away. Another train had just arrived and women of several ages rushed up to kiss a beefy man carrying two heavy valises.

"Why, Flo, I do believe you're looking for him," Joan said. Brewster har-har-haared again, and some Italians smiled at them.

"Act your age," she said, pursing her lips and using a shake of her silver hair for emphasis. The accent of her native language still came through in her r's and vowels. "I'm thirsty. I want a Coca-Cola." She held out the lira toward Brewster. "Is that enough, do you think?"

He started figuring. "Let me see. Five hundred. Seven hundred. Eight and some. . . . And there's seventeen hundred to the buck . . ."

"No," said Joan. "It's—"

"Never mind," Florence said. "I have traveller's checks."

She tried not to be irritated when Brewster intoned his usual warning.

"Well, you don't want to change much, Flo. It won't be worth a hoot day after tomorrow. Liras, I mean."

Joan made her usual comment about money. "So she buys herself something extravagant tomorrow. She's got a right. She can't take it with her."

Fine, thought Florence. Remind me I've got more years behind me than before. That's a good reason to waste money. I should have stayed in Ohio.

She pointed towards the platform and said there must be something to drink out there. Vendors always sold refreshments through the windows of the trains. Brewster said he'd wait in the lobby. Joan got short with him. It wasn't even two and André had said to meet him at three, but Brewster simply responded, "You can't be too safe. You don't want to get lost over here, do you?"

Florence's accent was stronger when she was impatient. "And what a catastrophe that would be! You'd think we were in the Congo! Why didn't we just stay home? Come on, Joan, let's go back out by the canal."

Brewster made a sour face and looked at Joan through the bottom of his bifocals. "You go on then. Get lost. See if I care." He lifted off his porkpie hat and wiped the inside of the brim with his handkerchief. "Flo was born here. I wasn't."

"I was not born here," she said firmly. "This is a different country."

The force of her words had intimidated him. His mouth twitched and he tried to divert the anger. "Maybe Flo's boyfriend whatzizname will be down there. He can help you get back home. I'll wait here."

Joan grabbed her arm. "Come on," she said. "We might as well have *some* adventure before we turn into old dinosaurs like Brewster."

Brewster plopped his hat back on his head and stuck out his jaw. He was like most Americans abroad, thought Florence; wondering why the money looked funny, why the food wasn't the same, why the people insisted upon acting like they did when all they really wanted to be was Americans. And yet, it was he and Joan who had badgered Florence to go along with them. Retired Americans always fantasized about travelling. Brewster and Joan had already wasted money on a battleship-sized Winnebago and a Carribbean cruise and probably spent most of those trips wishing they were back home, but not admitting it. Florence had wished she were back in Ohio from the moment they crossed the Pennsylvania border heading for the airport. Being born in Europe was not the same thing as its being home.

Joan and she went arm in arm down the stairs in front of the station, one step at a time. Joan said Brewster acted more like his father every day, and that he was getting tighter, too. Like he needed to stretch out his money for the next fifty years. "My stars," she said, "he irritates me sometimes!"

Something about it made Florence laugh. "That's just his way."

"You don't know what it's like. Timmy was always a card. Wouldn't it just be the end of the world to get stuck here!" She swept her hand toward one of the gondolas sailing by.

Timothy, Florence thought, wasn't always that easy to put up with.

"Momma always used to say men are only fit to live with when they are working. I'm just too old to put up with his retirement." She was amused to be saying something so wicked.

Florence watched the water taxi gliding behind the roofed dock. "When you live alone, you get lonely," she said. "When you live with somebody, you can't stand them. Timothy was too much fun all the time. Sometimes you want peace, a place to hide."

Joan giggled. "You can't live with 'em and you can't shoot 'em!" She noticed how loud she had said it and covered her mouth. A round-faced man with gray at the temples smiled at her, and Florence felt her stomach tighten as she momentarily thought she knew him. From long ago. He was back to bargain with her again. She squeezed Joan's arm. Her eyes widened. She shouldn't have come—*he was hunting her*. But he drew on his cigarette and called out to someone coming out of the station. A young vendor came up selling pamphlets, giving her time to recover. His English was poor and Joan smiled much too largely and shouted, "No thank you! No thank you!" as if he were deaf. He spun and attacked the crowd coming off the taxi.

"You know, I think Brewster's jealous," said Joan.

"Jealous?" Florence thought she meant of André, who had a flirty way with Joan and all the women, which Florence had always taken as part of his job as a guide.

"Yes," she said. "Brewster is jealous of you."

Florence stopped. "You are Timothy's sister! Brewster is my brother-in-law! You've had too much sun."

Joan patted her hand. "There is more to his kidding about your 'boyfriend' than kidding. Don't get upset. He's only wishing. It isn't like Brewster's a rooster anymore."

Florence chirped, "You *have* had too much sun! You'd never talk like this in Cadiz!" She wiped under her glasses with the end of the purple scarf she'd bought near the Doge's palace. She suddenly felt sorry for Brewster up there alone, making sure they didn't get abandoned to the cannibals of Venice, and said so, but Joan tugged her toward a café, saying that Brewster wouldn't be really happy unless he was left alone up there to worry. Florence tried to look in the booths selling miniature gondolas, postcards, and plaster lions of St. Mark, but Joan was virtually shoving her. "What a coincidence!" she said, much too chipper. "It's Mr. Renault!"

Florence sighed loudly. Since Timothy had died, everyone seemed to imagine she was pining away in her bungalow. They joked about "fixing her up" (as if she were broken!) with this widower or that, the principal who had always lived with his mother. Those awful evenings! She'd done most of them to keep Joan quiet, though she needed "dates" like a broken hip. It was so stupid to her to talk about a sixty-three-year old woman having "dates." She hadn't had anything like a "date" when she was growing up, and she certainly hadn't been tossed at a man in the way that André and Joan had shoved her at this man Renault every time there was an empty seat next to him. A widower from Baltimore, he probably didn't like it any more than she.

He reminded her of a white-haired Harry James. Thinner though, with very white hair, not a speck of gray. In the café he was smoking as usual, his fingers were as yellow from it as Timothy's had been, even in the coffin. His piercing eyes were fixed on an ornate building across the canal as if he were looking through it. The boat taxi pulled away and stirred the air. She smelled his Old Spice cologne.

"Why, Mr. Renault," said Joan, "my stars, what a coincidence! Florence was just coming down to have a Coke. Weren't you, Florence? Are you alone?"

He turned as if he were about to ask, "Who does it look like I'm with?" Instead, he extended his hand quickly and said, "Sit."

Florence couldn't think of anything to say. She fumbled with the chair, brushed off the seat, and sat, both hands on her purse. Her breasts felt enormous when she sat. They pressed the purse against the tablecloth and made her feel even more awkward.

Joan was still standing. "Here," she said, "you buy me a mineral water. With no bubbles. And ice. And I'll get Brewster." She put coins on the table. Renault shoved them back at her.

"No," he said. "My pleasure. No."

Joan wouldn't take them. "I'll get Brewster. He's alone up there. You two can chat." She scurried away. Florence wanted to order her to stay, but didn't.

Renault put the money in front of her and told her to give it to Joan later. She nodded but did not look at him. She had a feeling like a hot flash, though it wasn't quite the same. Joan wasn't coming back and he knew it. She'd only ordered mineral water because she knew it was so cheap. I'll just die of embarrassment, Florence thought. The silence was getting lengthy, though, so she held up a five hundred lira coin with its silvery ring around a brass center. "Isn't this pretty?" she said. "I'll have to remember to keep one of these. You'd think we could have different colored coins like this."

"Yes," said Renault. He looked at her with no expression. She lowered her eyes again. She *was* going to die. The waiter rescued her momentarily. Renault ordered in Italian, then he touched her arm. "Would you like something to eat? A snack? You do want ice in your Coke?"

"Yes. No—that is, no thank you to the food." This was ridiculous. She said nothing for a while after the waiter left.

Renault watched the canal. She asked him if he spoke Italian, which was stupid because she'd just heard him.

"Enough," he said. "It was handy to me, once."

"You have been in Italy before?"

He scrutinized her, lit another cigarette and said, "Many years ago."

"My husband was here during the war. Maybe you knew him? Timothy Quinn. He repaired tanks, he said."

He grinned. "There were many people in Italy then."

She flushed again. In another life, she had almost lived there. The fat Italian lieutenant had wanted to ship her to his home in Brindisi, or so he'd said. She shivered. This was what she had feared about Europe. It was all still here in the cracks of the cobblestones, the smell of the soil. In America you could forget, pretend it never happened. You were reborn when you touched the soil and the past was reduced to a vague nightmare.

Renault said his wife had died five years ago. She said she was sorry, but his voice grew almost rude. "We didn't get along. My son can't stand me. I thought marriage might soothe my old age. What was another broken promise?"

She didn't quite understand the final remark, but didn't ask for an explanation. "Timothy and I had got along very well. He should have been more careful with his diet and given up smoking. You ought to give it up, too." Why was she saying these stupid things?

But Renault laughed. "I am seventy. What pleasure is there for me but tobacco?"

She sipped her Coke and said it had been good to live near Brewster and Joan. "It's hard for a woman alone," she added, then stopped short, trying to think if that had sounded like a suggestion and hoping it hadn't. "They were there for me when I needed them. Joan is a whirlwind. I think Brewster's enjoying this, but he wouldn't've done it if Joan hadn't worked on him. He still doesn't like the idea of going behind the Iron Curtain."

There was a sudden fire in Renault's eyes. He leaned forward. "It will make him weep with happiness that he was born in America." He snapped the tabletop with his fingertips to punctuate the end of his remark.

The sharpness scared her. Not the words, she had said

them many times herself, but the feeling. Renault turned and watched the canal.

"The pictures in the brochure were very nice," she said.

"Of course they were. Advertisements."

"Well, then Joan will never get Brewster out of Cadiz again! He thinks there's ptomaine in every dinner and terrorists in every airport!" She had a laughing fit. "No, if it's terrible, he'll enjoy himself. I can picture him saying, 'I told you so, Joan. I told you so!' Maybe that's why he finally bought the tickets." She wiped her glasses where the tears had pooled and said she was sorry. "It struck me as funny. 'Brewster the rooster.'"

Suddenly, there was a slight twinkle in his eyes, the first friendliness she had seen in him. "Don't get me wrong," she said, "I love Brewster dearly, but—"

"I think maybe the waiter gave you pretty strong Coca-Cola!" He then looked past her and said he thought he'd seen André waving that damned yellow paddle. Renault paid, insisted on it, then took her by the elbow. André was shouting "Byzantine Odyssey tour! Here! Gather here! Byzantine Odyssey!" Halfway up the stairs Brewster and Joan were watching. Joan wickedly pursed her lips in her silly "caught ya!" look; Brewster stared and blew his nose with an enormous handkerchief. Florence gently pulled her elbow from Renault's grasp.

Her sleep had been troubled. She had not thought until yesterday that the tour would stir her ghosts. Perhaps it was the fear of what she would feel in returning to Trieste. Or was it memory at all? The Trieste of 1945 was a tense city about to explode. Uniformed British, American, and Yugoslav troops passed each other warily. The quiet streets had seemed nothing like that as the bus brought them to their hotel. She hadn't recognized a single building. But she had turned in her bed, her arms and legs strange creatures that knew no comfortable place to rest. She thought of Mark Renault's hand on her elbow, the dark of his eyes. It was as if she had known him but couldn't place him. She had tried to convince herself it was the change in food, but that had not helped her sleep.

She went down early for continental breakfast and lingered over *caffelatte* until the third cup began to upset her stomach. On the agenda was the Piazza dell'Unita d'Italia, the Cathedral of San Giusto and the Miramar Castle where the insane Charlotte had pined for her Maximilian. She watched the door of the dining room and realized that she was hoping Renault would come down early and the two of them could get away before Brewster and Joan came down. Renault had wandered off on his own in Rome, Florence, and Ravenna and she hoped he might ask her along. Why did Brewster and Joan seem so out of place? Brewster had spent his life being careful. He shuddered whenever he saw anyone taking a chance. He wrote a letter to the editor once about what a waste of money it had been to go to the moon. Timothy had argued with him about it. For no particular reason Florence sided with Brewster. She was embarrassed at the memory and lowered her eyes toward the rich coffee.

Brewster was Cadiz, Ohio, the hiding place, the town where she had fled with Timothy Quinn to deny there was a past. Every morning in every hotel Brewster had asked for "American coffee" and, of course, afterwards told the waiter exactly how unAmerican the coffee was, whether the poor man could understand English or not. She had a vision of Brewster in the Miramar Castle talking about why the Japanese were so successful and Joan shaking her head about some "lovely antique" which she imagined was just like something or other her grandmother had once owned. What was the point of being in Italy? Why go all the way to Trieste to say the things that were so comfortable in Cadiz, so meaningless here? Florence's heart beat rapidly as she thought she heard them coming down the stairs. She fumbled out a tip and left a note at the desk for André. She would meet them at the station.

An hour later she found herself at the beach. She pulled off her shoes and took off her sun hat. She walked for a long time, then bought a lemon ice, sat on a concrete wall, and watched the sea roll in, feeling the Adriatic run fingers of breeze through her hair. She thought of Renault, somewhere up in the city, perhaps visiting someone he knew during the war. Perhaps they had Trieste in common. Perhaps that was why he disturbed her. Maybe he had been a prisoner at the internment camp whom she had only seen once or twice. She remembered walking through the gate so like the gates of the concentration camps, thinking perhaps the British and the

Americans were going to do what the Germans had done, not just force them back into their native countries.

She closed her eyes tightly, as if to squeeze the memory back into the darkness in the back of her mind, and lifted her feet from the concrete wall. The sea breeze slithered up the legs of her polyester slacks and she had a desire to strip off her blouse and dive bare-chested into the waves. Imagine trying to swim without getting tangled in these floppy old things! she thought. The people would think I had water wings!

An old man in a beret nodded at her laughter as he plodded past. He would have been here in 1945. Her laughter stopped in mid-breath and she closed her eyes again.

Later, on the train platform, she could feel her skin glowing. Joan kept offering her Noxzema (they had packed *everything*) and Florence kept turning it down. She wanted to sport that burn, the way women on the beach move their shoulders to jiggle their breasts "accidentally" and say *I am young; I am alive.*

Joan and Brewster had ruined their day, they said, fretting about her. Brewster had wanted to call the police. An argument between André and the Yugoslav conductor interrupted them. After a little of this, Brewster was getting bumptious and Joan was complaining about her varicose veins. Someone said, "The conductor says there are not enough First Class seats." It was Renault. He had materialized at Florence's side as if out of air. "The man says he can't help it."

Brewster said that if they made him ride with the chickens, he'd demand every cent of his money back. Florence thought "Brewster the Rooster" and laughed. Brewster looked at her quizzically, so she quickly asked Renault how his day was. He shrugged. "So much has changed."

She had a yearning to tell him about the beach and how she had felt there, but knew she couldn't explain it. He started to push his way to the front. He seemed excited, impatient, but not irritated.

Brewster pointed with his chin down the platform at a short, fat woman wearing a black scarf on her head and carrying two overloaded sacks. "If they think I'm riding with the bag ladies, they've got another thought coming."

"She isn't a bag lady, Brewster," Florence said nastily.

"She's a peasant." The woman had reminded her of someone on her street when she was a child.

"I don't like the looks of this train, no way, no how," he shot back.

"We won't be on it long," said Joan, trying to calm him.

When André waved his yellow paddle and asked for six volunteers to ride in Second Class, along with Mr. Renault who had already offered, Brewster began to argue. Florence raised her hand and Brewster took off his porkpie hat in disgust, thinking she'd volunteered the three of them.

The second class coach smelled of cigarettes and the linoleum floor was sticky. The first compartment was filled with olive-skinned people. The second had two of the volunteer couples, who were trying to speak to an old couple who had no English. Florence nearly fell over a pasteboard box someone had placed in the corridor, then saw that only Renault was in the third compartment. He was smoking a cigarette and peering out the window as if he had been there for days.

"Are these seats taken? she asked.

"There is no reserved in second class."

"Perhaps we will have the compartment to ourselves," she said, then avoided his eyes because of the way it sounded and quickly took the seat opposite. There were drab green curtains and screws were missing around the ventilator. The seats needed cleaning. "This isn't so bad."

The iciness of Renault's eyes flustered her. "Yes," he said. "But you can see the difference instantly." He circled his hand. "No Italian train is this degraded. The worker's paradise!" He made a noise as if he tasted something bad in his mouth. "We'll be going into the past now," he said. "You'll see. Tito's paradise!" He made that noise again.

She turned toward the corridor almost as a reflex, as if someone might be listening. She had felt that way ever since they had landed in Rome. A young face was peering in. The boy was in his late teens or early twenties and carried a paper bag. He said something in Serbo-Croatian and gestured at the empty seats. "Do you speak English?" she asked, but Renault spoke in Italian and waved him in.

A couple bustled in, each carrying a purple plastic bag. The girl was blonde, round-faced, and a little overweight. The

[48]

boy had dark curly hair and a hawk nose. They chattered to each other and moved various items from one bag to another. The girl repeatedly adjusted the collar of her shirt, which was buttoned to her neck. The boy dug out a bottle of orange soda and a paper bag with packages of cookies and chocolate sticking out. They then placed the plastic bags in the overhead racks and settled in opposite each other, lighting cigarettes.

The girl asked Florence a question. The Slavic sound of the language was like something in a dream. It was like Slovak, the language of her childhood, but not like it. Florence stammered.

"She wants to know if you speak German," said Renault quietly.

"Oh, no." She shook her head at the girl. "I—no. No German." She would not allow herself to remember how much of that language she had learned long ago.

The girl glanced at her boyfriend. Something had struck her as funny, Florence thought.

"I suspect," said Renault, "they would prefer to be alone. If there were an empty compartment they would have taken it. Perhaps they would have made love on the seats."

"Anyone could come down the corridor," she said, and Renault indifferently said it happened all the time. She thought how she had nearly been alone with him and blushed despite herself. The couple's talking swirled around her and she felt a momentary dizziness. The sun, the lack of sleep, the awareness that some of the words were nearly identical to Slovak. She shouldn't have come to Europe. She had only agreed because they would not be passing through Czechoslovakia, nowhere near Bratislava. She had thought that Trieste would not be too hard to get through for one day, but it had shaken her more than she had at first recognized.

Now she felt like a dog paddling in an ocean of Slavic sounds. Nothing seemed to keep her afloat. She should have stayed with Brewster and Joan. In Cadiz. With only English speakers. She had always wondered why they always told the same stories to each other. As if everything interesting had happened already and there was nothing new to say. Since Timothy died Joan or Brewster would start on another "Do you remember when . . . ?" and Florence would rise to go home.

The comfort of English words repeating trivial stories had seemed asphyxiating. She hadn't wanted to spend the last decade of her life in that monotony and she knew she had encouraged Joan into the trip simply because she wanted something, anything, new to talk about. Now fears she had buried for years were crashing against her. She stared out the window at the adjacent railway cars and tracks without speaking for a good while.

The Italian border patrol checked the cars rather superficially, then moved on. The girl and boy chattered and laughed. Renault was silent, his eyes narrow as if he were watching for something. The train slowed to a stop at another station. "We are in Slovenia," said Renault. "One of the six republics of mighty Yugoslavia." She did not understand his tone and wasn't ready to speak again. Men in uniforms inspected visas. Renault held up his passport with a twinkle in his eye and did not answer the man when he asked a question. The man studied him and his passport photo, then handed it back without expression. Shortly the train moved on into the closing dark, and stopped again. She saw a sheet metal building, a rail switch, and a man looking under the cars.

The girl fidgeted with her collar again and whispered to her boyfriend. The smoke in the compartment was dense as fog with Renault and the two Serbs drawing on their cigarettes until they glowed like flares. Florence noticed the girl's sweaty odor. The compartment was closing in. She tried to open the windows. The joints in her fingers burned as she grew exasperated with the latches. The boy stood, reached over Renault, and slid it open. She noticed how the uniformed man on the gravel outside had watched them. Her fingers were dirty from handling the window. On the window frame was a black film that had been accumulating for years.

She distracted herself by scanning the tour booklet. She could have gone to France and Holland, but Brewster had resisted until June, when all the places were taken, so they had snatched up three cancellations on the "Byzantine Odyssey": Rome, Florence, Ravenna, Venice, Ljubljana, Belgrade, Budapest, Bucharest, Istanbul. Brewster didn't really approve but Joan got excited about the possibility of a side trip to Medjugorje, where she said the Virgin Mary was talking to some teenagers.

"What are we waiting for?" Florence asked abruptly.

"Customs," Renault said. "They like to get you out in the country for this." He winked. "No witnesses."

His wink made her feel a little more in control. "We'll be late."

He shrugged. "These people have no sense of time."

The girl and the boy were meantime leaning toward the compartment door and listening.

Renault gestured toward them with his head. "They are smuggling."

"Excuse me?" she said.

"Smuggling."

It took a moment to sink in. Barbed wire. Work camps. "No! Not drugs! We should move out of here."

He touched her hand. "Relax. It's not drugs. I don't think so. Anyway it has nothing to do with us."

She glanced up at their shopping bags. She had read of Americans getting thrown into foreign jails, even though they were innocent. The passport meant nothing. What should she do? Brewster would turn them in. He would stick out his jaw and let everyone know. But Renault's calmness made her hesitate until a bullish man in a brown uniform appeared in the doorway. He was holding a pad that looked like a state trooper's ticket book. He said something she took for a greeting, and she was surprised when not only the boy and girl answered him, but also Renault. The man studied Renault for a second or two, as if he suspected him. Renault stared back without blinking, as if challenging him, but the man spun quickly on the boy, firing a sharp question.

The boy was intimidated. There was no question of that. He was trying to appear calm, but his voice quavered. The man riveted his eyes on him, said something else, and the boy listed a number of things, counting on his fingers. The man pointed at the bag in the luggage rack. The boy said something else. The man stared at him harshly, then poked his thick hand into the plastic bag with the cookies. He pulled out a chocolate bar. The boy explained. The man threw the chocolate into the boy's lap and wrote on his pad. He tore off the slip, grunted, and flicked it at the boy. The ticket fluttered to the floor.

The boy's mouth opened as if he were astonished, but the man's stare was so hard, the boy only glanced at his girlfriend and wiggled his fingers into his blue jeans. He pulled out a wad of colorful money and began counting. He didn't have enough. After a few exchanges, the man thrust the money into his jacket pocket and turned on the girl. He similarly questioned and intimidated her by taking calculated looks at her shopping bag and ultimately assessed her a large fee, which she paid with a wry smile. Both the boy and the girl slumped into their seats, utterly drained.

The man now shot a question at Florence and an uncontrollable quiver started in her thighs. When had this happened before? The man in a uniform looming in the door. The cold superiority of his German. The Death's Heads on his black collar. She felt like she was going to wet herself and when she gaped trying to find feeling in her lips and tongue, Renault interrupted. He was utterly calm, giving the customs man stare for stare. "You have nothing to declare, do you?" he asked her, patting her knee. "And your luggage is in the baggage car. This is what I told him."

She nodded toward the guard, yes, yes.

The guard exchanged more words with Renault, who loudly said *Amerikanka*, twice. The man checked her passport, then fired questions at Renault, who smoked calmly and answered with almost a sneer. Her words tumbled out: "Do I have to pay him? I will pay him what he wants. Will he take lira?" Money wouldn't work, she thought. They take what they want: money, jewelry, porcelain, people.

Renault did not take his eyes from the man, but brushed off her question with a flick of his wrist. The guard scowled, tossed back their passports, and thumped out of the compartment. Renault was smiling. "He was hinting he might search our valises. He could keep us here for hours, you know, but he was just doing it to show he also picks on tourists. It was for them." He cocked his head toward the boy and girl. "They need our hard currency too much to give us much trouble. Their economy is a catastrophe." He expelled a short puff of air as if disgusted. "He was Slovene. He thought he was tough. I pissed him off because I said 'good evening' in the Serbian way. These two were very careful to say it in the Slovenian way, but he took it out on them anyway."

Florence's mouth was dry. Her heart was thumping and she touched the beads of cold chill on her upper lip. The young couple leaned into the corridor, then back. The girl began to laugh. The boy shushed her. He leaned toward Renault and asked him a qustion. "*Da*," said Renault. The boy slapped his head and leaned back.

"They did not know I could understand them," explained Renault. "Earlier he was teasing her about her bust."

The boy was red-faced, peeking between the fingers of his hand. The train jerked. They were moving. The girl crushed her cigarette on the floor, stood, unbuttoned her blouse, and began to pull the tee-shirt under it over her head. Florence, eyes wide, thought the girl was going to show her breasts or something, but there was a black shirt under the overshirt, then a blue under that and pink under that. In all there were five over the final shirt, which was khaki-colored and decorated with the emblem of the U.S. Marines. The boy unbuckled his belt and peeled off two pairs of jeans. They were smuggling clothes. Renault explained they could sell them for a big profit in Yugoslavia.

The train was now up to speed and rocking roughly. The boy twisted the top off his big bottle of orange soda, took a long swallow and passed it to the girl. The girl sipped and offered the bottle to Florence. She said, "No thank you," at first, but the girl poked and offered again.

She thought of germs and how she wasn't supposed to have sugary drinks, but she felt too limp with relief to resist. The train was moving again, as it had thirty years before, and she was free. She took the soda in both hands raised it in a gesture that she recognized as the way her father had lifted gifts to say thank you. She tipped back the bottle and swallowed three big gulps that nearly choked her as the bubbles rose in her nose. The girl smiled. With the slightest trace of amusement on his thin lips Renault said, "You were thirsty." The boy tore open his package of cookies and they all shared them silently. Renault nibbled and peered serenely out into the dark.

They were all sharing a communion, Florence thought.

The mystical fusion of those who, for reasons known only to God, have escaped. The boy and the girl couldn't have understood this—they would have felt they were lucky—but their quietness indicated they sensed it. And Renault? He had a wry acceptance on his face. Why does one boy go to jail and another get away? Why does one family die before a firing squad and another elude it? If you lived long enough, if you were one of the survivors, you knew there was never an answer to questions like these and it bound you to anyone who knew it, too. Renault knew. He and Florence were like twins who know each other's pain while miles apart. They had a connection stronger than love, and it terrified her.

Florence was still tired from the train's late arrival in Ljubljana as she climbed into the tour bus in front of the Hotel Kompas. A nice girl with black hair and a gap in her front teeth greeted them pleasantly. Breakfast, at which Brewster had complained about the loud talkers in front of the police station outside his and Joan's window, rested even heavier in Florence's stomach when the bus began to rumble forward without Mark Renault. In a strong accent, the girl gave a quick history of the city and began describing the Austrian Succession style of the older buildings. Florence pretended to be listening so that Joan wouldn't cross the aisle and take the empty seat next to her, but she often turned to the glass and closed her eyes, dozing.

The tour was a blur. They rode past the National Museum, the Modern Gallery, and the Opera. There was a performance that night and several tickets might be available. Joan tried to talk Brewster into going, but he said he didn't see why he should waste money to see "some cow in a helmet screaming." They went on past the Tomb of the National Heroes and the Parliament. After they had climbed back into the bus, they were driven to the town center where a large square was dedicated to the poet Presheren, who the girl happily said had called Slovenia "a little piece of heaven."

Some of the tourists went to look at the Franciscan Church, but Florence found a bench and watched the cars and people on each side of the river by the square. Where had Renault gone? Why? Why did she care? She was too old to have a crush, surely. She told herself she was merely concerned that something might happen to him wandering alone, but she envied his independence, also. A piece of a tune came to her. It was from a movie Timothy had taken her to when she docked in New York. Nelson Eddy was wandering through the Alps. He had a big walking stick and a rucksack. He sang a sort of duet with an echo, something about the free life for me, but he ended up marrying the princess anyway.

The group moved on to the university, peered inside the National Library, then crossed the river at the Bridge of the Shoemakers into the oldest part of town. They strolled through the cobblestone streets toward the town hall, but Florence fell behind. The narrowness of the streets, the old portraits in a photographer's window, the antique clocks on display began to look familiar. When the group suddenly turned a corner and got away, she had the sensation of being lost in time. She had climbed out of the hiding hole again and the Nazis had taken everyone away. A bicycle broke the illusion as it lurched out of an alley. She scurried to catch up. The girl was explaining that there was a map of the city carved in stone inside the town hall.

Brewster suddenly pointed at the red flags on the building. "What's it like to be under Russia's thumb?"

The girl was confused. "He's asking about the Soviet flags," said someone. Now the girl was offended, rather than perplexed, but she politely explained that the flags were Communist party flags, not Soviet flags, that Yugoslavia was a non-aligned nation. Maybe this was all Communist lying, but Florence didn't know. Can you say lies for years and not make them turn real? If a woman pretends to love her husband for thirty years, does it matter that maybe she didn't? If she acted like she loved him, even if only to take refuge in his kindness, she would be a better wife than most.

"Looks awful like the Russian flag to me!" said Brewster.

Florence spun on her heels and walked quickly out of sight of the hall. Why had Brewster come here? He knew nothing about it and didn't really want to know about it. He would never understand what she had been through, what thousands, millions, had been through. You didn't get that from riding around in a big-windowed bus. You didn't get that from sitting in the belly of a B-17 for however many missions and then coming home to an America that had not been disembowelled. She had never spoken of it, never tried to explain. What was the point? All the flags on Ljubljana's town hall reminded her of when the German military officer had called them into the square in Bratislava and read them their orders from the balcony. Afterwards, she had hidden as her father had instructed, and she was now ashamed of it. She was ashamed that she had taken the young Timothy Quinn's proposal, left her bloody land, and had tried so adamantly to forget. And worst of all was the shame that she, unlike the rest, had not died.

She walked with her head down, quickly, indifferent to where she was going. She didn't care if she ever saw them again. She passed through a farmer's market by the river. Vendors called to her, waving vegetables. Faces floated by. She walked more quickly, bumped into a man with a cane who had suddenly stopped, then made for the street leaving the square. She collided with another man.

"Ah!" he said, grabbing her shoulders, "you are charging like a rhinoceros."

She looked up at Mark Renault and pulled away.

"I am sorry," he said. "I did not see you. It was my fault."

"No," she said, "no. I—I was confused. The narrow streets. I think we are supposed to go to the castle."

"That is the way, but if memory serves, it is a very steep climb."

"Thank you," she said.

"Good day," he said.

The words tumbled out as he turned. "Would you show me?"

"I was going to the cathedral," he said. "That way."

"Oh." They hesitated for several seconds, eyes locked as if trying to understand something.

"It should be very pretty," he said. "If they didn't loot it."

Without a word, she nodded and walked up beside him. They walked for several yards before she finally said, "They took us to the National Library. It was very strange on the outside, like it was made of leftover bricks and stones. Inside was like a tomb."

"Yes," he said, "all that black stone."

"You've been there?"

"It almost didn't survive the war. A German plane crashed on the roof."

She didn't remember the guide saying anything about a plane, but then, she had been in this strange, distracted mood all day. She forced herself to make conversation. "The tour girl said that their poet called Slovenia a little piece of heaven."

"They repeat that hooey all the time," said Renault. "If heaven is this nice, how bad could hell be?"

"You don't think it is pretty?"

"It is no different than it ever was, except where they've slapped up those wonderful concrete apartments that are the pride of Communism. I spent the day going all over, looking for something. A dagger—one that had been through the rebellion against the Turk and the Balkan Wars and had to be sold to pay for an escape."

"You are a collector?"

"No. The dagger has no historical value, except to me."

"Have you seen the cathedral before?"

"Not as a tourist. I am not much for churches." He sucked his cigarette down further than anyone she had ever seen. "You are much too inquisitive, dear, and I have told you too much."

"I'm sorry," she said. "I mean no harm."

He shrugged and nothing else was said as they walked. He seemed to have settled into a mood as dark as hers.

But when the cathedral appeared in front of them, Renault rushed forward, then just as oddly stopped in the middle of the street. His face showed no emotion. He flicked the tiny stub of his cigarette away without taking his eyes off the building. His head moved slowly as if he were sweeping every inch of the facade, as if he were trying to memorize it. He did not move even when a loud motor scooter passed him.

She tried to see what he was interested in. The cathedral didn't strike her as being very distinguished, but she, too, was caught up in staring at it. Some baroque features of the Town Hall in Bratislava came back to her, flourishes on the cornices that she had stared at as a child. She quickly joined Renault in the middle of the street, but did not interrupt him.

"The door," he said to himself. "The exit."

She turned. There seemed nothing special about it. Heavy. Dark. "Yes?"

"Come," he said. He took her by the arm and in his excitement nearly dragged her. The door swung open easily, as if it had just been oiled. Their eyes adjusted to the dimness, then all the gilded carving seemed to issue light from inside each scallop shell, florette, and wreath. An old woman in a booth by the door nodded between her racks of postcards. She seemed as if she had been there since the church was built.

Florence was dizzied by tilting her head to peer up at the paintings in the high vaults, but Renault had already gone up the aisle. The altar recess was flanked by two statues with miters and a dozen cupids carrying a garland flew on the wall at the rear. Florence crossed herself, but Renault stood in the central aisle drinking it all in, leaning back, losing himself in the complexity of the gigantic chandelier. When he broke off his rapture and twisted his torso to her, his smile frightened her. His eyes glowed like red-hot iron. "It is the same," he said. "The same!" His voice echoed and the woman in the booth leaned forward angrily.

Florence awkwardly moved forward, turning completely around to see the organ pipes dripping with baroque ornament—gilded angels and cupids and curlicues. To her left was a small chapel. The pulpit was carved in dark wood and decorated with gold scallops. It was the crucifix, however, that caught her attention. It gave her a feeling of déjà vu, though she knew she had never been in Ljubljana, even in her escape during the war. Christ's body was the color of wet driftwood, though his loincloth was gold, like the wreath behind him and the pair of cupids above his arms. There were gold disks behind his head, his hands, and his feet. The oddest thing about it, however, was that the arm bar was raised at the ends, forming a "Y" rather than the conventional Latin "T."

She hardly noticed Renault had returned to her side. He moved forward, lowered himself to his knees and crossed himself in a slow, tentative way, his hand rising high off his chest between touches. He then made a noise which sounded like a chuckle, though she was sure it couldn't be. He clasped his hands in front of him, touched them to his head, and made the noise again. He feverishly rose, turned his back on the crucifix, and moved to her.

"What do you think, eh? What do you think? Am I a good Roman Catholic?"

"The Christ is so bony," she said. "You can really see the suffering. He looks—" she said carefully "—like a concentration camp survivor."

Renault's animated expression instantly hardened. His eyes were sharp, as if she'd insulted him, but his expression quickly softened.

The strangeness of his half smile drew her out of herself. "You have been here before?"

"The door," he said. "You always meet old friends—," he gestured at the Christ, "—at the door."

She blinked.

"At times," he said, "Ljubljana was so surrounded by barbed wire it was almost a prison camp, but we had friends nevertheless. The Vatican express. If you could just remember how to cross, if you could just remember the Latin 'Hail Mary,' they helped you. The fools!" His eyes told her that he, like she, knew what it was to betray himself.

"I had help, too," she said numbly. "I lived." The words softly echoed and she started, as if it were blasphemous.

He cradled her cheeks in both hands and tilted her face up to him. For a moment she thought he was going to kiss her, gently. Giving, not taking. Like Sergeant Timothy Quinn had kissed her when no man except her father had ever kissed her that way. "Poor Florence," he said. "You are sad today."

"I—I am tired. I feel confused. I—"

He dropped his hands and pulled her with him. He stopped before the confessional booths. Enthralled, he reached out and ran his thin fingers along the side. "The curtain is different," he said. "Nothing else."

"I'm sorry," she said, "I don't know what is happening to me today."

"Go in," he said.

"What?"

"Go in." He gave her a gentle push. "It is good for the soul. This is the door out."

"Out of what?"

"Out of personal trouble. Out of Yugoslavia. Out of everywhere."

"But the priest isn't—"

"Is God deaf? Go in."

She resisted for a moment, but staring into his eyes sharp as glass, she was unable to formulate any words, as if she had forgotten all her English.

"Is God deaf?"

She went into the dark cabinet, hearing nothing, seeing nothing. She set her purse at her feet and crossed her arms, digging her fingers into her elbows. She saw faces in the curtain. Her monocled father humming a Gypsy melody to help her sleep. Her mother with a touch of flour under her nose. Her grandfather, his eyes half-closed as he corrected his students' grammar. Her brothers Anton and Josef. It had fallen upon the baby of the family to save them all. The only daughter. She had gone to the SS-Captain who had propositioned her and bought their lives with her body. He kept her like his pet spaniel and promised her she would see all of them soon. If they ever knew, they would have cursed her. Wherever they were, now, they did not speak her name. They had been killed on the afternoon she had gone to the captain. The only life she had bought was her own: the very life she had offered to sacrifice.

And then why had she gone on living? Once the captain had traded her to the fat Italian lieutenant, why hadn't she had the courage to kill herself? She had known then that all her family was dead. What gave her the right to live? What gave her the right to live by satisfying the same men who had exterminated her line? By Zyklon-B, or bullets, or starvation—she had never known—they had killed her parents and brothers. By the captain's gonorrhea they had destroyed any hope of children. Why had she lived? Why? She lifted her head from her sobbing and touched the screen to the priest's compartment. To live was a sin: the worst sin of all.

But you could lie to yourself. You could look into the gentle eyes of Sergeant Timothy Quinn and you could tell yourself that God had meant you to live. God had meant you to listen to Timothy's plea to marry him on the night before all the others in the internment camp in Trieste were repatriated. Buying time, he'd called it. It was against Army regulations, but neither his lieutenant nor the other men on guard duty were very careful at the camp. Doors were left unlocked when corporals went for a smoke. The interned, by treaty to be shipped back to their homelands and Stalin's firing squads, had a way of disappearing. Why not Floritza Hurban? You bought the time. You feigned love. You forgot. How could you think that leaving Cadiz, that coming back to Europe, would not make you remember that you should have died?

Her nose was plugged from crying. When she gasped for air, she smelled cigarette smoke. The little door was open to the priest's chamber. The priest said nothing. Would he smoke?

"Bless you, Florence."

She pressed her throbbing eyes. "Leave me alone. You shouldn't be in there."

"I wanted to see it from the other side. I like to know where the mirrors are hidden, what's up their sleeves. Why shouldn't I? Do you believe in God?"

She wiped her glasses and nodded. "Yes," she said.

"Then why is he such a bastard?"

"I was a fool to come on this trip."

"Yes?"

She didn't continue.

"I have found it very informative. All is as I have imagined it for years. Can you believe it? When you retire you sit around so much. You sit alone and you think maybe things have changed back here. You look in the mirror and you have changed. Cars have changed. Clothes have changed. Everything else has changed."

"Yes," she said. "I thought it would be . . ."

"But it festers. Oh, yes, you notice the concrete and steel buildings in the pamphlets, the smiling people with nice clothes—they are even selling shoes and such in the United States. You pick up something nice and it says "Made in Yugoslavia" and you think maybe everything is better there. Maybe this Communism is working. But then you see it. I thought I might have been wrong, but there is no doubt." He coughed. "I am going on to Belgrade for one day, then going home."

She blew her nose.

"People have cheap clothes. They patch their sneakers. They come out at dusk to sell tin jewelry and horrible, smelly hamburgers. The ice cream is so thin! The workers' paradise. South Slavic heaven. They are just peasants in cheap polyester. European prices with African wages. They get what they deserve. Pah!"

All of a sudden it sank in. "You are leaving the tour?"

"I've gotten all I want. Belgrade will be no better."

She looked around the dark chamber as if she might find what she was supposed to say. She suddenly put her hand on the screen. "Take me with you."

"With me? I can't do that."

"Then stay. You'll miss Budapest and Istanbul."

"They don't interest me, just further back in time."

She didn't know what he meant. A panic was growing in her. She felt like she was on a raft and the single spot of light was drifting further away. "Take me with you then."

"My dear," he said, "you cannot imagine how foolish it is to fall in love with me."

She tried to think. What was she saying? What was she doing? "It isn't love. I feel something about you, that is true. I don't know anything except that we share the pain. We could help each other. I don't know why, but I feel that."

"I can't fulfill any dreams," he said. "Old age clings to me like a bad smell." His voice dropped, as if he were quoting something. "Who is left who can wish anymore? I'm leaving. Alone."

She was too far gone. She leaned her forehead against the screen. "I will make love to you. I know how to please a man."

The answer was a long silence. "I'm sorry," he eventually sighed. "I'm past that. It isn't you—it just doesn't interest me." His voice took on a frightening whisper. "I am in danger here, Florence. If they knew I was here I would be dead in a few hours."

"What? I don't understand. Who?"

"They are so stupid, though. So incompetent. They couldn't handle me if I were delivered on a silver platter."

She leaned down and tried to see through the screen. Suddenly she knew that he wasn't fully in the present. He was like her, flashing between the present and past, going around corners and misplacing forty years. She remembered his reaction to what she had said about the Christ and she knew. He, too, had been one of the victims. They had kept him and tortured him and somehow he'd survived.

"You've come back to see your ghosts," she choked out.

There was a vague red light as he lit another cigarette. It burned her eyes.

"I was imagining a boy—well, not a boy really. He just seems like a boy, a boy in his thirties."

She held her breath, listening.

"For all the terrible things that had happened to him, he still seems like a boy because of what would happen. This boy is running, night after night. He has heard there is a door in Ljubljana, an exit out of hell, and he must get there before it closes. He doesn't allow himself to be seen. He goes from ruin to ruin in the fog, in the rain, and he steals food from anyone, anything. His only hope is to get to the priest in Ljubljana who can get him to those who will smuggle him to Argentina, Mexico, Canada, the United States. Anywhere across the ocean. Someplace safe from the barbarians. Maybe he even hopes he will be part of a new war against the barbarians. Who knows?

"But there is a sunny day in Croatia. He feels giddy. He walks openly in the sun and bumbles into three armed men. The boy remembers enough Italian, he has always been good at languages, so he pretends to be a deserter going home to his family in Turin, and pretends his Croatian is so poor he doesn't understand them. Amazingly they fall for it. The fighting is nearly over. They offer him boiled potatoes in a broth. The hunger overcomes his good sense. They gather around the little iron pot. The oldest man bows his head to say grace. He crosses himself. The boy crosses himself. It is automatic. But he does it the wrong way. He crosses to his right first instead of to his left. They know he is not a Catholic."

He was silent for a while. She could barely make out the profile of his chin. "He is captured?" she asked.

"No," he exhaled. "The boy had a Ruger. As they jumped for their rifles, he shot them. Two head shots—the boy was good at head shots. The third one in the chest. The boy put him out of his misery with his ancient knife. All for some potatoes. But the potatoes kept him alive until he could cross himself again in the proper Roman way and the good Franciscan father would be convinced he was merely another of the persecuted Romans. It was a little incident, a nothing in the scheme of things. A little lesson in deception. Three more quick deaths among millions. Nothing even in the boy's life, less important than when he had to sell his father's knife. But sometimes he will remember it, even dream of the taste of those potatoes."

"They say," she whispered, "that ghosts can't hurt anyone. The war seems like only yesterday to us but it was a long time ago. No one is after you."

He chuckled. "You don't believe that. If you believed ghosts can't hurt anyone, you might convince me to stay. But you know you are lying. I must leave before they accidentally find me. If they were searching for me, they'd never find me, but if they're not—who knows? I just want to leave this rubbish pile, go home, and die in my rowhouse in Baltimore. Perhaps I will take up a hobby. I will hammer nails." He laughed sharply, then his voice became deeply subdued. "The exit from hell just opens to another hell. You want to find happiness, find someone else who wants it. Find someone who loves life. I don't give a shit for it anymore."

She pressed her face against the screen and silently wept. She felt stupid, humiliated. How could she have offered herself like that? Like he was the German captain who could save her family? How could she have imagined that she might help him forget whatever tortures he had suffered forty years ago, when she could not forget her own? And yet, she could not help hoping that he would change his mind, that he would hold her like the gentle Sergeant Timothy Quinn and lie to her and tell her she was still beautiful, that all of Floritza Hurban had not been stolen by the war.

The curtain was swept back by a heavy hand. The old woman leaned her head to one side and asked a question. Florence wiped her eyes and picked up her purse. "Seex," said the woman. She held up fingers. "Seex. Later." Florence touched the talking screen. The little door was closed. She came out and checked the priest's chamber. It was empty.

"Where did Mr. Renault go?"

The old woman twisted her lip. She pointed at the priest's cabinet. "Seex." She held up her fingers again. *"Shest."*

She could not find Renault. She climbed the cobblestone street narrowing to the path to the castle. It was in the process of being restored. She saw some of the tour members in the bar off the main gate and made for the high tower to avoid them. Her tiredness made her dizzy on the third landing, but she clung to the rail and kept plodding until she came out into the daylight. She interrupted a young couple whispering and nuzzling. The red roof tiles angled off immediately below and ordinary modern apartment blocks were beyond. Somewhere down there Mark Renault was running from his past. A poor Jew imagining that the Nazis were still after him, imagining that the dead would never forgive him because he had betrayed them by learning to cross himself in order to survive. The sadness was in everything—the air, the stones, the sloppy kiss of the boy and girl.

She moved on to dinner at Machek ("The Black Cat") at the preappointed time. Brewster complained about a piece of gristle in his paprikosh and tried to get André to translate his griping for him. Later Brewster warned everyone against the traditional Slovenian cream cake—"stuff grows on whipped cream"—and insisted upon ice cream, which he then said was too thin. Renault never showed up.

She watched for him in Belgrade. The tourists went to Tito's House of Flowers, chattered happily over the McDonald's sign downtown, had a boat ride on the Sava and Danube rivers, and lunched at the Znak. Afterwards they strolled through the Cathedral of the Archangel Michael, an eerie, smoky church, with hundreds of candles in large tubs of sand. They went through the Serbian Orthodox museum across the street, then ambled into the Kalemegdan, a huge park on the point between the confluence of the rivers. There were ice cream vendors and the tomb of a sultan. There were men playing chess and village women selling doilies. Graffiti marred the ruined walls, the monuments, and the statues. But there was no Mark Renault.

When Brewster had left to go through the Military Museum, Joan and Florence wandered among the ruins of the old fortifications. Near the Deftedar's Gate, Florence glanced up and noticed the silhouette of a thin man smoking. She couldn't make out his face really, or even the color of his hair the sky was so bright behind him, but she knew it was Mark Renault. He was staring down and across, maybe at the tunnel they had just emerged from. Something about his shadow froze her. He was smoking and staring. "What is it?" asked Joan.

She looked toward Joan and back, but in the time of the movement, he had disappeared. She scurried forward but saw nothing. The poor man, she thought. How many victims were there still counting the days?

"Florence," said Joan, "what is it?"

Florence stood and listened to the distant sound of a boat's horn on the river. "Nothing," she said. "Maybe the crying of a ghost. Thousands have died here."

Joan took her arm kindly. "Are you all right, Flo? Is the food agreeing with you?"

"I think . . ." said Florence quietly, "I must go to Bratislava."

"Bratislava? Where your family was from?"

"Then I can go back to America," she said. "Only then."

Margarita, like the Drink

♦

(Guayaquil, November 17–18, 1968)

Dark droplets fell from the prisoner's arms as he swung gently on the leather straps that splayed him. The odors of mildew, blood, urine, ozone, and shit were so heavy that each came unmixed to the nose, swirled by, then was replaced by another. With one hand Mark Renault tilted the light dangling from its cord and studied his map. His white hair seemed to phosphoresce near the bulb. Tinto, his bodyguard, leaned over his shoulder. "Iquitos to Ambato," said Renault. "It's a long trail."

"There is nothing out there," said Major Echeverria stepping into the light. Echeverria and the dangling man could be brothers: both gaunt, both hawk-nosed from some common Incan ancestor. "It is more logical that they would bring weapons along the coast."

The prisoner lifted his head and blinked, his eyes the only points of light in the dark corner. He is afraid we don't believe him, thought Renault. Good. "It is daring," he whispered. "It is exactly what they would to. They think destiny is on their side. They do it and think of Mao's Long March. He isn't lying; you have broken him. At the very least he believes what he is telling us."

"That does not mean it is true."

"We shall pass it along, Major, and let the company decide that. But I know when a man is broken. You have learned well. You don't need me anymore. Soon I will move on to another

[67]

country. They will not let me retire until I have taught my art in every country in Latin America."

"The travelling professor," the major said grinning. "Why would you wish to retire? You have absolute power in these chambers. To inspire fear is better than to receive love."

"Quotations?" Renault gestured at the stained concrete walls. "What about 'better to rule in hell'? You were born to this, Emilio. You will be a grandmaster."

Echeverria seemed to take the words as a compliment, but Renault's tone was tainted with exhaustion. "It is better than fucking," Echeverria said. Amused, he glanced at Tinto.

"And like fucking," said Renault, "at first it is terrifying. Soon it is pleasure, and gradually a need."

"A need?"

"Finally, however, you do it only because it is what you have always done."

The major's smile was wry. "As you say."

"If you live long enough, it will happen, major. But perhaps you will be lucky and die young."

The major licked his mustache. Inducing fear was automatic to Renault. A few words, and even a swaggerer like Echeverria felt a shiver. Perhaps inducing fear *was* better than sex. Making someone give himself over to fear was like forcing a virgin's legs. It was new every time. The major touched the map and drew a deep breath. "How do they get the guns to Iquitos?"

"The river, of course."

"Across the whole continent? Through Brazil? Señor . . ." The major smiled.

"This is how they think," insisted Renault. "They know the army watches the coast toward both Colombia and Peru. They know that you have been seizing the tuna boats and they know that it isn't just to protect your two-hundred mile limit. To your east, however, is this huge area. Brazil, Peru, and Ecuador each claim this region, but none of you actually controls it."

"How do they know we won't send our soldiers into the mountains to assert our claim?"

"Because that would draw in the Peruvians and the Brazil-

[68]

ians and there would be a stupid Balkan-style war about which the United States would be very unhappy."

The major pursed his lips. He appeared to want to say "What do we care how the United States feels?" but he also knew how they might express their feelings: with Marines. And if they did, it was impossible to know who they would choose for their new "democratic" government. "If the United States would recognize our claims in that area, we would have a free hand."

Mark narrowed his eyes. "That isn't the point," he said. "Do you want to grow up to be a general or spend the rest of a miserable life being re-educated by some Cuban teenager with a whip?"

"Very well," he finally said. "We will move into Ambato. We will look for these rebels he has told us about."

"And you will find them. The man is broken. Why do you doubt yourself? Michaelson will tell the Peruvians to move on Iquitos."

"I do not trust them."

"Michaelson will manage it," said Renault. "He will tell them the weapons are intended to supply *their* rebels." He opened the map one more fold as the major drifted away from him, stepping over the row of automobile batteries on the floor. Tinto leaned closer to Renault, lifted a handkerchief from the pocket of his tan suit and held it over his mouth and nose.

"Water," the prisoner mumbled. "Water."

Echeverria stopped in mid-stride and stared at the man for several seconds. The prisoner dropped his head. Tears began to course down his cheeks, washing a meandering line to his chin. A string of bloody saliva dangled from his split lip. He shivered silently. Echeverria moved indifferently to the spigot on the far wall and took the tin cup from its wire hook. The water screamed from the pipe in spurts. When he closed the spigot, a rumble moved through the pipes, fading into the upper floors of the ministry. He looked up as if contemplating all the clerks whose only knowledge of the dungeons below them might be this inexplicable noise in the pipes. He then moved to the table where two of his soldiers, bored, smoked short cigarettes.

He gently moved the electric switch away from the sergeant who had been in charge of it and gestured with his hand toward the bottle of cane whisky next to the lieutenant. He poured a couple of ounces in the water, then took it to the prisoner, straddling the battery cables. Renault was still studying his map.

The leather straps suspending the prisoner creaked as he extended his neck. He did not wince as the liquid dribbled over his split lip, but sucked at it greedily. Echeverria placed his free hand behind the man's head and held it to help him drink. Nonetheless, most splattered on the pavement, speckling the battery cables and the major's trousers. Echeverria paid no attention. He bent and placed the cup on the floor.

"Thank you," wheezed the man. "Thank you."

Echeverria caressed the man's shiny cheekbone as one might pat a puppy, as if he might pull him closer and kiss him on the mouth. The man smiled, the blood on his teeth nearly black in that light. The major lovingly took the man's ear between his thumb and index finger. He then snapped the .45 from his holster, put it against the prisoner's forehead, and fired.

The report rang the inside of the room like an enormous bell. Renault covered his head and bent over as if he'd been struck in the belly. Tinto reached for his pistol and whacked the light with his head. The two soldiers jumped back from the table, knocking the cane whisky against the wall, the electric switch to the floor, upsetting their chairs. Whisky dribbled down the concrete.

"*Pizda te materina!*" Renault shouted, but he was unable to hear himself. He looked up from his crouch. The force of the shot had ripped the prisoner's head from the major's caress and the body swayed on its straps. The swinging light cut an angular shadow from the dead man's nose and the dark triangle rotated like the marker on a sundial. At twelve was the bullet hole, small and not much more disgusting than a wart. At six, the mouth was still smiling. Blood oozed down the wall. There wouldn't be any back to the head. It would have been scooped out as if with a spoon.

Renault's ears rang. He diddled the ear holes with his fingers. Echeverria shrugged placidly and holstered the gun.

"*Kako sta radish?* Idiot!" Renault charged the major. "What are you doing? We might have gotten more out of him? Names, places . . ."

The major said something he couldn't hear.

"The bullet could have ricocheted!"

Echevarria repeated himself. "*You said he was broken!*"

"But we might have gotten more!" Renault grabbed him by the lapels, scratching the knuckles of his right hand on the collection of medals over the major's heart.

Echeverria tore the hands away and shoved Renault back. Tinto eased forward. The soldiers stood. Echeverria's voice came through low and weak. "He told us enough." Renault's eyes were wide, bulging. He could feel the veins pulsing in his head. A flicker of fear passed over Echeverria's face, but he controlled it. He spun and cocked his head indicating his soldiers should follow. He paused in front of the dead prisoner and grasped the battery cables clamped to his scrotum. With one quick snap, the major ripped them loose and flung them to the floor in front of Renault. A small piece of flesh hung from the jaws of one clamp like a piece of chicken skin in the maw of a cat.

When Renault looked up, the grinning lieutenant was closing the door behind them. The fine gesture, thought Renault. The Latin preference for poetry over success. All failed peoples were that way.

Tinto crossed himself, turned away from the prisoner, took three steps toward the back wall, then came back to say something. Renault couldn't hear it. He placed his hand on Tinto's shoulder and shouted above the ringing, "It doesn't matter. Maybe he told us enough." Tinto stared at the skin in the clamp. He was turning a little green.

Renault momentarily didn't understand his distress. Tinto had watched more than one interrogation. Ten days before, the questioning of the teenage girl turned in by the Indians near Otavalo had been much longer, much more brutal than this. It had taken a quart of lime brandy just to endure it, but Tinto had even egged on the army men when the brandy took hold. On the other hand, this was a part of a man in the clamps. All these South Americans seemed to think the universe revolved

[71]

around their cock and balls. An enemy wasn't beaten until he was humiliated sexually. Death was not enough.

Something from the war stirred Renault's memory. Possibly this was the first time that Tinto, strutting tough that he was, had ever seen a piece of a human being. A corpse was something different from a piece of a corpse. A boot with a foot in it and no leg. A finger lying on a rock still wearing a wedding ring. Gleaming white buttocks, severed above and below, and somehow landing on the turret of a burned out tank. Which had Renault seen first? And when? A corpse had some integrity in its death; it had some identity. But a piece was anonymous. It was a reminder that you are a few pounds of meat, a bag of bones, a hank of hair. Could anyone think of a severed finger, an ear, a chunk of heart having a soul? A piece of a man exposes you for what you are: a mouth that cries for food, an asshole that expels it, and some other wet gobs to keep both ends going. Then there's a brain, of course. A brain that lies to itself and keeps repeating, "I'm God. I'm immortal."

"Let's go," he said to Tinto. He pulled at the boy's arm. "Let's go." The bodyguard's face, shiny with sweat, returned to its normal Incan stoicism by the time they reached the courtyard. The night air was heavy. Guayaquil always felt like it was under water. Two soldiers glanced into the dark green Chevrolet and opened the iron gates. The clanking of the heavy lock was sharp, and Renault knew his hearing was coming back. He put his fingers in his ears and wiggled them. The act was like scratching an itch: it didn't do any good, but it was comforting.

"Home?" Tinto shouted, turning on the air conditioning.

"Yes." He looked at his watch. It was past eleven. He lifted the wet shirt away from his chest and leaned forward. "No," he said. "El Club Internacional." He pointed at the glove compartment. Tinto's teeth glowed pink as the neon light of a hotel was reflected from them. He made a difficult Y-turn on the narrow cobblestones, then handed Renault the fifth of clear lime brandy. The deep swig burned like kerosene. The stuff had little taste, but it was cheap without being the cheapest local drink. Sometimes it burned the smell of that room, of the ozone and piss and battery acid, out of his nose. The smell always reminded him of that endless night in which, according to ancient custom, he had had to sit next to his mother's coffin and protect her body. From what? From being forced back to life. From being forced to go on. He handed the bottle to Tinto, who also took a long drink as he entered one of the main streets. Renault saw a beggar on crutches thrusting his cup at a man in a suit. The man swatted at him with his panama hat as if annoyed by a fly.

"Who will you have?" Renault asked, taking another drink.

Tinto moved his head from side to side, as if considering the possibilities, then laughed, showing his gums. The boy was forgetting the interrogation.

"Catarina? Twiggy? Who?" Renault prodded him with the bottle.

"Carmella," he said.

"Carmella? Not again. You must try around. You are young."

"Carmella. I like Carmella. She has—" He made a large cup with his hand. He laughed again.

"Do you know what Americans say? Eh? More than a handful is a waste. Shows what they know, eh? Carmella!" Renault rolled down his window and shouted, mockingly, in a high-pitched, feminine voice, "Car-mella! Car-mell-ah! Tinto is in love! Tinto loves you, darling Carmella! Please, Carmella, have Tinto's babies! Car-a-mell-a! Please, my Car-a-mell-a! Take care of my Mickey Mouse!"

Tinto laughed and took the bottle from Renault's hand. Renault flopped back in his seat and rolled up his window. They were entering a suburb where the street lights were less frequent and no one walked the pavements. Renault noticed a jeep in the shadows. Two soldiers leaned against the grill, smoking cigarettes, submachine guns slung from their shoulders. Out the rear window he noticed a mid-fifties Ford a hundred yards behind them. Tinto turned on the radio. A Spanish version of "She Loves You" was playing and Tinto turned it up loudly, bouncing on his seat as he drove. The music didn't sound like the Beatles, more like some lounge singers gone mad. The tires squealed. Tinto took a deep drink and passed the bottle back. Renault put it between his legs and held it by the neck, as if protecting a glass erection. As Tinto became more animated, Renault became more somber. "Never love a woman," he said to the night. "Never."

"Yeah, yeah, yeahhhh!" sang Tinto.

They pulled through the chain-link gate. Imitation Roman statuary lined both sides of the circular gravel driveway. When the car crunched up to the front, Renault squinted as if he wasn't sure where he was. Tinto opened the door, moving his hips as if already dancing to the music coming from inside. Renault stuffed the bottle into the seat and noticed the nasty look the doorman, dressed as a conquistador, gave Tinto. They would never have let someone who looked so much like an Indian come into the club if Renault hadn't brought him. The first time, the madam, Mamita, had tried to make Tinto wait in the car. Renault, however, had made a scene and they had acquiesced. It was only another indignity the *norteamericanos* were always imposing. The other patrons seemed to understand and did not complain, though they always muttered about it in low, sneering voices to the whores.

"Señor Renault! Such a pleasure! You honor us!" The speaker was a stocky man with a pencil mustache and hair pomaded into a finger wave. "The mining business is satisfactory, I assume?"

"Excellent," said Renault sharply. He did not look at the manager directly, but scanned the room. He never entered a room without scanning it. Most of the women were wearing black garters with stockings and brassieres with cut-outs that showed their nipples. One wore a tight silver pantsuit and another a white jumper with black boots. The local men were dressed in black tie, except for one young man, who, like Tinto, wore a black shirt and a red tie. Unlike Tinto, he was not wearing a shoulder holster. All of them looked in Renault's direction as if an important celebrity had entered, except for three Americans at the café table nearest the bar. They were wearing the khakis standard among oil surveyors. One of them had passed out on the table. The music seemed to be Aznavour and had nothing to do with the psychedelic slides being projected on the back wall.

The manager put his hand on the upper part of Renault's arm and whispered so close he could smell his mouthwash. "Señor Renault, I have something very special for you. At great expense I have had it brought. You asked me several times if I could get it and now I have. My cousin personally brought it all the way from Cleveland in the United States." He glanced up sharply at Tinto, who was moving from table to table.

"Carmella? Where is Carmella?" The brandy had hit Tinto hard. After the interrogation Tinto had wanted it to hit hard.

"He is in love with Carmella," said Renault with amusement. For a moment the manager looked like he might throw the both of them out, then his eyes flickered with the same fear that Renault had seen in the major's. It no longer pleased Renault to see it, as it once had. Peasants! he thought with distaste.

"It is Carmella's night off," said the manager.

"Too bad," said Renault.

"I will find a nice girl for him," said the manager.

An Indian, thought Renault. One who can't be tainted. "Make certain she has a front like a Buick."

"Excuse me—? Ah! I understand."

"And you have something for me?"

"Something more precious than a virgin."

"Well?"

"Slivovitz."

"Slivovitz? Real slivovitz?"

"I remembered you said you were born in Cleveland and then I thought of my cousin Jaime. He bought it there and I compensated him. . . ."

Renault took him by the back of the neck and shook his head affectionately. "You are the best, my friend. The best! You shall be rewarded for this. Enough for you and your cousin. Thank you, my friend. Thank you."

"Perhaps something to eat?" He patted Renault's damp midsection. "You need your strength. These young girls are a test, no?"

"No food. Send Mamita to me in an hour."

"Certainly."

He was seated at his usual table slightly behind a potted palm, his back to the wall, on a tier where he could watch the entire room. A layer of smoke hung over the patrons, so that when the women stood and walked from table to table, their heads swirled the cloud. The place was rather refined, except

[75]

for the whores' outfits. It might have been Maxim's or "21." The men in their tuxedos were deep in conversation, barely distracted by the girls on their laps or hanging on their necks. They lit their cigarettes with the candles in red globes on the table, gestured as if arguing about Saturday's soccer match, and seemed in no hurry to go through the archway leading to the back rooms. Only the Americans, except for one who had passed out, were at all rowdy. They occasionally whooped, or took a nip at one of the girls' pasties. The fine, good people I work for, thought Renault, grimly tossing back his third slivovitz.

He found himself once again thinking of suicide. The boredom. What country was this? Why was he here? He remembered the long, thin thighs and vague eyes of Annaliese Dorst during the war in Belgrade. She had been bored. Two months after the invasion of Normandy, he had been reading a copy of *Signal* a Waffen-SS captain had given him. There was an article about how she had shot herself flamboyantly on a balcony in Paris. The point of the short article was that she had made a tragic mistake in thinking that the landing would have any effect on the outcome of the war. He had known instantly that the theatricality of the gesture was not like Annaliese, but he had not then been certain why. Now he knew what he had always seen in her violet-blue eyes: boredom. "Who is left who can wish?" she had once said. The Third Reich had meant nothing to her except an opportunity to do things peacetime did not present. She had known the true meaning of things better than all of the living, who went on deceiving themselves with false meanings. Suicide: She had quoted Schopenhauer on it. Suicide: Only cowards did not see it was the answer. And what a fine joke it would be upon the Franciscan priest who had helped Marko Renovich escape to South America! He remembered kneeling before the priest in the church in Ljubljana, crossing himself in the proper Roman fashion, and hearing the priest say, "Your life will be spared, my son, to drive the Bolsheviks from our lands. Your life will be saved." Renault lifted his head from his brandy and laughed.

Tinto was arguing with the manager, who was having a hard time controlling his temper. He gesticulated with upraised palms, waved over another girl, and moved his hand to show Tinto her body. She threw back her shoulders and gave her breasts a shake. Tinto pushed her away. The girl said something nasty and the manager ordered her away. Mamita then came out of the door behind the bar. She was a thickset woman, big but not fat. Her hair curved down to a point on each side of her face in a style they called a "Jackie." Her full-length evening gown was low cut and covered with silver sequins. Renault said *"Zhiveli!"* to himself and tossed back another slivovitz. He was getting dizzy and he wanted to sing. Slivovitz always made you want to sing.

One of the Americans startled him. "What is that?" he asked in English.

Renault looked up at a gaunt, sunburned man. "Excuse me?"

"Oh, I'm sorry. Name's Ferdy McMillan." He stuck out his hand. "Are you an American?" Renault did not take his hand. "My friends were just wondering what you were drinking. We saw the funny shaped bottle and wondered if this was something special."

"It is slivovitz."

'Slivah—what?"

"Plum brandy."

"You mind if I try some?"

"Yes," said Renault. "It was gotten with some difficulty."

"Just a little."

"Rejoin your friends," said Renault. "I'll buy you another round of beers."

"Keep your fucking beers," said the man. "Asshole! Try to be friendly and . . ." The man left mumbling. He went back to his friends and talked loudly, pointing back at Renault.

"Shall I throw them out?" It was Mamita. She had evidently handled Tinto, who was not in the room anymore. Her great skill was that she could handle anyone. If she had been in the U.N. there wouldn't be this Cold War, thought Renault, and I'd be dead. Thank God it's the idiots who run things.

"No. They're drunk. You don't want to anger Americans."

She made a slight movement with her head and three girls who had been leaning against the bar homed in on the oil men. The Americans were quickly distracted. "We'll get them upstairs and then they'll be gone soon enough. I would be rich if only Americans came in. They drink fast, fuck fast, and don't leave with any money." She cackled.

"I'm an American," said Renault, tossing back another slivovitz. "I've got the passport to prove it."

Mamita wryly grinned. "*Ja wohl!* From Cleveland is it? Or Chicago? I forget. I think you yourself forget at times. You are a rare American. Your Spanish is impeccable for one thing, true Castilian. And who ever saw an American with this wonderful white hair?" She reached up and gently ran her palm over his temple.

"Americans are all kinds," he said. "Where is Tinto?"

"He's happy," she said. "Do you want a bath tonight?"

"No," he said. "Only the usual."

"There is a slight problem," she said hesitantly.

"Problem?" he said sternly. He wasn't certain he really wanted it, but it was more important that she obey.

"I can take care of it." she said quickly. "I thought so. You have that look. You always want the usual when you have that look." She lit a cigarette from the candle. "I think you look even more like that tonight. Maybe it is this drink of yours."

"What look?" he said.

"This look," she said, gesturing toward his rough face. "You get fire in your eyes. Like you see Death but will spit in his eye. Like a matador facing an untrustworthy bull."

"Hmmph! A man my age has to work himself up for a girl. A man my age cannot trust his bull to hold his head straight."

She pursed her lips and tossed her head to say, "Shame on you." She slapped his arm. "You are a liar, Mark Renault. That isn't what is in your eyes," she said. "Not at all. Perhaps you will tell me, sometime, no? I am frustrated to meet a man I cannot read. You have shadows. Perhaps you will explain them to me?"

She probably thinks I'm Martin Bormann, he thought. Sorry, dear! Bormann had power. I am merely a zombie who does the work of others worse than myself. He poured himself another drink and tossed it back. He tensed his neck in a shiver as it burned its way down. He stared at her and said nothing.

"Well, sometime," she said, rising. "Come to the upstairs room in ten minutes." She left.

A drop of sweat ran down his nose and exploded on the

table. The air conditioning couldn't overcome the slivovitz. He wanted to sing the old songs. *"Beli shebog u chashi miri-she—"* He stopped abruptly. The forbidden language. The language of donkeys. No one had heard him. One of the Americans had pinched a girl. The manager was watching, but did not interfere. Those peasants songs, those stupid primitive songs, no better than a Gypsy's fart. They weren't any good unless sung with a dozen others, arms linked, drunk to the ears. Sung so that you can forget what a stupid, primitive, manure-smelling fleabag you are. Feelings and thoughts were getting too tangled. Had ten minutes passed? It must have. Katy and Esmerelda would be waiting. It wasn't polite to keep ladies waiting.

His left foot was asleep when he rose. Holding on to his table, he shook his leg and limped toward the archway. The youngest American noticed him, but seemed embarrassed, as if he didn't want this white-haired old man to see the whore licking at his ear and tugging at his belt to get him into the back room. The big-mouth was whispering to his whore and blinked his glazed eyes angrily when she didn't seem to understand. My slivovitz, thought Renault. He will steal my slivovitz. He limped back to get it, took two tries to get the cork back in, then carried it cradled against his chest. The manager winked at him as he left the room.

Through the brocaded curtains was a corridor lit with soft pink light. It always reminded him of a funeral parlor he had seen in Miami the month after the Bay of Pigs. He wasn't sure the frosted glass fixtures shaped like engorged lilies weren't the same as they had been in Miami. A boy no older than twelve came out of one of the rooms carrying a silver tray with two empty beer bottles. Someone was taking his time in there.

The long staircase with its white baluster was to the left. Only the most wealthy or trusted customers were allowed up there. Normally a wiry man with a shiny suit sat on the bottom tread smoking cigarettes, sometimes sharpening his oversized knife. His ashtray was on the floor, but he was not there. The climb seemed long, tiring. Was the air conditioner working? Renault felt too sweaty to move. He stopped about halfway, held the rail, and watched the whore lead her young

American into one of the rooms under the stair. He must have noticed Renault, but he sheepishly avoided looking up at him.

Near the top he heard Mamita lecturing someone. A girl talked back. The sound of a slap cracked off the walls. Just above the top step he could see Mamita poking her finger into a girl's shoulder. "Perhaps you want to go back to San Juan de la Florida? Perhaps you enjoy planting potatoes? Another word out of you and you are on the streets. Understand?"

The girl had long black hair and *café con leche* skin. She wore the usual black garters and open nipple brassiere. She held her cheek with one hand, her head lowered to one side, and did not seem to be crying. In the open doorway behind her, Katy leaned against the door frame, arms crossed, the gap between her two front teeth visible even at this distance. Her white satin robe made her skin seem even darker. That and her hairdo reminded Renault of the Supremes. She pointed with her chin at Renault and said something to Mamita, who immediately turned and blocked Renault's view of the girls as she approached him.

"Ah, Señor, right on time. Tonight will be special for you." She reached her hand out to him, but he remained three steps down. "I see you are protecting your drink. Good for you. It was much trouble to get. Though it is always a pleasure to serve a man such as you."

"Where is Esmerelda?" He leaned to look around her, but she moved to block him again.

"She is not well, not well. A tainted seviche. We are taking care of her and she will be quite well by tomorrow."

"You should have told me."

"Come," she gestured with her hand. "Katy is still here, and a totally new girl: Margarita. Like the drink."

When they introduced themselves, the girls always explained their assumed names. Katy, like the actress who loves Gary Cooper in *High Noon*; Esmerelda, like the Gypsy in *The Hunckback of Notre Dame*. The whores always knew movies. They always seemed to think that if they took actresses' names the customers might think they were as beautiful. Taking names separated their old and ordinary lives from their new lives, and like nuns they assumed the names of their saints. What was the saint of his new name? Marcus Brutus? The

Mark of Cain? He chuckled to himself. Marko Kraljevich who served his country's enemies? This dreary and anonymous new life of his! To be alive was not to live. The corridor reeled. He closed his eyes.

He stepped forward and lifted the new girl's chin. She glanced at Mamita for an explanation, but he jerked her chin straight. "You will do as I expect."

Her lip quivered. "I can please in many ways," she said timidly and unemotionally.

He slapped her quickly and hard. The lines of his fingers marked her cheek. Her eyes were wet, but she did not weep. "My way! Only my way!"

He stepped back as if he were on the deck of a ship and it had just swayed. His fingers stung. There should have been pleasure in controlling her, in frightening her, in slapping her; that was what he was supposed to feel. Where had the pleasure gone?

"Margarita is young, but she is experienced. She is very *horny*." Mamita used the English word. "She wants to try everything. Don't worry, Katy will teach her anything she doesn't know. You will watch her learn. I wouldn't offer this to anyone but you." Of course! he thought. Mamita tugged his upper arm. Katy came forward and took his other. He relaxed and they led him toward the room.

"Margarita is the daughter of an important landowner in Quito," whispered Mamita. "She was raised in a convent. Her family thinks she is only an innocent girl. Doesn't she look pure? Look at those sweet lips, those demure eyes. She is tender as a rose bud. She would do this without pay. She does it strictly for pleasure."

Renault closed his eyes and let them lead him as if he were blind. Too much slivovitz. Too much talk. Why didn't Mamita stop? Didn't she remember she had said almost the same things about Katy six months ago? What had happened to him that he no longer wanted to believe these stories? He just wanted to get on with it. How could it matter who they were? Who he was? I am saving the Latins from Communism, he thought. My weapons are battery cables. When he opened his eyes, Margarita was in front of him.

"Good evening," she said. "You are a handsome one." She

seemed to search for something to say. She glanced at Mamita then very consciously licked her broad lips in an artificial passion. She reached up and caressed his ear and slid her fingers into his white hair.

She flinched as he twisted away. "Don't touch me, Margarita," he said quietly. "Not yet." Why did he feel sorry for her? Why did he hate her? The slivovitz. It always deranged you. First you lost the feeling in your toes, then you could believe opposites. Slivovitz was more than just a brandy.

Mamita left them, closing the door behind him. It was the usual room: mirrored ceiling, French Provincial wardrobe and dressing table, white wallpaper with pink fleurs-de-lys, a huge round bed, and his chair—the wing chair in the corner by the shuttered window. Margarita sat on the bed, resting her elbows on her thighs, and holding her hands together out in front of her. Katy crossed to the bureau and turned on the fringed pink lamp. She checked her "Jackie" in the dressing table mirror, then repointed the curl at her cheek by licking her finger and thumb and smoothing it. Margarita studied something on her thumb, perhaps a small cut.

There was a tapping at the door. Katy said something under her breath. The boy leaned in with his silver tray. "Drinks?"

Renault remembered he was still cradling his slivovitz. He raised it.

"A glass? I will bring you a clean glass. Ice? Something for the ladies?" The boy obviously worked for tips. Or perhaps if someone wanted a boy, Mamita would arrange it.

"A Cuba libre?" Margarita asked Renault. She knew the game. The customer always paid for the rum, but it was impossible to tell whether it was in the glass or not. He nodded. He had his part to play, too. While they waited for the boy to return, Renault reached in his shirt pocket for a cigarette, but they were all damp with his sweat. Katy offered to call the boy back—there was an electric button by the headboard—but Renault said no. It must be near dawn, he thought. He needed to sleep. He was surprised that his watch said one-twenty.

Katy opened her satin robe and lifted a cut glass bottle from the dressing table. She poured a golden oil on her palm and rubbed it on her calves, her thighs, her belly. Margarita glanced back at her and asked Renault, "Where did you learn Spanish? You speak very good Spanish for an American."

"I have always been good at languages," said Renault.

"I am hoping to learn English. I know many words already."

"Travel," he said. "I have travelled all over the world."

"You are a very interesting man," she said.

"Please," he said, placing his bottle on the floor next to his chair. "I don't wish to speak. I know you are trying to be friendly, but that is my preference."

"Certainly," she said. He shouldn't have done that, he thought. Talking helped her calm herself. Ah, to hell with her, she wasn't getting paid to be cared about.

The boy tapped again, left the tray, and leered at Katy's open robe while Renault tipped him fifty sucres. Katy sneered at the boy, showing him her teeth, and he left. "Street mutt," she said. Margarita poured Renault a half glass of slivovitz, enough to kill a dinosaur. He sipped it, then sat it on the window ledge. Katy saw he was ready.

She dropped her robe to the floor and again poured oil into her palm. She sat on the edge of the bed, rubbing the oil on her feet and ankles and between her toes. With both hands she massaged her calf, rubbed her knees with the tips of her fingers, then poured oil directly on her dark thighs and slowly rubbed it in. She stood then, spread a streak across her belly, and circled the inside of her navel with her pinky. She stared straight ahead, as if she were alone and did not know Renault was there. The strawberry scent of the oil cloyed the room. She was now taking both hands and tracing two slick circles around each firm breast, over the slight corrugations of her ribs, bringing her hands almost to her armpits, then over the top and down the bony cleavage.

Renault glanced at Margarita, who crossed herself. He almost laughed. It won't save you here, he thought. There is no Ustashi priest who will show you the escape route. This is where the losers run to. She saw him see her, and knew she was supposed to be aroused by Katy. She swivelled, rested on one arm, and crossed her legs. He could see soft black hairs on her thighs. She seemed to be straining to look aroused and her eyes would flick toward him to see if he approved. Strangely, he felt an obligation to please her, to make her feel that she was deceiving him, making him believe she was utterly degrading herself for him. He was feeling, if anything, less than she: dizziness, some heartburn—he had missed dinner! The oppressive dampness in his clothes, on his face, in his groin. For the moment he owned her and he, in turn, was owned by Michaelson and his superiors. Margarita would fuck until she died. Would he? Would they ever let him retire?

Katy had closed her eyes and was oiling her purple nipples. She tilted her head back slightly, as if she really were one of the Supremes and might sing. She hissed between the gap in her teeth and squeezed both breasts, burying her fingers in their soft sides, leaving circles where they had pressed. Quickly taking more oil, she smeared it over her buttocks, then brought both hands around to her belly and slid them down into her crotch. The oil glistened on her pubic hair as she bent her knees and slid both hands down her groin and over her dark lips. As she drew her hands back, there was a glimpse of pink. She brought them down again, reached all the way through and back to her rear, then with a moan dragged both index fingers through the slit.

She did not look at Renault, but turned on Margarita as if surprised to see her watching. She reached out and caressed Margarita's face, and some of the long hair clung to the oil on her hands. Margarita's cheekbone glistened where Katy had touched her. Katy sat on the bed, hunched her hips up close to Margarita's, took her head, and kissed her forehead. After studying her closed eyes for a second, she kissed her on the eyelids. They rubbed noses, then she put her hands over Margarita's ears and kissed her deeply on the mouth.

Margarita opened her eyes, startled, but did not break the kiss. She glanced at Renault then closed her eyes and awkwardly placed her hands on Katy's gleaming shoulders. Renault shifted slightly. Prostitutes did not kiss, or at any rate they did not kiss their customers. A kiss was too intimate. Kisses were not for sale. That was why this moment usually gave him a sensation like his heart had jerked a cord connected to his testicles. There should have been even more pleasure in Margarita's surprise, because it did not seem to be performed. He was aroused, he told himself, but not caught up. He needed a cigarette, but they were doing their job, so he didn't interrupt them. He reached for his drink and sipped.

Katy was unfastening Margarita's bra. The girl's breasts were heavier than they had appeared. Big for a girl of—what?— sixteen? Fifteen? Maybe they meant she was older than she looked. They were not, however, the breasts of a woman who had nursed a child, and the women did that early here. They were children, then they were mothers, sometimes at thirteen, or even twelve. There was no luxury of an in-between. Or was it possible that Margarita *had* been raised in a convent? Could she have been all that Mamita had said? Could the way she was now biting her own lip as Katy lapped at her lifted breast mean she was now deep in passion?

Ridiculous, he thought, sipping again. Bitches!

Katy had laid Margarita on her back. Margarita shifted backwards on her elbows and swept her own hair out from under her. Katy undid the straps on her stocking, kissing the inside of each thigh. Margarita lifted her hips so that Katy could pull off her panties and then languished, arms over her head, her legs slightly parted toward Renault. Katy took the oil and began massaging Margarita with it, slowly working her way down from her neck to her belly. Margarita opened her eyes halfway, reached up and stroked the small of Katy's back. She closed them, biting her lip, when Katy's thick fingers reached into her dark pubic hair. The hair covered a third of her belly and revealed nothing of her opening, it was so dense. Katy's fingers, however, spread it. She smoothed down the hair and began to flick at the wet inner lips with her index and middle fingers.

Why did he look away? He tried to think of all the women he had known. Of how secret and sacred this opening had once seemed. It distressed him that he now paid so much to do this, all the while knowing it was a game.

He lifted a loose slat in the shutters and saw a big-boned woman tottering drunkenly along the chain-link fence in the alley behind the Club Internacional. She had blonde hair, probably bleached, and was wearing a tight, miniskirted shift. The light was funny in the alley so he couldn't really tell the color of her shift, or whether she was as light-skinned as she seemed, but she might have been a foreigner. He glanced back at Katy, who was thrusting three fingers into Margarita, then continued to watch the woman. She rolled against the fence dizzily, then looked both directions. She bent over. He thought at first she was going to throw up. Instead, she hiked her miniskirt up over her hips and pulled off her panties. She squatted, legs far apart, her long pale thighs and rear bright in the dark alley. He thought about that big-boned woman lowering herself upon him, squatting upon his penis, and riding it. He felt himself hardening, pressing against his zipper, and when she finished peeing and began hopping on one leg to get her panties over her shoes, he dropped the slat and looked back at his whores.

Katy's face was deep into Margarita's crotch, and although Katy's hovered just inches above Margarita's nose, Margarita was thrashing her head from side to side, clawing red lines on Katy's thighs, pressing her hips upward against Katy's mouth, and babbling, babbling.

She was really coming. For real. In truth. She was raised in a convent. She was only after pleasure. He wanted to believe that now. He could believe that now. He unzipped himself. In a moment, when Margarita finished her spasms, Katy would lead her to him. The two of them, mouths still wet with each other, would kneel before him as at communion, and after teasing the shaft of his penis, Katy would place Margarita's mouth upon it.

The pressure was building in him. His cock was armed and the safety was off. He would shoot Margarita as if she were a traitor. He would blow her brains out with one great explosion of his sperm and spatter bloody chunks on the pink wallpaper. And in that moment, a timeless, exquisite moment, everything would cease to exist: the past, the present, Guatemala, Colombia, the endless round of suspected Marxists, the self.

Everything.

Lisa, the Partisan

◆

The rumor was that Field Marshal Baron von Weichs would retreat from Serbia across the Drina and regroup in Bosnia-Herzegovina before continuing north. Harassed by Bulgarian and Russian troops and partisans of every stripe from mere Albanian bandits to devout Communists, the officers seemed to Marko to be rather proud of how well they had managed the long retreat from Thessalonika, though not happy. "There are no medals for masterful retreats," Major Grauer had ruefully stated over dinner, "the only consolation is fewer of your own dead: fewer ghosts in the night." Grauer swallowed another large mouthful of ouzo and said, "At least we have little interference from the Führer. Since the assassination attempt, he is too busy ruining our defense of Poland, Italy, and France to bother with us. Too busy hanging generals . . ." Grauer's aide Werner tugged his arm and silently leaned his head toward Marko.

Grauer pulled his arm away. "Our Serb will not tattle to Herr Hitler, will you? Tito has a price on Marko's head, Werner. They call him 'Bloody Marko,' 'The Traitor Marko.' "

"What a man says in his cups is less important than what he does on the battlefield," said Marko. He was having trouble chewing his horsemeat steak, but he had no intention of being dismissed before he finished it. He had managed to locate it, after all. They always referred to him as "our Serb," as if he were a breed of dog. That, he had resolved with himself, was insensitive on their parts, but that only. Most of his country-men had been stupid about their place in the world as a whole. The choice had been (and still was) Asia or Europe, barbarity or civilization.

"There's nothing left but to get out alive," said Grauer. He was staring at the stone wall of the farmhouse as if he were seeing through it. The tic he had developed around his right eye over the last six months began to dance. "There's nothing left but to get out of this Godforsaken country and hope that the western Allies get to us before the eastern. Do you think I shall make a good dairy farmer?"

"Even if we surrender," said Werner, "Germany will need an army."

"Not for me. I never want to smell gunpowder again."

"The war is not over yet," said Marko.

Grauer mused, then said nothing. "I suppose you won't have any home to return to."

"There will be a war against Communism. The British Empire will never share the world with the Russians."

"So you've said," said the aide, "but I still say Britain and America will squabble over the spoils."

"Yes, well," said Grauer to Marko, "until that misery comes you may have a week left on Serbian soil."

Marko considered his answer, but came up with nothing. He had thought about it before, from the day when Tito and the Reds had captured Belgrade. Possibly, if there were civil war between the Chetniks and the Reds, the Chetniks might find him acceptable. Once Mihailovich and his royalist parti-sans recognized that the real war was between Europe and the Bolsheviks, they would have to forget their animosity to the Germans, even to the Ustashi. "Serbia was held by the Turks for five hundred years. Can it be that patient again?" He let it hang as a rhetorical question, but he was not certain of the answer. He had chosen Europe, but given the stubborn stupid-ity of most of his countrymen facing the choice of Europe or Asia, they could choose Serbia, missing the point altogether. Now, except for this particular corner of Serbia, they had Bulgarians and Russians slitting their throats while they did all they could to frustrate their only protection, the Third Reich. It was insane and disgusting.

Marko had just finished his steak when Grauer lifted the ouzo bottle and said, "That is the last of it." He spoke with the same voice he used in announcing the combat death of one of his friends: somewhat surprised, but mostly weary. He and Werner had nursed the twelve bottles carefully since evacuating from Greece, as if nothing could happen to them as long as there was still ouzo left in the major's oak chest.

"We shall soon be in the Fatherland," said Werner. "Anisette is better."

"If they still have anisette," said Grauer, yawning. He would soon be asleep in his chair, thought Marko. The major could sleep anywhere, instantly. Marko envied him. He envied anyone who could sleep. Perhaps tonight. A belly full of meat, several glasses of ouzo. Perhaps tonight. The farmhouse was dry. It was surrounded by troops scattered for nearly a kilometer in each direction. Why not? It was as if thinking about sleep made it impossible to sleep. He did not think it was fear. He had never been able to sleep when he lay beside a woman, either. Maybe it was just that he missed his own bed. With women he had never been in his own bed. He did not like their smell lingering in his sheets after they were gone, so he was always in their beds, some child crying in the next apartment, the maid picking up teacups in the next room as if it were the most ordinary thing in the world for her mistress to be fucking a young officer.

And then there was Annaliese Dorst. His heart still raced when he thought of her. You could never relax around her. The languor of her ennui concealed her desperation to escape it. You could not know what she would do next in her endless search for something, anything, that was more than mildly entertaining. It was like sleeping with a queen cobra. Whatever fear was in him was replaced by the intensity of lying with such a deadly creature. She knew where your mental carotid was and let you know she was carrying the razor to slash it. He had asked her once if she had amused herself with other men. Annaliese had laughed. "Would it terrify you to know that my last lover was castrated by the Gestapo?" He had not believed her; by then he knew that a shocking remark, a lie, was merely her most effortless way to put an edge on sex. It was impossible SS-Colonel Dorst had not known; perhaps she had told the old man about it herself, simply to stir him up or to amuse him—he had heard of odder things and Annaliese was far from usual. But if she had told the colonel, or he knew, would he have spoken so highly of Marko to General Nedich? Would Marko have been made personal liaison from Nedich's civilian occupation government to SS headquarters?

About the time he heard that the SS and the Wehrmacht were at odds in the Balkans, someone had decided he would be useful working intelligence with the army. He had been sent five times into the Serbian countryside to parley with Chetniks and twice into Macedonia to assist the SS in locating undesirables. On the second occasion, a trainload of Jews had been shipped with the assistance of the Italians, and SS-Colonel Dorst was certain the Italian brigadier general had deliberately misrouted it. This same general had "lost" another train previously, attributed it to the incompetence of a Neapolitan captain, and shrugged it off. Dorst thought perhaps Marko could inquire of the various people near the switching points. If the Jews were located and it could be proven that the general were deliberately losing them, the brigadier general would be reported to Berlin and through the ambassador to Rome, or so Dorst said. Marko traced the train to the line for Elbasan, but whether it reached the Albanian city was uncertain.

When he reported back to Dorst, however, the colonel seemed barely interested. Was it therefore political maneuvering that got Marko permanently assigned to Army Group F away from Belgrade, Annaliese, and his promising career in Nedich's government? When he had been ordered to Nedich's office at eleven-thirty at night, he had thought his affair with her had been discovered, perhaps even that she had confessed it in order to be entertained by the excitement it would cause. But, no, it must have been a political maneuver, maybe to place Marko as a spy among the Wehrmacht, or to make the Wehrmacht believe he was there to watch them. A colonel with the power of the SS behind him could wreak a much crueler revenge. The trains left for the concentration camps every day. Another passenger would not be noticed.

As he paced in the dark, a cigarette cupped backwards in his palm to conceal its glow, he thought of all this, as if reasoning could take away his desire to lie with her. He had not been with a woman since the crooked-toothed whore in Skoplje. Too long ago. Perhaps a woman, any woman, was all he needed and then he would be able to sleep. The sweet release. He inhaled the smoke deeply and hunched his shoulders. The night chilled him. The stars were veiled by mist. A good night to sleep. Should a man with a price on his head sleep well? He leaned back against a tree. He should sleep like a baby. Who was this peasant Tito without the British and the Russians behind him? Ha!

The sputtering of a motorcycle interrupted his thoughts. New dispatches, orders for tomorrow. But the hubbub outside the farmhouse was louder than usual. a whistle was blown and several soldiers were running. A night attack maybe? Marko squeezed out the end of his cigarette and carefully placed the butt in his breast pocket.

"Where is our Serb?" Grauer was yelling.

"Find Marko," said Werner.

"I'm here!"

"Where did you go?" asked Grauer sharply.

"A smoke," said Marko. "A walk." He leaned his head toward the woods.

"Perhaps he—" said the dispatch rider, eyeing Marko.

"You said five kilometers," said Werner.

"He could have told them."

"Be quiet!" said Grauer. "There wasn't enough time. I'll need ten men, and you, Renovich."

"They killed some men," Werner said as he passed Marko.

"How many?" said Marko.

"Three," said the dispatch rider. "But they—" His eyes widened as what he had seen rematerialized before him. He couldn't continue.

A truck came out of the dark grinding its loud gears. Grauer pointed to the back. "Take off the canvas. No talking, no cigarettes. It could be a trap."

"Yes, sir," said a sergeant.

"Is there any indication of a larger force?"

"No, sir," said the dispatch rider. Grauer grabbed the man's dispatch pouch and took him into the farmhouse to send a report on the activity, then the truck pulled away, the ten men, Major Grauer, and Marko in the rear. They were already moving when he remembered he had forgotten his father's dagger. He felt awkward without it, as if he were only half dressed.

In the dark with the truck's lights shielded the jostling was disorienting. Sometimes it felt as if they were travelling sideways. Grauer bounced against Marko several times and—incredibly—Marko thought he heard him snore. The exhaust was pungent. Petrol seemed to smell odder each time a precious supply got through. Against the black sky only the blacker shadow of trees was visible. It seemed hours before they had gone the five kilometers. When the brakes squealed to a stop, everyone held his breath. An infantryman had waved them down. His breath formed clouds that obscured his face in the shielded lights. They scrambled out of the truck and formed a silent circle, rifles leveled, staring tensely into the tight darkness around them.

Grauer ordered four men into positions beside the road, two in each direction. He sent four more ahead into the woods. With the remaining two, he and Marko moved up the slope. "The dispatch rider stopped to piss," said Grauer. "He heard a moan. It was probably the death rattle." He paused for a moment checking that the position was secured, then turned on the battery lantern.

Three men had been stripped and splayed backwards on adjacent trees. Their arms and legs had been bent back around the trunks. Burns that at first glance looked like bullet holes formed a swastika on the chest of the left man. The man on the right had been flayed over his rib cage in parallel stripes. The man in the center, raised slightly higher than the other two, had been split open from the bottom of his rib cage to his groin. His bowels lay in a stinking pile beneath him. Their genitalia were gone. Their eyes were gone. The light flickered as Grauer's hand shook. He lowered the light and turned away.

"Did you see the blood?" he rasped to Marko.

Marko did not answer.

"Most of that was done while they were still living. Dead men do not bleed."

Grauer clenched his fists, leaned back, and roared like an animal. The cry echoed off the hills. "Take them down," he said to the corporal nearest him and when the man hesitated, he struck him on the shoulder. "Take them down!"

The two men scurried up to the bodies. Grauer turned from one side to the other, so angry he couldn't speak.

"Calvary," said Marko. "It was a joke."

"A joke? A *joke?*"

"The next contingent that would have come down the road tomorrow would have seen them."

"They are not visible from the road! They did it for pleasure."

"Oh yes," said Marko quietly, "they enjoyed it, but in daylight the men would be seen. A warning. They are laughing at the Third Reich."

"What is wrong up there?" shouted Grauer. "I told you to get those bodies down!"

"We were checking for traps, sir." The corporal got sick.

"They are nailed," said the other timidly.

"What?"

"Through the arms and legs. Big nails."

Marko took the lantern. "One of them is young. He doesn't look over seventeen." There was a sucking sound as the soldiers pulled an arm from the nails.

Grauer paced like a wild animal. "I think I knew the soldier on the left. I decorated him for his service in Greece." He raised his hands and made another animal noise through his clenched teeth. "The partisans did this?"

"I suspect. There is little difference between partisans and peasants. Both are equally cruel."

"Albanians? Serbs? A Bulgarian patrol?"

Marko had no answer.

Grauer raised his hand and chopped it across in front of him. "It doesn't matter. What is the closest village? I want it decimated: ten for one, no, twenty for one. I want it leveled! Damn them!"

The soldiers had managed to get one victim down, but had missed some of the nails in his leg, which stayed in the air as they lowered the rest of him. "My God," said one of the soldiers. He crumpled to his knees beside the body.

"What is it?" said Grauer. "What?"

The second soldier spread his hands trying to form words. "The eyeballs—they are, they are in their mouths."

Grauer hissed through his teeth. The smell of ouzo filled the air. He clutched his arms across his chest as if trying to contain his anger. "And what do you expect me to do about it?" he finally sputtered. "What do you expect in a war? Get them down!" He turned to Marko. "Is this some sort of signature?"

"I do not know."

"What kind of people are you, damn you, what kind?" For a moment Marko thought Grauer was going to strike him.

"Cruel people," said Marko. "Like all people. Saints do not make good warriors. We will get our vengeance." Marko recalled one of the ancient Serbian ballads about Kraljevich Marko. In it the hero gouged out the eyes of the teenaged shrew Rosanda because she had insulted him.

Gradually Grauer's features softened and he settled onto a stone, his head in his gloved hands. His voice was weary. "Oh, yes, and we are good at vengeance, aren't we, Bloody Marko?"

"We do what is necessary."

Grauer peered around. The sky was getting lighter from the moonrise. "Just when you think you've gotten used to what you do to the enemy, just when you've forgotten the men who were shot next to you, who were blown to pieces next to you, God sends you more ghosts in the night."

"These men's killers," said Marko, "were not God. Give me a dozen men and I will take our revenge."

"I cannot put you in command of German soldiers."

"Then put someone else in command. A small group who can move fast. Let me do to them what they do to us: move quickly, strike, and disappear."

Grauer resisted at first, but ultimately agreed. He assembled a patrol of seven men under Sergeant Bader to probe the area with Marko. They were under no circumstances to engage any forces larger than themselves. They were to return no later than dawn of the next day, when at least thirty civilians would be executed for the killings.

Marko studied his maps until sunrise. They were, he estimated, about twenty kilometers from Valjevo and east of the Skrapezh river. Would the killers have gone toward the river or into the hills? The river offered nothing, he decided, but the greater possibility of stumbling into the German army, setting aside that they might have been looking for water (not likely) or set on some other objective (Why bother with torturing the three?). According to the maps, the hilly area was relatively unpopulated. A good place for a partisan camp, he thought, or an Allied supply drop.

They started immediately at sunrise, passing the three gory tree trunks and climbing the slight ridge above the road. They followed it for half an hour, then skirted a meadow downwards. There were empty hay racks at the end of the field and Marko noticed that the dry grass had been trampled in a narrow path. He followed it into a copse of acacias that had been stripped for livestock food. Sergeant Bader was in no hurry and Marko kept getting ahead of the group. "You will walk into a hornet's nest," warned the sergeant.

"Well, then you will be warned of the trouble, won't you?" Marko replied. "You are not very excited by hunting, are you?"

The sergeant gave him a grumpy look. "Do not tell me how to soldier, Serb."

Marko went ahead into the trees. He heard a stream to his left and saw dog tracks, but they did not seem recent. A plane passed over and he peered up into the canopy of leaves on the off chance it was indeed an Allied plane dropping supplies, but he saw no parachutes. When he reached the edge of the trees, there was a low stone wall. He crept up behind it and looked with his binoculars. Another field, the ruin of a peasant shack, and a rolling ridge beyond. The field had been neglected for several years. A few woody plants had risen above the dry grasses. The earth felt damp through his trousers.

It was nearly ten when the soldiers caught up. They sat behind the wall, sipped from their flasks, and chewed grass. The sergeant demanded Marko show him where they were on the map. "My guess is," he said, "we are in this vicinity."

The sergeant checked the sun. "I think so. Don't try to lead us into a trap, Serb. You will die, I promise, before I will."

Marko stared into the man's eyes. "I have served the Reich better than most Germans. I have done things that you would never do."

"Just remember who gives the orders here."

Marko reached into his pocket for what was left of his cigarette. He rolled it between his fingers to restore its shape, then lowered his head and lit it. He inhaled the smoke until he felt it in his belly. He offered the cigarette to the sergeant. Bader eyed him suspiciously and took it. He took a puff and handed it back.

"You are on the wrong side in this war, Serb. The French, the English, they will make the punishment after the First War seem like an afternoon in a beer garden."

"There is still a chance the Reich could win."

"A chance," said Bader. He stood. "Find us a farm, Serb, I am getting hungry."

They skirted the field, checked the ruined shack, then clambered through the trees to the top of the next ridge. The next valley was small and was mostly wooded over. About half a kilometer down, however, Marko spotted a low cloud of smoke. He raised his binoculars. "A village," he said. He checked this map. "It is not recorded here."

"A partisan camp?" whispered Bader.

"There's a chimney. And the roof, what I can see, seems old. It may just be an unmapped village."

"We will come up slow," said the sergeant.

"They will know something," said Marko. 'Peasants know everything that happens in their vicinity. They sniff it out, like dogs."

"But will they talk?"

"Everyone talks for me."

Bader sneered. "So I have heard."

"And do you want the men who killed your comrades?"

The sergeant turned to give instructions to his men. They spread out in a line, guns ready, each in sight of the man to his left and right. As they steadily moved closer, the village revealed itself to be seven ramshackle buildings not nearly as hidden as they appeared at a distance. Eyes fixed on the primitive shacks, the Germans were aware how open they were on the downslope. Bader raised his hand to stop the movement and signaled two men to circle the enclave. He waited several minutes. Low smoke curled over the raggedy thatch roofs and along the paths between the buildings. A bony, sand-colored dog walked out, lifted his head toward the intruders and sniffed the air. He strolled back without barking. The silence was eerie. There was no sign of any people and Marko remembered childhood tales about the *vila*, spirits in human form who lived hidden in the mountains. Bader raised his hand and the patrol moved across the stream that divided the trees from the camp, and onto the barren soil, packed hard with centuries of walking, children playing, and the nervous pacing of dogs.

The Germans held their line to within a few meters of the first buildings, then scurried up and pressed their backs flat against the wattle-and-daub walls. The soldier next to Marko had beads of sweat on his upper lips, despite the chill. The boy looked no older than sixteen. Bader poked his head out and quickly drew it back. He signaled for Marko to do the same. Even the dog had now disappeared. Bader surveyed the tree line behind them, then signaled men to go behind each building while he, Marko, and the rest moved up opposite sides of the common path.

Bader kicked in the first door. No one. Marko kicked in the next and went inside. The hearth fire was nearly out, an insect was swimming in the cooling soup, but there was no sign of a sudden disruption: no broken crockery, no overturned stools. In the opening between these buildings and the next was a donkey cart half loaded with firewood. The donkey watched them carefully. Bader touched its snout. "What do you think?" he asked.

"They left in the middle of everything. Jews, maybe?"

"Christians. There was a brass cross in that one."

"The SS rounded them up?"

Bader shrugged, then jerked, leveling his Schmeisser sub-machine gun. Marko crouched. It was the men Bader had sent in from the back.

"Anyone?" asked Bader.

"No one," said the corporal.

"I do not like staying here. This place is too easily sur-rounded."

"There was soup in that hut," said Marko.

"They could have poisoned it and left it for us."

Marko looked incredulous.

"Stranger things have been done, Serb," he said sternly. "Did you see any chickens up in that end, corporal?"

"A coop, but feathers and fresh blood only. Someone got them first. Schindler found about half a dozen eggs, though, in the last house."

"You cannot poison eggs," said Marko.

"We'll boil them and move up there for lunch—"

Something had rustled. Bader spun. "What was that?" he whispered. He raised his gun.

"The dog?" said the corporal.

Bader signaled them around the storage shed. He faced the door and nodded to Marko.

"Come out!" said Marko. "You're surrounded."

"Leave me alone!" said a reedy voice in Serbo-Croatian. The Germans raised their guns. Marko raised his hands to signal it was all right.

"Don't make the Germans angry," said Marko. "Come out."

"Leave me alone!"

"What is he saying?" asked Bader.

Marko cocked his Ruger and eased up to the shed. He flipped the unlocked door open. An old man was huddled in the back. A hoe and two adzes had fallen against him. "Come on out, grandfather," said Marmo. "We will not hurt you."

The old man's eyes were white in the shadow.

"Come, come," said Marko kindly. The old man glanced from side to side. Marko extended his hand. The old man pushed aside the tools and slowly emerged, blinking. The corporal shoved him aside and quickly eyed the shed's contents. "There, there, grandfather, why do you hide from us? You wouldn't be a partisan would you?"

The old man cackled, his single yellow tooth glinting. "I am General Draga Mihailovich and this is Chetnik headquarters!" He cackled wildly.

"What is he saying?" asked Bader.

"He is either an idiot or is crazy."

"Ask him where the people are."

"My warring days are over," said the old man. "They came to demand I serve. Ha! I can hardly walk when it's cold. In the war with Bulgaria I had four horses shot from under me . . ."

Marko squeezed his biceps. "I'll bet you're strong as an ox. How much wood do you cut down in a day?"

"Not as much as one of those," he pointed at Bader's machine gun, grinning.

"What is he saying?" said Bader. "He is delaying us."

"What is your name, old man?"

"Peter!" His eyes widened. "King Peter!"

"Well, King Peter, why is the palace so empty? Where did everyone go?"

"You took them. This morning. I was in the woods pissing. If the water would just come faster for me you would have got me, too. I think I have a stone."

"It was not us, King Peter, and I think you think that we are stupid." He raised his pistol and pressed it against the old man's forehead. "That would be a mistake."

The old man still looked amused. "For most of time no one bothers us. For centuries no one. Now in one day everyone comes. My grandfather was once visited by a Janissary here. The Turk was lost. He was very polite and paid for his meal with gold."

"Who were they? Did they have German prisoners?"

"Like these men? No."

"What did they want?"

"Everyone. My entire kingdom. All my chickens. My big rooster Dushan."

Marko lowered his Ruger and turned to Bader. "The partisans must have taken everyone. Perhaps they drafted them."

"Were they Chetniks? I heard the old man say, 'Chetniks.' "

"He did not say. It is more likely to be Reds. Or bandits. Maybe some of our friends the Ustashi trying to kill more Serbs."

"The Chetniks do not like to stir us up this way. I have heard they feel more threatened by the Reds. I do not know whether it is true."

"It is." Marko looked around. "Wait. Reds like to indoctrinate the people. This place is too open. I saw a discarded children's boot behind that house. The partisans have no use for children. They did not draft them."

"Maybe they took them out to kill them and blame it on us."

Marko went back to the old man. "Grandfather, we believe

the partisans mean harm to your family. We are here to rescue them. Where have they taken them?"

"I was pissing in the trees, I—"

"A secluded place. Big enough for all of them. A place that could not be seen easily." Marko grabbed his shirt. "Why are you helping the partisans? Where are they?"

"I help no one. They left by the path." He pointed.

Marko shoved the old man away. He thumped against the shed door and tottered, nearly falling. "We will follow them," said Marko.

"That is my decision," said Bader.

"That was in your orders."

"An army marches on its stomach. We will eat first."

Marko quietly said, "I will kill King Peter."

"The old man? That is my decision. Leave him alone."

Marko knew Bader didn't care about the old man; the sergeant had been at war too long for that. He simply wouldn't allow Marko to have any control. Maybe he had more contempt for Marko than hate for the enemy. "He may locate us for the partisans. You cannot trust these peasants. His own family may have done that to the soldiers."

"I am in command. We'll take him with us. He knows the lie of the land."

"And slow us down more?"

"My orders are not to be questioned, Serb."

"Very well," said Marko curtly, "but an officer would have known it was necessary."

They hard-boiled the eggs, and, with a round loaf of gritty bread the boyish private found in a cupboard, they climbed out of the village and took half an hour to eat. The old man had been very slow ascending the slope. Without explanation, Bader ordered the corporal to take him back into his village and tie him inside his shed. This was not kindness, said Marko. If no one came back, "King Peter" could starve to death or die from the night cold. Bader ignored him. The sergeant was doing it only to prove he was in charge. Stupidity like this, Marko thought, not knowing who is loyal, could make you lose a war. There were millions of Slavs who would have fought for the Reich if they had only asked them.

The patrol had gone on for only ten minutes when the two

men sent out front came back. "To the left, sir," whispered the baby-faced one. "There's a plum grove where two streams come together. The farmers are on the ground and a partisan is reading to them."

"How many?"

"About a dozen villagers. Only six, maybe eight, partisans. Two are near the road, watching. They did not see us."

"Very good, Schindler."

"Shall we take them?" asked the corporal.

"We may be outnumbered. There may be others. Is there high ground?"

"Some."

"Take Erich, he's the best shot, and climb up there. Kill anyone who tries to run. Fifteen minutes?"

"Yes, sir."

"You and you and the Serb will in exactly twenty minutes capture or kill the men by the road. But no one escapes. We do not know how many more may be in the area. The rest come with me."

Marko moved off with the two men. The one was a cold-eyed, washed-out shell of a man with a few prematurely gray hairs in his bushy eyebrows. The other was a rail of a boy who ambled along as if his shoes were too tight. Still, they were clean, thought Marko. The war wasn't over until the Germans couldn't get clean.

The trees were sparse. There wasn't enough cover. The three of them were close enough to hear the stream and someone speaking in the plum grove. The two sentries had their backs turned, but fifty meters lay between. Marko looked at his watch. Seven minutes. "What do we do?" said the boy.

"Drop them," said the other. He gently slid the bolt on his Mauser.

"Give me your bayonet," said Marko, removing the swastika from his arm. He rubbed soil on his face, unbuttoned his tunic and concealed the bayonet under the back of it. He handed his pistol to the boy and made certain that the flap of the holster was obviously open. "How good are you with that rifle?" he asked the boy.

The boy made a strange face.

"Ah," said Marko, "then remember I am the one without a gun."

He stood and walked down the middle of the road, his head lowered, his gait forced, as if he were exhausted. One of the sentries saw him out of the corner of his eye and slapped the other. They spread out on opposite sides of the road and leveled their rifles. About fifteen meters away, Marko lifted his head and stopped. He jerked as if he were going to run, then raised his arms to his side, and smiled. "Comrades!" he said. "Thank God!"

The sentries glanced at each other, but did not lower their weapons. Marko scurried closer.

"For a second I thought you were Chetniks. Thank God! I've wanted to see that red star on your caps for days."

"Identify yourself!" said the sentry on the left.

"The SS was shipping me north for slave labor, or worse. Thank God! Now I am among friends!"

The sentries maintained their distance. Marko covered his face and dropped to his knees, heaving with great sobs. "Thank God!" he crossed himself. "Thank God!"

The sentries looked at each other again. "Stop that!" said one, but slowly the barrels of their rifles dropped. They eased forward.

"Thank God! Thank God!" He could see the toes of their boots. The rifle of the one on the right was in the crook of his arm. The one on the left hovered near Marko's ear. Marko peered up the barrel into his eyes. The man was round-faced, heavy browed, definitely Serbian. He reminded Marko of the oldest Andrich son from his village. Marko's hand dropped slowly behind him. "I barely escaped. I strangled the Ustashi guard with his own helmet strap, pulled it back and twisted until—"

His left hand flicked out and grasped the rifle. His right drove the bayonet up into the other's groin. He pulled the rifle and felt the shock of its discharge. He tore the bayonet out of the sentry's belly and swung it to cut down the other. The first man fired into the ground and dropped. The second desperately jerked on his rifle. Marko hacked at the hand pulling the rifle. The partisan kicked him in the chest, but the force of it almost made him lose his own grip. Marko twisted, rolling onto his back, still hanging on. There were shots. The sentry buckled backwards, his dying hands never letting go of his weapon.

In the grove was the sputtering of a machine pistol and random firing.

Marko blinked, then followed the two Germans into the grove. When he caught up, the fighting was over. Peasants were flat on the ground. A white-haired one was on his back, staring. A praying woman was covering her child. A partisan lay head down in the stream, blood issuing from his torn neck. One of the Germans was kicking and pushing a partisan who had tried to flee. The peasants scurried on their hands and knees and clustered in the center. Three of the five partisans still alive stood defiantly in a row. Another was grimacing and holding a bloody spot on his limp sleeve. The fifth, a woman, could not stop the trembling in her lip.

Squeezing the sprain in his left wrist, Marko kicked through the leaves. The air was redolent with decaying vegetation. He was just behind the sergeant when he looked up at the partisans again. The trembling one leaned up against the man next to her. It took him a few seconds to realize that one of the defiant ones was also a woman, but when he did he couldn't take his eyes off her. She was gaunt, stony-faced. Her nose had been broken once in the past, and a scar gleamed white on the tip of her chin. The faces of women he had helped the army round up in Skoplje, Kumanovo, and Prishtina passed across his mind, but when he remembered her chin had once been soft, that her dry and cracked lip had once been pink and moist, he knew her.

"Jelena?" he whispered.

"What?" said Bader

Marko walked forward as if entranced. "Jelena. I thought you were dead. Everyone in Krushka thought you were dead. Where did you go? How did you—?"

"Jelena? Who is Jelena? They call me Lisa. You, what they call you is traitor, 'Bloody Marko.' Where is your hammer? Are you going to use your hammer on me?"

"That is propaganda. I was translating, that is all. I had no choice. This is war. The peasants would not talk. Your friends should think of that."

"What is she saying?" asked Bader in German. "Are these the ones who killed our soldiers?"

"Why not tell him we are?" said Lisa. "You are going to kill us, so why not fabricate a reason?" The trembling partisan woman squealed and buried her face in the man's chest.

"How could you join the Communists? Jelena . . . Why didn't you let me know you were alive?"

"Because Jelena was dead. You made certain of that. Could I have gone back to my father? He would have beaten me to death, or handed out the stones for all the old women to do it."

"But you could have come to me."

"You? You who tagged off after Bronkovich for fear I would tell what you had done to me."

"You loved me," he said angrily. "I loved you. That was pure and that was good and then you pretended I did not exist."

She sneered. "We were never lovers. You hurt me. You stole my life from me." She shifted her head. "Now you can kill me again by this stream, eh? Only this time use a bullet. If you touch me I'll vomit in your face."

He lashed out with his fist. It struck her hard on the cheekbone, the force lifting her off her feet. She flopped like a parachute losing air.

"Well?" asked Bader. "Well?"

Marko stared at the blood on his knuckles as if looking at someone else's hand.

"What did she tell you? Well? What is the matter with you?"

Lisa stirred. Marko ripped his arm away from the sergeant and went to his knees beside her. "Why do you hate me?" he pleaded. "Why?"

She held her cheek and tried to focus her eyes. Blood had dribbled onto her lower lip.

"Under your dying bourgeois system," said the biggest partisan, "she was a whore. When we have finished, there will be no whores."

Marko leapt at his throat. "What do you mean *whore!* You shit! What do you mean?!" The man reeled back, trying to peel Marko's hands from his throat. They crashed back into the stream, stumbling, nearly falling into the cold-eyed corporal. The man's back thudded against a tree trunk, then Marko twisted him away, shoving him to the ground. He kicked him twice in the back, then whirled, eyes wild, and churned back through the water to Lisa, who was up on one elbow. He looked down at her, panting.

Her voice was slurred by the swelling in her cheek. "I tried to kill myself. I walked on the railroad tracks praying that a train would come along and finish me, but nothing came. That is how I spent my wedding night, Marko, the wedding night you ruined."

"I *loved* you. It was you who wanted to go ahead with marrying Bronkovich. You!" He held his head in his hands. "Oh God! I looked for you. I looked everywhere. No one had seen you. Your father told everyone you had made your way to the Morava and drowned yourself 'like a good girl.'"

She laughed. "There were Gypsies, then Sarajevo, then the alleys in Dubrovnik. The Italian men, the German men, the English with their canings, the French men and their wives. Who knows what else? I was brilliant at it. A baronet offered me marriage. Ha! I tried one night to see how many I could do from dusk to dawn. Fifteen, Bloody Marko. Fifteen! I was sore, but I didn't have to work for another week. Fifteen! It could have been more. Everybody liked Lisa. She did anything. I was sore, but they could never have hurt me as much as you did. Perhaps I should be grateful. You gave me a profession."

"Stop it! Why do you say these things to me? Why?"

"Because I want you to know how well you have helped the cause. The Communists talked me out of that life, said it wasn't my fault. Now I give them whatever they want when they want it. I do *so much* for morale. And my generosity is appreciated very much."

Marko's hands clawed his pockmarked face. He quivered as the rage built.

She laughed, lay back and flapped her legs like wings. "*Very* much!"

His boot crashed hard into her ear. Her head snapped to one side. He kicked it again and again, moving her entire body with the force. On the fourth or fifth kick, he missed, awkwardly spun, and crumpled back. Bader was on him, clutching at his breast pocket.

"What is it? What is it? God damn you, Serb. What is it?"

Marko sat panting, staring.

"What did she say, Serb? Are these the ones who mutilated our men?"

An older peasant man moved forward on his knees. "Please," he said, "explain to the Germans! The Partisans were trying to force us to help them! They killed my brother to make the rest of us join them! They were forcing us!" The corporal pushed the man back. "Please!"

Marko's glassy eyes turned to the peasant. "They are all guilty," he said. "All of them."

"What?" asked Bader.

"They are all guilty." He panted. "All!"

Marko pushed aside Bader's hands and stood. He crossed to the corporal, snatching the Ruger he had given him earlier, and spun. He fired into the male partisan. He moved to the trembling woman and silenced her scream with one shot. A peasant woman plucked up her child and started to run. Then the others jumped up. The startled soldiers opened fire. Bullets shattered arms and thighs and chests, and the iron smell of blood burned the air. More than a dozen bodies lay still and the only sound in the dense silence was Marko's empty Ruger, clicking, clicking, as he desperately tried to pull one more bullet into the chamber.

Bader swung his Schmeisser and struck Marko on the arm. Marko looked at him numbly. "You are empty, Serb." Marko studied his hands, his wet and muddy trousers, the blood on his boots. He looked at the body of the man who had fallen backwards over Lisa. The partisan's mouth was wide open like a child's trying to catch the rain.

The sergeant spoke wearily. "You men should have held your fire until ordered. You could have hit one of our own in this confusion. This shit did not happen at the beginning of the war. I commanded real soldiers, then. Don't you think there would have been some value in interrogating these prisoners?" He expelled a tired stream of air.

One of the peasant women moaned. She had been shot several times in the back and wasn't moving. Her pale child lay dead and gaping under her arm. Bader walked over to her. "Finish her off, Schindler."

Schindler did not move.

"I said finish her."

"I would rather not, sir."

Bader blinked.

"I don't like killing women. Let the Serb do it."

Bader shook his head. "And what was all this?" He nudged the woman's side with the tip of his boot. He nudged her head. "She is done," he finally said.

The corporal with the bushy eyebrows bent over and searched a pouch carried by one of the partisans. He pulled out a string that looked like a necklace of dried sliced apples and stared curiously.

"Ears," said Marko.

"Ears?" said the corporal, turning it.

"Our three still had their ears," said Bader. "Drop those and look for any maps or writing. Quickly! Even Tito's grandmother could find us after all this noise. Let's go. Hurry! We want to get home for dinner."

The soldiers searched the bodies and headed out to the road. Bader gave Marko a sharp push to get him moving. During the long walk back, Bader wordlessly released "King Peter" from his shed. Marko glanced back and saw the old man had squatted and was watching them fade into the woods as if he were watching a receding storm that had destroyed a year's crop. The peasants went on forever, animals who would never seek to better themselves, wallowing in their bestiality as if it were silk.

They reached the main body of troops an hour after dark. They sat behind a light panzer and ate stale biscuits with the tank corpsmen. No one spoke but tank men, who gave up trying to make conversation after several minutes. Every time Marko lowered his eyes, he could feel the patrol members staring at him.

They had seen horrible things in this war—done horrible things—but they were still astonished by the blood madness they had seen in him. They were afraid he might snap again, he knew. They were afraid that the force which seized him could never distinguish between enemy and friend, could only kill until it was exhausted. They did not know that it was not madness, but anger, rightful anger. He could kill without madness. He could kill mechanically, like a soldier, the way he ought to kill. Today, however, he had let it get away. "They think I am Death himself," thought Marko, but they could not understand how relaxed he now felt. How utterly limp. He had killed the past. He would sleep tonight, as he had not slept for years. The past was dead.

And no one would disturb him. No one in the old epics, he remembered with satisfaction, would ever waken Kraljevich Marko. Friend or foe, Serb or Turk, they were afraid to.

Ilya, the Witness

◆

When Marko tried to enter the officers' mess tent, a burly private with sagging eyes blocked his way.

"Excuse me," said the private, "I am very sorry to report there is a shortage of food. You are to eat with the enlisted men."

Marko could see the officers inside the tent. Lieutenant Kerner tapped Major Jäger on the shoulder. They seemed to be making a point of letting Marko see their amusement. "This is what you told me yesterday."

"The shortage hasn't changed."

"The food looks plentiful."

The private shifted to block his view. "You know how it is. Officers eat far too much."

"I am not all that hungry; I will have only a cup of tea." Marko tried to move past the private, but he did not budge.

"Don't force me to get nasty, Serb."

Marko stared at him for several seconds.

"Is there a problem, private?" Lieutenant Kerner had moved to the door. His amusement was obvious.

"No, sir," said the private.

"SS-Colonel Dorst specifically said that I was to live among the officers," said Marko.

"Yes," said Kerner. "How unfortunate that he is in Belgrade and does not understand the situation."

Marko raised his hand as if tipping a hat. "Let us hope these shortages soon end."

"Of course," said the lieutenant.

"I shall make certain SS-Colonel Dorst hears about your sacrifice." With another tip of the head, Marko strode away quickly. He heard the officers laughing in the tent behind him. This was the third time. There was little difference in this camp between what was served in the officers' mess and what was served the enlisted men—and they knew he knew it. Except for the diversion of supplies to Barbarossa, the invasion of Russia, they seemed short of little. British Egypt would likely fall by mid-September, Stalingrad and Leningrad before winter. Under those circumstances, the American entry into the war would mean nothing. National Socialism would be secure and the future would lie before them like a vast healthy city of marble and steel.

He wanted to understand the pettiness of Wehrmacht officers like Kerner and Jäger. After all, they too were part of bringing in the new era. They were likely frustrated to be here in the defeated Balkans chasing after the rag-tag resistance— bandits with an excuse, he called them—while their brothers were accomplishing Napoleonic victories in Egypt and Russia. Or perhaps it was this distrust between the SS and the Wehrmacht he had heard about in Belgrade. Marko's role as a personal liaison between General Nedich's government and SS-Colonel August Dorst might have made the more traditional army men suspect him of being a spy, rather than a translator and advisor. Still, it was all stupid.

He joined an infantry squad gathering around a large pot of pork and noodles. "Smells good," he said pleasantly.

Sergeant Bittner, an emaciated man with a narrow nose, was sitting on a collapsible camp stool. "They threw you out again," he said.

Marko was irritated to admit it. "I think Jäger has something against me."

"Jäger thinks he's God's nephew," said a private.

"They don't want you to hear their plans," said another man.

"Plans? Ha!" said the man stirring the pot. "They don't sneeze without permission from Berlin."

"It is not good to be flippant about your superiors," said the sergeant.

"Excuse me," said the stirrer. "I meant no disrespect." He waved at an insect that was pestering him. "I meant they are very careful to be obedient." He had a pixie look in the cock of his eyebrow. Several soldiers laughed.

"Well, you make certain you are as carefully obedient," said the sergeant. "The war's not over yet."

"Is it true, Sergeant Bittner," asked a boyish private, "that we will soon be sent to the Black Sea?"

"I've told you a thousand times, Klepper: *Stop listening to rumors*. If we're sent, we're sent."

"It will be cold there."

"I could use a little cold," said the stirrer. "This heat kills me."

"The Black Sea is Russia's beach," said another soldier. "What kind of geography did you learn?"

"I hate being cold," said the boy. "This weather is fine for me."

"We'll send you to Rommel," said the stirrer, dipping out a bowl of food for himself. "You'll have all the heat you can stand."

Marko chewed a large chunk of the pork. "The officers are not eating as well as this," he said, swallowing.

"If you say so," said the sergeant. "Gives me gas."

The boy sucked a noodle in off his lower lip. "Serb. Tell me about these Chetniks."

"The Chetniks?" Marko eased himself down onto a patch of dried grass. "They are fools who do not know when they are beaten, but they will change their minds."

"Kill them all, I say," said the sergeant. "Make room for some good Bavarian farmers."

"It is the Reds we need to worry about," said Marko. "The Chetniks will come to see this."

"You'll tell us what *we* need to worry about? And who do you think are *we*?" snorted the sergeant.

"All who are part of the new world order."

"The new world order is a German world order, Serb."

Marko blinked. The short-sightedness was everywhere. His first two assignments outside of Belgrade had been to parley with Chetnik leaders. He was fairly sure that one of the two groups would eventually come to see that General Nedich's cooperation with the Axis was the only way to save Serbia from Communism and the old primitive ways of life. It should have been obvious. One of the Chetnik leaders, however, had seemed more concerned about the activities of the revitalized Ustashi, the pro-fascist Croatian group who had gone after Serbs in the mixed areas. Marko had tried to reassure the man that the SS was taking steps to discourage these excesses, just as SS-Colonel Dorst had reassured him when he had seen reports of the atrocities. The Ustashi had eliminated a number of pro-Communist enclaves. The peasants had brought it on themselves. None of these thoughts gave him an answer to what the sergeant had said.

"You misunderstand," said Marko. "When Rome conquered, it gave the indigenous population citizenship. Many Serbs, many Hungarians, many Greeks, many people of all nationalities know that Germany is showing us the way. We can be as devout National Socialists as any German." He leaned forward passionately. "We have strong arms and solid backs. Let us help you!"

"Must we have a political speech at every meal?" said the man who had been stirring.

"I'd watch your mouth," said the sergeant, placing a finger to his lips. Out of the corner of his eye, Marko thought he saw him toss his head in Marko's direction. "This man saved a good German woman's life in Belgrade." His tone was ironic.

"But of course, Herr Sergeant Bittner!" he said. "I was merely wondering about the human aspect of the Serb's story. The politics of this man must be all stirred around with his personal ambitions, eh? I merely wonder why he sets out to impress us at every meal. Perhaps he wishes to sell us something and get rich."

Several soldiers looked down to cover their smiles. "I could have been a wealthy merchant," Marko said, "but I saw that nothing you can sell changes the world into a better place." Marko sat back and angrily dipped his spoon into his food. What more did he need to do to prove himself? What? He *had* after all, saved not just Annaliese Dorst, but perhaps many soldiers, and this was his reward?

"God save us from the dreamers," said a corporal.

"I think I need a woman," said the boy. Most of the soldiers glanced at each other with bemused disbelief.

"You need your mother," said someone.

"No! Some ass! That's what I need a woman for!"

"Wait until you grow some hair in your crotch," laughed the stirrer. "Women feel more comfortable with a little wool."

"He doesn't want her to knit him a sweater!" said someone.

The boy interrupted the laughter. "You think I haven't, don't you?"

"No, no," said the sergeant, "that's why Germany needs room to expand. Your bastards are filling the nation. Close your mouth on your spoon and don't get any ideas about ass. These Slavs will cut your balls off."

"The partisans like to use whores," said Marko grimly.

"See?" said the sergeant. "He should know."

"I need a woman," protested the boy.

"Your woman's at the end of your wrist," said the stirrer, and all the soldiers laughed, some of them sputtering white flecks of food into the air. The boy angrily ate with his head down. Marko felt sorry for him. Eventually, he would grow into being just another of the men. With him it was just a question of age. What was it with Marko?

The private who had blocked Marko at the officers' mess suddenly rounded the truck parked in the trees behind them. "What are you doing here?" he barked. "You were told to eat at the enlisted mess."

"I enjoy the company here," said Marko.

"Major Jäger wants you at his cottage immediately. From now on, go where you're told. I don't have time to search for you everywhere."

Sergeant Bittner peered up at the private. "You wouldn't want to miss your afternoon tea."

The private hardened his face to avoid reacting to the sergeant. For a second, Marko thought maybe Bittner was annoyed by the private's manner toward him, but no, this was some older dislike between the two. "We may be moving soon," said the private. The sergeant belched.

Marko stood, but before he left he leaned over to the boyish private, patted his shoulder, and whispered, "I hope you find your woman." The boy turned away as if he thought Marko was mocking him.

He went into the sparse cluster of trees where the four wooden cottages were concealed, then passed through the gate of the barbed wire perimeter without challenge from the sleepy guards. A soldier opened the cottage door for him. Just as he was about to step across the threshold, he noticed a fat woman sitting on a stone with her back against a tree. Though she looked like a peasant woman, she was oddly dressed, with too much make-up and an ill-fitting shift. A noose around her neck was tied to the trunk and she never took her eyes from the helmeted soldier pacing and watching her.

"Come in, Serb," said Lieutenant Kerner. Jäger was behind him. A young girl, maybe twelve, sat in a chair in the middle of the room. Her hands were big-knuckled and powerful, but the skin of her cheek looked like a baby's. The slight pout of her pink lower lip reminded him of a girl he had once loved. "This is Ilya," said Kerner. "Her mother says she knows something about the partisans who tried to blow up the bridge on the Treska."

The botched attempt had intrigued the Germans for a week. An alert truck driver taking seven Italians back to their regiment had spotted the green detonation cable snaking up the opposite bank. They saw three men who fired a few shots to cover their escape, but the explosives failed. No one could see quite what the point was in wiring that particular bridge, except maybe as a diversion for something more important, but what that would be had remained a mystery.

"Good day, Ilya," Marko said in Serbo-Croatian.

The girl simply blinked.

"Her mother," explained Kerner, "has been helpful for some time. She's a widow. She makes her living in a whorehouse in Skoplje, hears things, and sells them to us. She sent her daughter Ilya here to work herself to death on a farm near Matka. Maybe she sold her to the farmer, I don't know."

The girl picked up on the names and looked up at Marko's pockmarked face. He touched her shoulder.

"What did the woman say?"

"She tried," interrupted Jäger, "to say she had been in the

country having a picnic when she saw two peasants sneaking food into the hills. She said if we searched the village we might find these partisans."

"This makes no sense," said Kerner, "if they are hiding in the hills."

"Ultimately she admitted she was lying," said Jäger. "She did not see it. It was something little Ilya here had seen."

"Find out where the partisans are hiding," said Kerner.

Marko nodded. He pulled a stool under him and sat knee to knee with Ilya. "Do you know who we are, Ilya?" he asked in Serbo-Croatian.

She shook her head.

"We are here to help you. We are here to help the whole world. We are here to help protect a pretty young thing like you from these partisans."

She blinked.

"You cannot know what I have seen. These partisans, they do not care about you or your mother or anyone. They will kill Germans and thereby force the army to punish innocent civilians. These Germans are not so different from you and I. They do not wish to hurt people, but these stubborn partisans, these Communists, they plant bombs and kill young German boys. If we can just capture these bandits, we can begin rebuilding, bring German technology and goods into our country. Imagine! Tractors, the newest breeds of animals, all sorts of farm machinery so that you won't have to spend your life bent over, hoeing weeds and picking vegetables. People will tell you this war is about something else, but that is what it is really about. Can you believe that, Ilya? These Germans are saving us. It was fools who declared war against them: Jews and Communists and traitors to their own people."

She peered at Major Jäger, who was lighting a cigarette.

"Your mother knows this. That is why she helps us. At great risk to herself."

The girl lowered her eyes and laced her fingers.

"Get her to talk," barked Kerner. Marko looked at him sternly. Jäger made a shushing noise.

"Lives are in the balance," said Marko. "Please, won't you help us?"

"I did not see," said Ilya. Her speech had been influenced by the Macedonian dialect, especially in the vowels.

"That is not what you mother told us."

"I did not see where they went."

"You saw them, but you did not see where they went?"

"Yes."

"Can you explain for me, Ilya?" He touched her soft cheek to lift her face. They stared at each other. Her eyes were the ox eyes of an ancient goddess, brown and deep. He wanted to kiss her. The feeling came over him like déjà vu. He felt her cheek tremble.

"Can I see my mother?"

"Explain for me."

She blinked. "Goran was angry."

"Goran?"

"My master. I spilled honey on his shirt. I thought if I picked him some berries he would be happier."

"I see." He knew the bastard had beaten her. She did not have to say it. How many times perhaps not even she remembered.

"I rose before dawn to milk the cows and hurried into the woods. The berries were mostly gone, so I went further. I was on a hill near the village when I heard them passing below."

"Who were they?"

"I don't know. But they were joking about Old Savich who lives in the village, and one of them was saying that if the three men were too stupid to blow up a bridge, why should they feed them?"

"You would recognize these men?"

"No."

"Don't be afraid."

"I did not see them, except from behind."

"Surely, Ilya, you would recognize them? Don't be afraid. The army will protect you."

"But I did not see them." She looked up at the Germans. "Please."

He took her thick wrist. "You really didn't see them?" She shook her head. "I believe you, Ilya. Don't be afraid."

"Goran will be very angry I was not working today."

"He cannot blame you for the army taking you away. Don't

worry over nothing." He paused for a moment, knowing that she would be beaten, her fault or not.

"Well?" said Kerner.

"She says she saw men taking the partisans food, but she did not see where they went."

Jäger threw down his cigarette and angrily crushed it. The girl looked at Marko for an explanation. "Get her mother," he said to Kerner. "That will make her talk."

Marko stepped between Kerner and the door. "She is talking. She does not know. Can't you see she is already terrified?"

"We will see about that."

"No," said Marko.

The back of Kerner's hand snapped across Marko's cheek. In a reflex, the girl covered her face and curled up on the chair.

"You question our methods, Serb?"

Marko's nostrils hissed as he clenched his jaw. His eyes were so terrible, so full of hate that the emotion flared out in front of him like a jet of burning gas. Kerner leaned back slightly as if to avoid being singed.

"Lieutenant!" said Jäger. "That was unnecessary! This is not the Kaiser's army!"

"This," said Kerner, recovering from what he had seen in Marko's eyes, "is not one of our soldiers."

"I have saved the lives of German soldiers," said Marko grimly. "I have killed for you."

"So I am in the presence of a great hero?"

"I have already done more for the Reich than you will ever do."

"Enough!" said Jäger.

"And for that you treat me like a dog," continued Marko. "You are a worse traitor than these partisans."

"*Enough!*" Jäger stepped between them. "This is no help," he said to Kerner. "Renovich, we shall take the girl to the village. She can point out the men she saw, then we will interrogate them."

"She did not see them."

"I do not believe this."

"Why do you have me here, then, Major? I tell you she is too frightened to lie. She is just another peasant girl living as a slave to some bastard who whips her when she looks tired. If you will simply give me some trust, I shall get these partisans."

"We'll bring the girl," said Jäger.

"She is far more useful as a spy. If she identifies the men, she is no longer useful to us. If she cannot identify them, as I am certain is true, then we will be tossing her away as a possible source of maybe more important information. We should reward her, Major, not destroy her effectiveness."

"He's just trying to save the whore for himself," snorted Kerner.

Jäger glared at Marko to keep him from reacting to the remark. "Very well, Serb," said Jäger. "We shall do it your way. Lieutenant, conceal the girl and her mother in the back of a covered truck. They shall not be seen. Gather twenty men to move on the village." He put his hands behind his back and leaned into Marko's face. "Get these partisans for us or we shall. Go ahead, Serb, prove your worth."

The location of the village in a deep ravine made it impossible to surround without being noticed. Jäger stopped the trucks and ordered a quick dispersal. They would enter on the northeastern side. Kerner, a sergeant, and seven men would drive straight through the center and secure the southwest end. As rapidly as possible, other men would move behind the buildings and watch for anyone trying to escape up the slopes. It was possible that someone who knew the Germans were not merely passing through would get away, but that couldn't be helped.

The village itself was little more than a dozen structures, including several barns, henhouses, and other outbuildings. There wasn't even a church, which was probably the reason the place was not on any of the maps. As the soldiers rousted the peasants from their dinners, Marko saw that the settlement was predominantly Serbian, with an occasional man and several women and children who had the round Macedonian face. A white-bearded man limped out of his home on a single crutch. Women clutched handkerchiefs to their mouths. The mature men—there was a conspicuous gap between boys in their adolescent years and men of middle age—walked stiffly and held themselves tall. Several of them spat on the ground.

They had been tough to stick it out here (for how many generations?) with the Albanians and the other competing ethnic groups nearby. Perhaps that alone would make it easier to get them to cooperate; they might hate the surrounding people more than the foreigners.

In a few minutes about forty people had been assembled. They huddled close in front of the largest house facing the dirt road, as if trying to keep warm. Several women clutched at the men's sleeves. Children buried their faces in their mother's skirts. Many of the men stood defiant, arms crossed.

Major Jäger stepped out onto the running board of his car. The boyish private hurried up to the car and saluted. "The perimeter is secure!"

"Thank you," said Jäger. He scanned the villagers. "A dirty lot, aren't they?" he mused. He spotted Marko beside the second truck. "Well, Serb?"

Marko picked up a three-legged stool from in front of the house, placed it in front of the villagers, and stepped on it to speak.

"Brothers," he said in Serbian, "do not be afraid. I am not here to persecute the innocent. The Germans are not here to persecute the innocent. The hardships of war are always on the minds of people such as you and I. Our people have suffered for a long time: five hundred years under the savage Turk, in the Balkan Wars, in the Great War, and now, unfortunately, in this one. If Yugoslavia had taken its rightful place at the side of Adolf Hitler and the German nation instead of resisting the inevitable, many innocent soldiers would not have been sent to futile destruction. Belgrade would not have been bombed. Yugoslavia would have been a conquering nation with the conquering heart of Emperor Dushan the Great, instead of a defeated nation which must rebuild its place in the world. Beside the Germans, we might have won Greece and Albania. But because some petty generals refused to see the wisdom of Prince Paul, for their own selfish reasons they placed a boy king on the throne and forced our friends to attack us.

"Brothers, even now, far away in Bolshevik Russia, the German army is winning a monumental victory. In the Sahara, the Afrika Korps has backed the British against the Nile and soon all of the Holy Land will be in our hands." He reacted to a cynical expression on one of the men. "Oh, you think this is far away. This has nothing to do with you and your plum trees and your children. You would be very wrong, my friend. When these battles are won, there will be no one to challenge the Third Reich. A thousand years of peace will lie before us in which we may care for our farms, raise our children tall and healthy and proud, free of the corruptions that the Bolsheviks, Jews, and Gypsies have sown among us. Without these animals stealing from us, we will have healthy children with good teeth, herds like you've only dreamed of, good meat, and enough grain to pave a million highways."

"And when is this great day coming?" the old man said quietly. A woman tugged him to remain silent.

"Soon!" said Marko. "Very soon! Our enemies are getting desperate. Thieves are no good face to face. So they send people in the night. They assassinate good German boys who should be home taking care of their mothers. They hide in the countryside stealing from peasants like yourself, promising what they can never deliver—the future. Do they care that their depredations may result in the punishment of innocent people? *No!* They provoke our friends again and again, and who pays for it? We do. In some villages they have stolen so much that children have starved to death. They have raped women hundreds of times all over Serbia and Montenegro and Macedonia and elsewhere. They have dashed out the brains of babies. Do their leaders punish such acts? *No!* They encourage them. It is written by their God Lenin that they should do these things. They are worse than the Turk. Less than the Turk. They bring barbarity to a level unsurpassed in history." He reached under his tunic and lifted his father's sheathed dagger. "This knife fought the Turk and the Bulgarian and the soldiers of the Austro-Hungarian emperor. Now it fights the partisans, our true enemies."

The old man coughed. Some of the men and women stared grimly; others were listening closely, looking for a way to get to tomorrow alive. Someone would give up the partisans, thought Marko. His talk was working.

"Well?" said Jäger. "Is your speech torture enough?"

"One moment," said Marko in German.

He put the dagger back in his waist belt, stepped down off

his stool and strode closer. "Friends," he said, "we know that the three Bolsheviks who mined the Treska bridge are being concealed by two of you. We have no interest in the rest of you. We want these bandits. The Wehrmacht guarantees protection for whoever turns in these criminals. You will be doing a service to peace and to your nation. Stop the Reds now and they will not be killing your children, stealing your land, and molesting your daughters tomorrow. Please, these soldiers are good men, much like you, but when their brothers are murdered their rage can be uncontrollable. They are identical to you in this; no different at all."

One woman stared up at her husband. Marko instantly knew that she knew the man could tell them something. He moved closer to him. "What about you, brother? Perhaps you have heard, in passing, something that might be helpful?"

The man sniffed, shifting his black mustache. "I am just a poor farmer. I know nothing about the war."

"Brother," said Marko, "the struggle is here! You must be part of it! Tell me what you know."

"I know that Germans piss and you drink it. I know Germans shit and you eat it. Does this help?"

Marko clutched the man's shirt in both hands and pulled him forward. His wife grabbed at Marko's arm and tried to bite it. He kicked at her and his boot thudded into her thigh. She toppled back, rocking with pain. With the sudden release, Marko and the peasant stumbled forward, the peasant losing his balance and falling on his knees. Marko shoved at the man with his heel.

"Shall I tell them to shoot you?" he shouted. "Shall I tell them to shoot you all?" Kerner had returned to the center of the village. He rocked on his boots and watched with amusement. The Germans were all watching Marko, he could feel it, and these ignorant pigs were making him look foolish.

"Well?" said Jäger.

"One moment," said Marko sharply. He leaned over the peasant. "Do you want all of these people shot?"

"Isn't that what you are here for? Why not make it quick?"

The villagers panicked at his words. They turned and embraced. Babies cried. Women shrieked and men shouted.

"Not me!"

"My God! My God!"

"It was him."

"He knows!"

"Spare the children!"

They were silenced by Major Jäger's approach. "Well, Serb? Where are the partisans?"

"They will talk."

"I don't have all night."

Marko glared down at the kneeling peasant, who seemed unable to stand the heat of Marko's gaze and turned back toward his fallen wife. "Separate them," said Marko.

"Are you presuming to give us orders, Serb?" asked Kerner.

"Separate the men from the women. They are trying to be courageous in front of them."

Jäger gestured towards Kerner. "I am willing to indulge him." It was clear from his ironic tone of voice that he was certain Marko would fail.

"Take the men into the barn," said Marko.

Kerner gave the order and the soldiers rushed forward to pull couples apart. An old woman clung to the old man's arm until the butt of a rifle thudded against her chest.

"If you hurt our women—" said someone.

"It will be on your head!" shouted Marko. He strode ahead and kicked open the barn door. A shaft of light slashed across the room from a vent in the loft. Motes glittered like stars as they swirled. The air was stifling, oppressive with heat and the smell of old hay and something winey: a dusty basket of withered apricots rotting in the corner. Under the loft, he made out an ox plow, an anvil, a wooden rake, and a decorated yoke. Other tools hung from leather straps on the wall. There was probably an old musket or two hidden in the hay above. Years of dull labor always killed the peasants' imaginations. They handled their animals so well because they had similar minds.

He stepped aside as the soldiers shoved the men through the door. Several stumbled and were lifted by the others. They huddled back in the empty corner by the apricots. Marko paced until Jäger said, "Well?"

Marko stopped and looked almost casually at the peasants. One licked his lips. The important thing, Marko thought, was not to look too anxious, to let the peasants know that the capture of the partisans would be a tiny thing, no more important than the swatting of a fly, as inevitable as the wind.

"The Germans have your women and children out there," he said very quietly. "They will use them to make you talk, brothers. Would you have them suffer because of your stupid pride? For your own good they seek out these enemies. And make no mistake, the partisans are as much your enemies as theirs. They wish to make your country nothing more than a province of the Soviet empire and you the slaves of the Communist party. They will take everything you own, as they did in Russia, and they will not give you the chance to save your women and children. They will rape and kill and will not give you the chance to live in peace that our allies do. These good men's patience is wearing thin. Mine is wearing thin. You are being stubborn against the very people who will protect you."

The peasants were expressionless. The silence made the stuffy air seem even heavier.

Kerner sniffed. "You are not being very persuasive, Serb. Perhaps we shall shoot a few of the prettier girls."

"I have warned them of that," said Marko.

"But it is different when they see it happening." If the peasants' understanding of German was weak, their sense of Kerner's tone was not. They glanced at each other and stirred sensing the danger closing in.

"Another moment," said Marko. Jäger nodded. Marko moved closer to the peasants. "Please," he begged, "do not force us! We are here to help you. If you refuse our brotherhood, there will be deaths. The dead will cry out to you from their graves and you will be at fault. Please let us work together. For God's sake let me help you!" He rushed up to the old man on a crutch. "They call you Old Savich, correct? You are the eldest man, eh? You are wise, they turn to you for advice. You know that these bandits are not worth the suffering of your people." The man's sad, watery eyes met his. He wrapped his arm around him and pulled him forward, away from the others. They lurched across the dusty floor out of the hearing of the others and stopped under the low loft.

"Old grandfather," he whispered, "you must trust me. You have lived long and can die happily in your bed if you give me these partisans."

"I am very old. I forget things," said the old man.

"You will see horrible things. Please. For your family's sake."

"They will kill us all anyway. You can't deceive an old fool. You know that we will all be meeting St. Sava before the day is out. God have mercy on me: today is my day to die."

"No," said Marko, "simply whisper—"

He felt a thud, as if some one had whacked him in the side with a shovel. He stumbled back, reeling in the shaft of light, blinded by a flash of pain that seemed to obliterate the world in its brightness.

"Knife!" roared a German. "Knife!" shots sputtered like the quick rattle of a snare drum. The smell of hot gunpowder filled the room. Marko heard the screaming of the women outside the barn and felt the anvil against his back, holding him up.

Old Savich was dead, on his knees, still oddly propped on his crutch. His chest, ripped open by the shooting, poured blood down his baggy pants. The ornate knife lay bloody and flecked with straw. He had plucked it out of Marko's own belt. Old Savich's face had no expression as he tottered, then finally dropped onto the knife. Marko looked numbly at the wound in his ribs and covered it with his hand.

The pain flared through him again. "You old bastard! You stupid bastard!" A soldier rushed up to help him. Marko pushed him away.

Kerner was almost laughing at him and Jäger crushed his cigarette like he'd never seen such a fiasco. "Now we try our methods," said Kerner. "You can go back to your appropriate role as translator. We will shoot them one by one until some-one talks. Then, you will be useful."

Marko whirled in a moment of dizziness, but did not fall. The stupid peasants! Stupid! They had made him look a fool. The Germans now thought of him as a fool. "No!" he shouted. "I will get you your partisans. I!"

"You should rest," said Jäger.

Marko staggered forward to the center of the barn. He pressed his hand against his side. He didn't know what a deep wound should feel like, but this jabbed only when he inhaled deeply. He was taking short quick breaths as he scanned the remaining men. He thought of the child Ilya: her pink lower lip soft as a flower and her hands hard and darkened by timeless days of work. "Which one of you is Goran?" said Marko. "*Goran!*" He grimaced from the pain.

The men drifted apart. Goran stood alone. "No," he muttered, "I know nothing. I know nothing."

"Take him," said Marko.

The soldiers turned to their major.

"How long must this go on?" said Kerner, but Jäger tilted his head in assent.

Two soldiers grabbed Goran by the arms. His boots slid, raising a cloud of dust as they dragged him.

"Over there," said Marko, pointing at the anvil. The soldiers held the farmer tightly. His eyes were wide. "Goran is a patriot," said Marko in Serbian. "He is going to tell us where the partisans are."

Goran shook his head. "I do not know, sir. By my mother's head, I do not—"

"Your mother's head? *Your mother's head?*" Marko spat in his face. "Where are the partisans?"

Goran mumbled and began to weep. A coward. A lousy, filthy coward. A man who would beat his women and overwork his horses. And his sons? He was the kind who would humiliate them in public, slap them, insult them, drink slivovitz until he couldn't feel his lips, then go charging off after the closest whore or even a sheep if he were drunk enough. How could Marko have thought people like this could be part of a great future? They were pigs, stupid, foul, disgusting pigs. He knew them—why did he deceive himself?—he had grown up among them. He took a large hammer off the wall. The Germans were watching. They would see Marko wasn't of this breed. They would see.

"Put your hand on the anvil."

The man quivered.

"*Your hand!*"

Goran struggled, but the soldiers held him. Marko hefted the hammer and repeated his order in German. The soldiers needed help. A third placed his bayonet against the peasant's throat while two others forced down his hand. Marko paced, hefting the hammer. The officers' eyes were riveted upon him. Kerner still seemed amused. Jäger looked uncomfortable.

Marko's feelings were like none he had had before. He was frightened in a way similar to that when he had first killed, but this was different. Killing was quick; the satisfaction evaporated with the light fading in the eyes. This moment begged simultaneously to be savored and yet to be consummated. There was some kind of hunger in it, a desire, a feeling as if this moment contained everything you had ever wanted. Revenge? Power? Love? Hate? The handle of the hammer felt smooth as the skin on a woman's thigh. He measured its weight and warmth.

"Stojan did it! Stojan knows!"

Marko glanced at the Germans and grinned. "Too late," he said. He spun and brought down the hammer. It thudded into the bones and slid, plinking the anvil. Marko's nostrils flared. He raised the hammer and brought it down. Blood flecked his face. He raised the hammer again. This time it struck steel and bounced away, ringing like a bell, the backward force causing him to stagger. The soldiers had let go to avoid the flying blood and dropped to one knee. Goran had collapsed, his mouth open, his eyes rolled back in his head. The soldiers gaped up at Marko, then at their officers. Jäger had twisted his face in distaste. Kerner still looked vaguely amused.

"You let him go," Marko gasped at the soldiers. "You let him go!" Sweat trickled through the blood on his face. He whirled on the peasants. "Who is Stojan? Who?"

A man bolted from the group. Two soldiers grabbed him and dragged him struggling to the anvil. "I won't talk," said the man. "God bless Serbia! God bless Serbia!"

"Where are the partisans? Where?"

Stojan turned pale. Marko reached to pull his hand to the anvil. Stojan kicked at him. The soldiers lifted him off the ground. His flailing legs knocked Marko back. Marko kicked him hard in the belly. When the man doubled over, retching, he lifted the man's foot onto the anvil and crushed it, once, twice, three maybe four times. He was drunk, he could no longer tell what he was doing, where his imaginings ended. He had yielded himself to some overpowering drug rising out of the darkness in his soul and he struck until his body had no more strength. It was then he heard Jäger yelling. "That's enough! That's enough!"

When he turned, the major took a step back.

"Don't you want to know?" Marko panted. He lifted the bloody hammer towards one of the remaining men. "You? Are you Stojan's friend? Are you the partisans' friend?"

The little man shook his head, no, no, and he quivered until he wet himself. The odor instantly filled the barn.

"I think you are Stojan's friend."

"There were three," the man said quickly. "They said they would kill us if we did not help. What could we do? Please! What choice—?" He collapsed.

"Their names were Smilovich and Vukadich," said another rapidly. "The third called himself Meso."

"Where are they now?"

"Stojan took them to a hiding place."

"We don't know where! Stojan never told us."

"You will remember," said Marko, smearing the greasy blood on the hammer head against the man's vest.

"Stojan's son knows," the man choked out. "Bogomil knows."

A tall boy about twenty years old charged at Marko. He brought the hammer into his shoulder and leveled him with one blow. "Is this Bogomil?" he growled. The men nodded.

"Where are they?" He kicked at the moaning boy.

"They left at dawn," he blubbered defiantly.

"You will show us."

"No."

"No? I will tell the Germans to spread your legs over the anvil. It won't be your hands I crush." Marko gestured at the soldiers.

"I will tell," begged Bogomil. "Anything!"

Major Jäger drew his Ruger and eased up to Marko like a man checking for mines. "They have told you?" He cleared his throat.

Marko stared at him without answering. He saw the hammer as dark with blood as the night sky. Particles of bone winked like stars. He winced at the pain in his side and saw his own blood in the tear in his tunic. It had drooled and mingled with the blood of the peasants. The drunkenness had come on him like arousal, quickly but in stages. It had left him instantly and he felt some vague shame at having been so exposed, so naked. He felt as if he had lied about love in order to fuck a woman and now he wanted to slip away while she was asleep.

"Well?"

"Well?" Marko returned. "The boy will lead us, but the partisans are gone." He walked past Jäger toward the barn door, his side throbbing.

"Shoot them," he heard Jäger say in an echo, as if in a dream.

"Sir?" said someone.

"They harbored partisans. Shoot them."

"I shall take the order to the rest of the men," said Kerner.

"No, leave the women. Just leave them."

Marko walked into the sunlight like an apparition, like some incredibly deformed creature who causes wonder and fear at his sight. The soldiers drifted away from him even when he was not close to them. The women stared at his bloody tunic. It was not until the shots rolled like thunder that the spell was broken and they began screaming and wailing.

The sun was setting. Marko sagged to the bumper of a truck. He heard Kerner tell some soldiers to clear out the barn, they might use it for the night. They set up pickets and confined the weeping women to one of the larger houses. Major Jäger sent someone with Marko's dagger. The soldier said nothing, approached hesitantly and laid the knife, its hilt stained with dried blood, on the truck as if leaving an offering to an angry God. Later a pudgy man came to bandage Marko's side. He worked quickly and did not speak. He tentatively wiped at the mingled blood of Marko and his victims. He seemed afraid he might hurt Marko or get burned if he touched him too long. In the morning the partisan's hiding place under a rock ledge was found. Only a few chicken bones were scattered around the black smear that had been their fire.

Four days after they had returned to their camp, a corporal newly assigned from Crete was telling two of his friends about two informers who had been found dead on the day he left Skoplje. He was telling all this with the weariness of any soldier who has seen brutality piled on brutality. Telling it was just another way to pass the time between terrors, though he said it partly to prove what a barbaric country they were in. The informers had been a prostitute and her daughter who had only just gone to live with her because her master had been killed. Both women had been found dangling from a lamp post. Their faces were mutilated. "Informer" had been written in blood on handkerchiefs that were spiked to their chests.

The corporal was startled by a sound that he mistook for a dog begging. When he looked across his circle of friends and just behind them, he saw it was the Serb this unit used as a translator—the one who spoke to virtually no one and about whom most of the soldiers spoke in hushed tones. The man squeezed his head in his hands and was weeping. "Ilya, poor Ilya," he repeated again and again. Was Ilya his sister? His girlfriend? The corporal shrugged and asked if anyone had heard anything about new boots. No one had.

Annaliese Dorst, the Wasp

◆

(Belgrade, August 10, 1941)

Holding Annaliese Dorst's gloved, limp hand as if he were about to kiss it, SS-Colonel August Dorst scrutinized Marko carefully over her shoulder, whispering quickly. His murmuring blurred as it echoed off the marble floors and evaporated into the dome of the foyer. Marko picked a fleck of lint off his uniform cap and tried to look indifferent, like an aide-de-camp waiting for orders, more interested in the gilded leaves on the half-Corinthian columns than in the father and daughter intimacies. Eventually, Dorst raised his free hand in a gesture of acquiescence, lowering his bald head slightly, as if admitting he could never really deny the girl anything. "Lieutenant!" he said pleasantly.

Marko approached.

"You are on time, Lieutenant. Very good. Shall we say that some of your compatriots seem to have retained the Turkish sense of time? I will remember your punctuality. It is beastly to keep a lady waiting." Annaliese extended her hand. Marko took it and lowered his forehead to just above it.

"I am honored," said Marko.

She said nothing and Marko saw no change of expression under her black veil.

"As I informed General Nedich, Annaliese is insistent. He recommended you, Lieutenant. I suppose it must be safe. There are occasional incidents, but—pfft!" The colonel flicked his hand. "I shall hold you personally responsible. Annaliese is my treasure."

"I will guard her with my life," said Marko.

"So you have said." Dorst smiled pleasantly and tugged at Marko's collar, now stripped of any Yugoslav army markings. "When the time comes, Lieutenant Renovich, with a new uniform, you could be a captain for us. What would you think of a Serbian SS brigade?"

"I would think it excellent. The Serb is a tough man, but he lacks training. The combination of German training and Serbian hardiness might produce troops to equal the Waffen-SS."

"Perhaps," said Dorst. His expression was a little sad: a mixture of nostalgia for Marko's enthusiasm and of the world-weariness that comes from having heard the intense speeches of many others who were only interested in improving their positions. All the same, he seemed pleased to see this Slav so devoted to the cause. "It is not such a bad world if young men still have faith. You see," he said to Annaliese, "a bright young man. A soldier since he was in his twenties. Going places."

"We should have been your ally, not your enemy. It is what I have always said. Putting the boy king on the throne to abrogate the treaty with Germany was the cheap trick of malcontents who cannot see where the future lies. This uniform should never have faced you. It should always have been at your side."

"Yes, yes," Dorst said somewhat impatiently, gazing at Annaliese worshipfully. "The coup was foolish. King Peter can now rule a hotel suite in Egypt."

"What shall he rule when Africa is ours?"

Dorst pursed his lips as if the inevitability of it bored him. "Lieutenant Renovich sided with our friend Prince Paul a bit too forcefully, it seems. He was on an arrest list my men discovered." He touched Annaliese on the shoulder. "Sightsee, my dear. I'm certain you'll find nothing to entertain you, but go ahead."

"You fret too much," she said. Her voice was low and her vowels were full, rounded, almost tangible. "Until dinner."

Marko saluted, the "Heil Hitler!" reverberating off the columns like the echo of destiny. Two SS privates swung back the doors and Marko rushed down the broad stone steps to catch up with Annaliese. Her thin figure moved rapidly and elegantly toward the limousine. Marko nearly stumbled trying to open her door. They had caught the heavy-browed driver (a corporal) and their bodyguard (an SS sergeant) napping and the men comically bumped into one another reaching for the handle.

"For God's sake," Annaliese said sharply, "I'd rather open it myself." Marko reached past her nonetheless, smiled and twisted the handle. When she climbed inside, he glared at the driver, who curled his lip in a sneer.

"You will take us around the city," Marko said. "Slowly, so that Fraulein Dorst may have a good look."

"Fraulein?" said the sergeant. "*Frau* Colonel Dorst. And the driver has his orders." The sergeant had no respect for a beaten uniform.

Marko was momentarily befuddled. General Nedich had said he was to give a tour to "Annaliese Dorst, the colonel's darling." Then he had added, "She's about your age." It had seemed that the general was talking about her as if she were another eligible young woman. Marko had agreed only because he thought it couldn't hurt his career to flirt with Dorst's daughter. He had even thought that if he could bear the girl he might set aside his oath to himself and marry her, as an investment in the future. He felt stupid and looked at the soldier.

"Open my door," Marko said.

"Do it yourself," said the bodyguard.

It was a cool day, not unpleasant, but without enough brightness in the gray summer sky to lighten even the cleaner building facades. Annaliese settled back in her seat, her head turned toward the window, resting against it like a weary traveller. Marko could barely make out her face. Her skin gleamed porcelain under the black veil. His first impression in the foyer had been of a black wasp. Her strong shoulders tapered to a tiny waist. Under the dress she was bony, he thought, not much of a woman at all. Perhaps she was older than her shape.

"How long have you and SS-Colonel Dorst been married?" he blurted out.

"What business is it of yours? Are you married?"

"No," he said. "I apologize for my bluntness. I under-stood—"

"You are well past the age. She died?"

"I was never married. I have—" How could he say he had once taken an oath without sounding melodramatic? "I have been too busy with my career. I left my village, joined the army and have had little time for socializing. There have been many things to learn."

"I learned a great deal from my first husband, particularly what to look for in the next." She did not elaborate.

He thought how curious the colonel's adoring her now seemed. To be that silly in public with your daughter was not nearly as distasteful as doing so with a frau colonel. He had noticed since his days working with the merchant Bronkovich how Germans doted on their women, often licking their hands, but it seemed particularly tasteless from an officer of Dorst's stature. Marko immediately disliked this shriveled woman who allowed an SS colonel to degrade himself to her, but knew it was essential not to incur her antipathy. A word over the pillow could easily destroy his prospects. He had been prepared to be charming to a daughter; a wife was a different matter and he was confused how to behave.

"Belgrade," he said pleasantly, "is a tolerable city, but no one would claim it has the charm of Dubrovnik. It is certainly not on the level of true cities, such as Prague, Vienna, Paris, or Berlin."

She nodded.

"I fear it may disappoint you."

"I am well-travelled," she said. "The less-frequented places interest me more."

"I see. And do you have particular interests? Churches, perhaps? Perhaps you would like to try Serbian cuisine. It is certainly not remarkable, by world standards—"

She turned abruptly and lifted her veil. "Please," she said, "these pleasantries bore me. My father was a diplomat, my first husband was an envoy, and Colonel Dorst spends too much time in uniform exchanging carefully chosen phrases. If you wish to speak to me, please do it directly, as you would to a friend or a sister." She removed her hat. "I hate all the formalities. I hate them even in myself."

He was struck by the smoothness of her face, so different from his own. It was as pale as he had thought, but also much younger than he would have expected. She was at least eight years younger than he, and maybe as much as thirty years younger than the colonel. Old man, young bride: like an arranged marriage in a peasant village. It revolted him. Her eyes, strikingly violet-blue, were sorrowful, or perhaps bored, but not imbued with the searching curiosity of young eyes. They did not seem to draw in what they saw, but merely to pass over the surface of the world as unmoved by it as the shadow of a cloud.

"As you wish, Frau Colonel."

The car ground into gear and lurched forward. She twisted her face with disgust and turned away. "Who is left who can wish?" she said. The rhythm of the line made Marko think she was quoting someone, but he did not know who.

"I understand," he said thoughtfully. "It is a shallow world without wishes, without dreams, without passion. One must love one's nation, one's beliefs, one's causes, or there is no reason to live."

"And you?" she asked tiredly. "What do you believe? What do you love?"

"Me?"

"You."

"I believe we are on the dawn of a great era. Germany has given Serbia, the whole world, a future."

"Ah." It was no surprise and she wanted him to know it.

"You do not believe me."

"I didn't say that."

"You think I am merely trying to wheedle my way into a comfortable position in the Third Reich."

Amusement played about her lips. "And you are not?"

"I was jailed within three hours of the coup. The anti-German faction was planning my trial on some trumped up charge. My beliefs are more important to me than merely—"

She placed a hand on his arm to silence him. "Listen to me, Lieutenant, what is your name?"

"Marko Renovich. At your service."

"Yes. Renovich, I will swear to you that whatever you say to me will never be repeated to my husband. Never. I will neither advance your case, nor inhibit it, eh? But I utterly assure you that if you continue playing the loyal retainer, I shall never allow you to be my escort again and August may draw what conclusion he likes from it. Do we have an understanding?"

She withdrew her hand from his arm and sat back. He thought to insist he was being genuine, but considered the risk of it too much. "Do you smoke, Frau Colonel Dorst?"

"Always," she said. "Another part of our understanding is that you call me Annaliese."

"Except in front of others."

"I suppose so. You *are* the conquered nation. Except in front of others."

"I am honored, Annaliese. Will you honor me further by calling me Marko?"

" 'Will you honor me further?' " she mocked. "Yes, yes, I will call you Marko. What is it that will make you speak like a human being, Marko? A drink? Surely you are more human when you are drunk. You Serbs love your liquor, I am told. What is it called?"

"Rakia—fruit brandy—is very popular in the countryside, particularly slivovitz, the plum brandy. I, myself, try to avoid getting drunk."

"Why is that?

"I do not like it."

"Why not? I thought all you Slavs liked your drink."

"We do," he said haltingly. "Most of them do. I do not. I have seen too much drunkenness. In my village. When I was young, I mean. I haven't been back since my mother died in 1932."

"Your village?"

"Krushka, in the Shumadia."

"And your family owned the village?"

"No one owns the village. Serbs have always been free landholders, not serfs. My family, alas, owns very little. There was a plague that carried most of them away."

She coolly reached out and touched the scars on his cheek. "Smallpox, obviously."

He snapped his head back as if her fingers burned him.

"Ah," she said. "I shall expect to try this rakia. And the other. And you shall be a gentleman and drink with me."

"Yes, Frau Colonel."

"Annaliese."

"Yes, Annaliese."

"The cigarette?"

"Excuse me, I nearly forgot." He fumbled open a silver case. She took one and held it while he fished matches out of his pocket. She inhaled the smoke deeply. Annaliese's mannerisms reminded him of Greta Garbo's in the first talkie he had seen many years before. Perhaps she was playing the actress playing the bored wife. Marko didn't like this. She was a spoiled brat who needed a good spanking. It was probably why she was already into her second marriage. Oh, some men might say she was beautiful, but Dorst should have known better than to marry her.

"What is this?" she asked, pointing out of the window.

"Only the front is intact. It was a merchant's home."

"It is more elegant than the royal palace."

"Yes, but I suspect the bombs have finished it." Marko grinned. "This man who owned it was an iron merchant, very powerful before the war, but he also was against granting Germany free passage to Albania and Greece and he said so, loudly."

"Where is he now?"

"He likely fled south. I have heard he might have joined Mihailovich and his Chetniks."

"A pity about the house. The destruction in general is quite astounding."

"It could all have been avoided. The Luftwaffe is like the arm of God. It delivered what was deserved on that Palm Sunday."

Annaliese sighed.

The car had entered a street blocked with rubble. The sergeant peered about suspiciously, as if the corporal had driven them into a trap, and raised his machine gun. He was startled by a head appearing out of the devastation, but the dark face vanished behind what was left of a shop front.

"A Gypsy," said Marko as if smelling bad meat. "Looting. He should be shot. They run loose in the devastation like rats."

In front of the glass dividing the front seat from the back, the sergeant settled down, lowering his weapon. He impatiently said something to the driver and signalled him to turn around.

"Would you like to chase this Gypsy?" asked Annaliese.

"I am unarmed."

"If you were armed?"

"They are vermin."

"And you would kill him?" Her eyes flashed.

He hesitated. She was joking, he thought. "I would be honored to kill him for you," he said with a flourish.

"Why?"

He didn't understand the question. "Because he is a looter. Because he is a Gypsy."

There was an amused curl to her lip. Maybe she *was* joking. "So, you liar, it has nothing to do with me."

"I would kill him for you. Yes. If you asked me. But also because looting is forbidden."

"And how many men have you killed?"

He looked away. The car was moving down a relatively clean street to a square. Wehrmacht soldiers had made a fire on the cobblestones and were sipping soup.

"How many, Lieutenant Renovich of the Royal Army of the Serbs, Croats, and Slovenes?"

"None."

She laughed.

"I was imprisoned as soon as the coup occurred," he said quickly. "I escaped only when the bombs started falling. The Luftwaffe saved me from a firing squad. Would I have killed Germans? I was beaten because I would not swear an oath to King Peter. I still have stiffness in my shoulder. It may be permanent."

She looked at the shoulder strap of his uniform as if trying to see the skin underneath. "You could have killed some of ours in the defense of your country, if you'd liked."

"I wouldn't have taken arms against Germany. This is not my country, not the way it is, not the way it has been. When it becomes part of Europe, then it will be my country. Now it is just a backwater. A place the Turks discarded. You would be appalled at how people live in the villages. No better than rats. They have no culture at all."

"I have read that Goethe learned your language simply so he could read your national epic. That would indicate some culture, would it not?"

"Well, I would think he was disappointed. I have heard these from the old *guslars* since I was a child. The ballads of Kraljevich Marko are vulgar compared to the *Chanson de Roland* or the *Niebelungenlied*. Marko is a lout and a traitor."

"Actually, I believe the point might have been more that Goethe learned the language in three days." There was a sudden flicker of interest in her eyes. "But you are the name-sake of this Marko. You insult the place you were born."

"I have no illusions about my people. I was born in the Shumadia, which means 'the wooded area.' My village was as backward as when the Turks left. But I had the sense to see the world. I am not now the ignorant, dirty-fingered peasant I was born."

"So. One of nature's noblemen."

"Excuse me?"

"You are a new Napoleon, born in the backwoods, destined for a palace."

"I have aspirations."

She laughed. He wasn't certain whether she meant it as ridicule or not.

"That is to say I have no desire to spend my life ignorant and poor. Not when the future can be so rich."

"I suppose peasant life is as dreary as life gets."

"Drearier. It is no life at all. It is not that I wish to put my beginnings far behind me as much as I wish to put an end to that kind of life. A new world deserves a new way of living. The Bolsheviks would have us all be peasants. That kind of sentimentalizing of misery must be ended. The National Socialist movement is bringing civilization to Serbia as surely as the British brought it to the Indians and the French to the Africans."

She was craning her neck at the Cathedral of the Archangel Michael. "No politics," she said.

"I'm sorry," he said. "What would you like to talk about?"

"Anything else."

"I would like to know more about you. Perhaps you will tell me about yourself."

"You *are* a bore," she said, but with a slight twinkle in her eye. "Tell the driver where to take us. I am getting hungry. And you need a drink, definitely, or you'll kill me babbling about Bolshevism."

Marko tapped on the divider and blew through the speaker tube. The sergeant plucked out the whistle plug. "Just up here, turn left," said Marko.

"I take orders only from the Frau Colonel."

Marko handed the tube to Annaliese. "Go where he says," she said.

The sergeant eyed Marko. "You are certain? Colonel Dorst instructed us—"

"Go where he says!" she snapped.

"Yes, madam." The sergeant clicked the plug back into the tube.

"I am not certain the café is open, though it was open two days ago. It is very near the Kalemegdan."

"Ah. The park. We shall walk in the park afterwards."

"It is a very large park. There are many trees. I would hope that the army has made it secure. But we may encounter a stray vagabond. I would not endanger you."

"This is a conquered city. You and August act like you are the ones who were beaten. If I cannot stroll in the park, then you are admitting you have not yet won."

Marko was a bit confused by her last sentence. He, after all, was wearing the stripped uniform of the beaten army, so, in some sense, even though he had cast his lot with the Third Reich, he was not the same as the SS-Colonel. On the other hand, perhaps it indicated that she had begun to consider him one of theirs, which was what he wanted. He could do a lot for them, certainly more than translating and taking their wives on tours. The Germans had put a new government in Croatia and would eventually need one in Serbia. The Germans were not prejudiced against younger men, they looked to the future, not the past. He imagined having his own ministry in that government. "I suppose if a woman shows no fear it proves that there is nothing to fear," he said pleasantly. "You are a very wise woman—Wait! Here. Stop here."

Marko was relieved to see six young Wehrmacht officers sipping beer at the two sidewalk tables. He had already been wondering where he would find Annaliese her food and drink if the place were closed. He even smelled the grilling of *chevapchichi* as he opened the door. The officers froze as they saw his uniform, then recognized the car and the colonel's wife as Marko took her gloved hand and led her inside. "Good day," two of them said as she passed. She ignored them.

The inside of the café was tiny and the three tables were empty. A picture of Vuk Karadzhich, the man who had standardized the Serbian language in the nineteenth century, hung over a dusty fireplace. The barman might have been his twin, and cultivated the resemblance by training his big handlebar mustache to look like Vuk's. Vuk, however, also wore a fez, upon which someone had pinned a small Hitler Youth medallion.

Marko spoke in Serbian to the barman. "This is the wife of a very important German official. She would like lunch."

"Tell him," interrupted Annaliese, "I would be interested in local specialties. He is not to prepare anything other than local specialties."

"The lady wants Serbian cuisine only," Marko translated.

The man was plainly flattered. He smiled at Annaliese and bowed twice. "I have a piece of veal I have been saving," he told Marko. "Commercial travellers would often walk down from the Serbian Crown Hotel to eat my Wiener schnitzel."

Annaliese heard "Wiener schnitzel," and tugged Marko's arm. "Tell him if he makes anything German or Austrian or Italian or French, I shall go out of my mind and have him shot."

A slight squint told Marko that the man understood more than he was letting on. Marko translated the remark as: "She is interested in the *chevapchichi* and perhaps a Serbian salad. Veal disagrees with her. Do you have the ingredients for a Serbian salad?"

"She may have all that I possess." He smiled and bowed several more times.

"And rakia?"

"Would the lady not prefer wine, instead?"

"Rakia. She wants to learn about us. Don't ask me why."

The man was bothered by the last remark, but didn't say so. He was grateful to have survived the devastating bombing, happy to be alive and still in business, thought Marko. All the posturing of Serbs about their independent natures likely covered an inclination to be defeated and controlled, inbred by five hundred years of Turkish rule. Marko brushed a chair with his hand and Annaliese sat. The sergeant followed the man toward the kitchen, but stopped at the curtained doorway, having seen all there was.

"If the meal is bad, shall we have him shot?" said Annaliese, holding up a cigarette in a black holder.

Marko lit it. "Under what law?"

"Under the law that dull cooking is a crime."

"We should have to shoot many more than him."

"True. It would cripple the war effort for lack of bullets."

"He is obviously a hoarder or a trafficker on the black market."

"I wouldn't shoot a man under a pretence," she said, staring at the portrait of Vuk. "The Third Reich now owns this nation. Why is it necessary to make up lies?"

"Very well," said Marko. "Your wish is my command." He remembered his earlier thought about the underlying inclination to obey and it made him uncomfortable to associate himself with this Asiatic inheritance. His obedience was not of that kind, he thought, not a matter of breeding as much as reason. He was not an ordinary Serb.

The proprietor brought a tray with two glasses and an unlabeled bottle. He had put on an apron which smelled of onions. "Rakia," he said with pleasure. "From cherries."

"Very good," said Marko as he poured. "It isn't polite to keep a lady waiting." The man bowed and went back into the kitchen.

Marko lifted his glass and clinked it against hers. "Prost!" he said. "To a lovely lady."

Looking straight into Marko's eyes—searching, maybe, searching for what?—Annaliese took a mouthful of the drink. Spreading her long fingers on her chest, she widened her eyes and stopped breathing. Marko put down his glass and reached for her. She coughed, exhaled, then waved her hand like a fan. Not prepared for the drink's strength, she had swallowed too much. "God!" she said. "That *is* a drink! Delicious! Pour me another."

The sergeant had come halfway across the room, thinking she had been poisoned. His jaw muscles were tight as he turned back to the kitchen. I must not be too friendly with this woman, thought Marko. The sergeant will fill the colonel's ear with any detail that looks bad.

After another drink, the salad arrived. The tomatoes were overripe, said Annaliese, but the minced peppers had just the right sting. Shortly after, the *chevapchichi* arrived. Annaliese picked up one of the little beef sausages with her fork, bit into it, then rotated it slowly, inspecting it. "These are a bit singed," she remarked.

"They are grilled in the primitive fashion over an open flame."

"They are all the more flavorful for it. You use the word 'primitive' with such a sneer. We would all be better if we could accept the primitive in us. I think we shall not shoot this man after all, not today."

"No? Then perhaps tomorrow?"

She smiled. "Perhaps we shall have an impulse tomorrow, one way or the other. Is it possible to act purely on impulse? What do you think? If everything were permitted, if you could do anything you wished, what would you do?"

His first thought was that the rakia had loosened her up. A flush was spreading over her pale cheekbones. How would Dorst react if he brought her back drunk? "I cannot know what I would do. Who can have absolute power? No one can do everything he fantasizes."

She speared a wedge of tomato and held it up dripping. "You are very wrong. I have always been able to do anything I wish. And now I can do even more."

"Then you must tell me what it is like. What do you do?"

She took the wedge of tomato whole into her mouth. A rivulet of its juice meandered through the powder on her chin. "Nothing," she said calmly. "I do nothing." She gestured for him to fill her glass.

He talked to distract her. "Nonsense. You are part of building the Thousand-Year Reich. You are rescuing the world from the barbarians of the East. You are saving my country from itself. How can you say you do nothing?"

"Politics," she winced. "I open my legs for the colonel when he feels up to it. Is this saving the world? Pour."

Marko glanced at the sergeant, who was watching them warily while nibbling at a chunk of bread. "Each person serves in his or her own way," he said carefully. "Wives are an important element in the struggle."

She snatched the bottle from him and poured for herself. "If you don't stop talking like that, I will have *you* shot. Drink! You are letting this delicious petrol evaporate." She raised her glass as if toasting the portrait of Vuk, then winked at the sergeant.

Despite Marko's fears, she drank little more. She quickly dispatched exactly what she needed to reach a familiar level of intoxication, settled into it as comfortably as she would a silken bathrobe, then sipped to maintain the condition. She ate more than he would have expected a woman with her figure to eat, though she did not eat lustily. She picked at it, constantly inspecting it as if she were looking for the good-luck coin baked into a Christmas cake, then condescended to a mouthful as if disappointed. It took nearly two hours to finish the meal, then she stood up abruptly. "The park," she said. "You will take me into the park."

"Do you think it is wise?" he asked, but she walked past him and out of the café. He glanced at the sergeant, who sucked at something stuck in his tooth. Marko shrugged helplessly. "Women!" he said. The sergeant wasn't interested.

Annaliese waited for a tank and three trucks to drive past, then hurried to cross to the Kalemegdan before a large contingent of infantry led by three men on horseback blocked her. Marko ran to catch up. The sergeant spun past the last horse, nearly bumping it. The Wehrmacht lieutenant on it shouted down at him. Annaliese noticed none of this, she was charging ahead on one of the pathways, and when Marko reached her, she calmly took his arm as if he had been beside her all along. He watched the bushes, neglected because of the war, and felt naked without a weapon. An SS private had been strangled in the Topchider Park near the old palace across the Sava river only two weeks before. It might have been an ordinary robbery, but everyone assumed it was merely because the boy was a German, and there had been reprisals: ten for one.

He apologized for the weeds in the flower beds and between the cracks in the pavement. He remarked that her countrymen would never allow it to continue to deteriorate. Once things had settled down the Kalemegdan would be as lovely as the Tiergarten in Berlin. Each conqueror rebuilt the Kalemegdan in his own way; this time it would be the same for a thousand years. By the time they had reached the high bluff overlooking the junction of the Sava and the Danube, he had explained much of the history of the park, the site of fortress after fortress, over a dozen since ancient times. Celts, Romans, Turks, Tzar Lazar, Dushan the Great, and so many others had built their walls only to have them reduced to the fragments scattered over the hill. He had thought that all this guidebook history would interest her very little, and though she kept urging him to continue she was certainly unimpressed. He continued only because he did not know what else to do. This woman would never speak well of him to her husband. There was no friendliness in the way she held his arm. As an amusement in a conquered city he was a failure, and though this ought to mean nothing compared to his commitment to the cause, it would mean everything to his future. His anger had been aroused by the drinks, and he only kept it from being released by clenching his right fist and babbling more quickly about the Vojvodina, the area to their north, now stretched before them.

He pointed out a fisherman dropping his nets into the river as if there were no war. A thousand years ago, he said, she might have seen nearly the same thing if she had climbed the parapets of one of the medieval fortresses. She had said nothing since entering the park and she startled him by suddenly taking her hand from his arm, turning her back on the view and staring up at the statue high atop the column beside them. A male nude with stylized musculature stared out over the Sava toward the swampy land on the other side, the confluence with the Danube, and the Pannonian plain beyond. One foot was in front of the other and his hands rested in front of him on the pommel of a huge sword.

"And this is?"

"*Victory* by Mestrovich. There is another statue of his in the park honoring the French for their help in the Great War. Perhaps your husband should order it removed."

"This is a fine work. Very modern."

"It was not made for the Kalemegdan. It was supposed to be in the center of the city, but there were typical provincial reactions because of the nudity. Imagine that. Nudity! It proves how backward our leaders have been."

She circled the base. "*Victory* should be nude, but he doesn't belong in the center of the city. He stands here with the smell of two thousand years of blood swirling around him. The victor always bathes in death. You can smell it, can't you? Think of all the ghosts roaming these broken walls."

"You are very poetic."

She shook her head. "No. I am very literal."

"Truly. It is an insight worthy of Heine or Stefan George."

"I am afraid George is quite out of fashion in Berlin. In any case I am not being symbolic. Only the noise of the city and this wind keeps us from hearing the dead, from smelling the blood dried on the mortar." She had spread her arms and twirled, her head tossed back, as if hearing a waltz, her dress clinging tightly to her narrow buttocks and legs. Her possession possessed him and for a moment he was convinced he smelled something, too. There was also a strange murmuring, like whispering, which he was always on the edge of comprehending. He suddenly knew that this woman was beautiful—not pretty, not physically ideal, not in the ordinary way in which he had been attracted to the many prostitutes and other women available to young officers. Annaliese perplexed you until you did not know how to react to her, and then, with all your preconceptions of woman stripped away, you saw her for the first time and were entranced. He understood now the devotion he had seen in Dorst, but when he noticed the sergeant standing on the pathway behind them he also knew that what he had heard was only the wind moving through the grasses and the ancient archways. What he had smelled was the vegetation decaying by the river.

She pointed away from the rivers. "What is down there?"

"The Roman well. Would you like to see it?"

"Let's go further along the top."

"There are several ruins this way: Roman, Turkish, Tzar Lazar's gate."

She walked ahead of him, her legs elegantly moving over the dirt path. Whatever excitement she had shown in her brief dance reverted to languid self-absorption. When she paused at the top of a short, curving staircase that had once led into a tower, or when she looked down into a square of weeds that had once been a chamber or a tiny courtyard, her violet-blue eyes were again passing over everything as if it were mildly interesting, but no more.

An old woman appeared near one of the walls carrying three tiny, overripe pears in her apron. He thought of his mother and the long night sitting by her coffin. Barbaric custom! When the old woman tried to sell a pear to Marko, he brushed her aside. Annaliese, however, turned back to her and bought one. The old woman was effusively grateful and Marko told her to go away. As soon as she was gone, Annaliese stopped at a gap in a wall and took one bite of the pear. Chin glistening with juice, she thrust it at Marko. He took a small bite, wiped his mouth with the back of his hand, and thanked her. "Please," he said, "you finish it," but she tossed the pear over the wall and down the steep drop to the river.

Farther on, they came to one of the old gates—the Defte-dar's Gate, if he remembered correctly. A long vault with a cobblestone floor passed under the hill. He didn't like entering the dim tunnel and told her it might not be safe, but she took him by the elbow and pulled him. He briefly thought she was trying to lose their bodyguard to get him alone. He wasn't sure how he should react to that. Old man, young bride. It was usually a bad idea to refuse a woman—they never forgive that—but it was probably a worse idea to accept an SS colonel's wife.

The tunnel was dank and smelled of urine. Halfway through, they saw a German gunnery sergeant just inside one of the alcoves in the walls on each side. He had a woman pressed against the wall, one hand inside her blouse, the other clawing up her dress. She watched Marko and Annaliese with a smile, her gold front tooth gleaming. The gunnery sergeant's face was buried in her neck and he did not notice them until he fumbled to open the buttons of his fly. He glanced back angrily and studied Marko's uniform. Marko turned away and tugged at Annaliese, who continued to stare as she walked. The soldier watched her coldly for several seconds then thrust his face back into the woman's neck. The woman winked at Annaliese as if there were some secret between them. Marko tugged her more forcefully and they left the tunnel.

"I apologize for that," said Marko. "I will report the man."

"You do not know his name," said Annaliese impatiently.

"But I saw his regiment patch."

"If you report him, I will never forgive you."

"But the slut could get information from him, could infect him, or lead him into a trap. There are reasons for him not to fraternize. As a military man, I—"

"Please! You are giving me a headache. You are more rigid than one of those ancient Prussian generals. Do you know how many pompous local guides my husband has arranged for me? Sometimes I think Hitler is smashing his way across Europe merely so that August can bore me to death with stiffnecks like you. But you, you are the worst. Normally they try to impress me with how wonderful everything from their country is: the food, the air, the pig manure. With you it is how wonderful Belgrade is going to be *after* we replace it. How magnificent it will be at the end of the Thousand-Year Reich. What Slavic romantic drivel! You won't ever see it! I won't ever see it!" She laughed, a high-pitched witch's cackle.

Marko spun away from her before he struck her. Is this what being loyal meant? Eating shit off the Colonel's plate? No woman had ever dared speak to him that way. He remembered one of the ballads of Kraljevich Marko. The hero had gouged out an insulting woman's eyes and thrust them into her bosom. He cracked his fist against the palm of his right hand. He spoke slowly, without turning to look at her. "I will take you back to your car. It is obvious you would prefer another guide. I will tell the colonel that I am not sufficiently—"

"Look!" said Annaliese, rushing past him. Down below, two men reeled out of the tunnel. They clung to each other's shoulders and spun together awkwardly, like a top losing speed. They tumbled to the ground, cursing. One was the sergeant assigned to guard Annaliese and Marko. The other was the gunnery sergeant. He flailed his fist at their body-guard's head, but only struck the helmet.

Marko shook himself out of his confusion and pursued Annaliese down the path. She, twisting her ankle, hopped on one leg and removed her shoes, but went on even before Marko could catch up. Legs flailing, the fighters had rolled over. The gunnery sergeant grabbed at the other's head to bang it against the ground.

Marko slipped and tumbled off the path into the grass. He landed on his rear, slid several feet, then used the downward motion to stand up. He swatted at the burrs on his trousers and barely had time to notice he had lost his cap when he saw the gold-toothed whore emerging from the dark mouth of the tunnel. She moved intently toward the struggling soldiers. When she pulled the long knife from her sleeve, it glinted.

"Look out!" Marko shouted. "Look out!"

The knife came down on the gunnery sergeant's back. It entered his shoulder and he straightened, only to have the bodyguard, unaware of what had happened, punch him. The knife was embedded firmly in his shoulder. It slipped from the woman's grasp. She gripped the handle again, but he reached back at her and the blade snapped with a plink that Marko could hear as he scrambled down the hillside, falling and rolling over grass and stones. "Look out! Look out!" The woman desperately stabbed with the broken blade, then threw it away as the gunnery sergeant tumbled to the side, his legs still tangled with the confused bodyguard's beneath him. She went for the gunnery sergeant's pistol. With one hand he held down the holster flap, with the other he flailed, but he was so tangled up in his pain he could do nothing more than frustrate her. She spat at him. She clawed at his hand on the holster. She struck him across the face with her forearm.

She was only a few meters away. Marko had hit the bottom of the hill with a roll and was charging, charging. Her hand went under the holster flap. It flew up. Marko was halfway to her. The Ruger came out. He was closer. The sergeant clawed at her hopelessly. Her dark eyes turned on Marko. He could see the "O" of the barrel. He leaped at her, feet first, and in the air saw the flash and smelled the powder. He landed on top of her. Her chest was between his thighs, and she collapsed like a rag doll folded backward at the knees. The explosion of the gun had stunned him. I am dead, he thought. She has killed me.

Their sergeant had extricated himself and took his machine gun from under him. He was flicking the mechanism to make certain no dirt was in it and panting, eyes large as boulders. The gunnery sergeant was groaning, squirming, trying to crawl away into the grass as his hand groped over his shoulder for the buried blade.

The woman's eyes rolled in her head as if the force of his jump had knocked her unconscious, but they widened as she looked up at Marko. "You pig," she muttered in Serbian. "You whore." She stretched for the pistol, but Annaliese had already picked it up.

He crawled off her, flicking dirt at her with his fingers. He numbly studied his hands, his chest, his dusty thighs. He was not shot. The bullet had ripped through the cloth adjacent to his shoulder strap, leaving a hole like a cigarette burn. He should have used his father's dagger, illegally concealed under his tunic, he thought, but he was not going to die. His legs were rubbery as he stood, but he was alive.

Their bodyguard had gone to the gunnery sergeant. "Are you all right, you fool? Are you all right?" A centimeter of the broken blade was sticking out of his shoulder and the back of his tunic was cut in several places, but there wasn't much blood. He settled to the ground on his side and said, "Shit!" Marko noticed the gunnery sergeant's fly was still unbuttoned.

Annaliese thrust the pistol into Marko's hand. It was warm. He numbly pointed it at the woman on the ground. She twisted her lower legs out from under her with a grimace. Then raised herself on her elbows. She seemed too calm. Marko glanced at the sergeant, and they both, as if having the same thought, looked up the tunnel and at the surrounding slopes and walls. There was no one.

"Who are you?" demanded the sergeant.

"Do I hear something?" she said in Serbian. "Pigs grunting. I hear pigs grunting."

"What did she say?" asked the sergeant.

"She called you a pig," said Marko.

The sergeant took one step and kicked her in the face.

Blood streamed from her nose. He kicked her again and droplets of it flecked the dusty earth. She spat. Her gold tooth gleamed in a wad of bloody saliva on her chest.

"Did you kill the boy in the Topchider?" asked the sergeant.

"I hear pigs. I hear pigs."

The sergeant glanced at Marko.

"She doesn't say."

The sergeant kicked her in the side. Marko thought he heard the ribs break. She gasped for air. "Pigs," she muttered through her broken teeth. "Pigs."

"When the Gestapo gets her, she will answer more questions than she can imagine," said the sergeant.

"No," said Annaliese. "Summary execution."

"What?" said the sergeant.

Annaliese came forward. "Summary execution. She attacked a German soldier."

"We will take her in," said the sergeant, trying to ignore Annaliese.

"No," she said. "The lieutenant here has never killed anyone. He risked his life. He should get the pleasure."

"Pleasure?" The sergeant studied her for a moment. "We cannot take it upon ourselves without orders. She might reveal useful information."

"She will be a fine example. I want Marko to shoot her." She touched Marko's arm. "Shoot her. I'll watch."

The sergeant was squinting. He seemed to think it was some kind of tasteless joke. The woman had raised herself to her elbows again and was smiling. Her gold tooth was sliding in the saliva down her blouse. Marko thought about how close he had been to dying when the woman had fired. She would have killed him, the sergeant, Annaliese, if she'd had the chance.

"This man should not be armed," said the sergeant. "He should give me the pistol immediately."

"No," said Annaliese sharply. "I have ordered him to execute her."

"Excuse me, Frau Colonel Dorst, but the wife of an officer has no authority to order anything."

"No?" The way she spoke it conveyed more to the sergeant

than just a threat. His face began subtly to relax. He knew that whatever the implicit threat was, Annaliese would carry it out. The sergeant hated her for this, Marko suspected, but knew he could not resist. "Well, then, I give him permission. He wants to, does he not? He is helping the Reich eliminate its enemies."

"I am a soldier, too," said Marko.

The sergeant sneered as if Marko mocked him. "I will go for help for this fool," he said quietly. He turned his anger on the gunnery sergeant hissing in his pain. "You see, shithead! This is why you don't let yourself be led around by the cock. Shit!" He headed into the tunnel.

"Well?" said Annaliese. Her voice was low. "Do it."

Marko looked at her. Her eyes were wide. She touched the upper part of his arm and he broke her gaze. The injured gunnery sergeant had closed his eyes. The Serbian woman was staring. Did she know enough German to know what was going on? Did she care?

Marko took one step forward. He aimed between her eyes. His legs, already rubbery, began to shake, and he needed to hold his gun hand by the wrist, it was so unsteady.

Annaliese's breath caressed his ear. "Shoot," she whispered. "Do it for a new world. Do it for me."

"Whore!" said the woman in Serbian.

Marko did not hear the gun go off. His ears roared with a neverending thunder. Was it his blood pounding? His heart bursting? Was it the dead spirits of the battlements chanting? He closed his eyes for what seemed like minutes. When he opened them again, he saw he had missed. The bullet had torn through the woman's jaw. He saw bone in the oozing blood. Still on her back, she was defiant, cursing at death in wet sputters as he lowered the gun again.

He jerked the trigger and missed her completely. Dirt spattered. He fired once, twice, three times into her chest and she fell flat, twisted and pulled with her hands toward the tunnel. Annaliese impatiently took the pistol from him. Her voice was clear and calm in the hurricane of noises he heard in his head, though what she said was unintelligible to him. She bent at the waist and placed the gun at the dying woman's head. The report cleared the noises from him. The body stretched and died. The trees stirred and Marko heard a bird sing.

Annaliese picked up the woman's gold tooth. She wiped and wrapped it in a handkerchief, and stuck it in her sleeve. "You did that badly. Ah, well, you shall do better." She smiled. "Virgins always have to learn."

Soldiers appeared from everywhere. Chaos swirled around him. Some were helping the gunnery sergeant, some were aiming at Marko. Annaliese raised the pistol in the air and identified herself. Marko blinked. It was nothing, he told himself. Nothing. Not pleasure, not disgust. His hand trembled as if killing were something terrifying, but it was nothing. A jerk of the finger and she died. She had been dead before Annaliese fired into her head. He had killed her. Stunned, he felt a gasp of triumphant joy, as if something he had longed for and never expected to have had dropped out of the sky. He had told himself since he was sixteen that he was no longer a boy, but now, just in his thirties, he finally felt like a man.

Someone pulled at his arm, but Annaliese shoved the man away. "Marko saved my life," she said. "Do not ruin the moment." Finally, an SS major came through the tunnel in an open car. He recognized Annaliese and thanked Marko grudgingly. There would be reports, but of course the Frau Colonel Dorst was free to freshen up and appear at her convenience. He offered them his car. Annaliese insisted upon walking.

Accompanied by four infantrymen, she led the dazed Marko back the way they had come, but when they left the Kalemegdan, instead of going to her car she led him up the street, in the direction of the old Serbian Crown Hotel. The banners of the Third Reich were draped over the entrance and armed guards flanked it. She had no need to ask for her key. A bellman rushed up behind her and followed them into the elevator.

"Where are we going?" Marko asked.

"To my suite. You need a drink."

"The café . . ." He wasn't sure what he was trying to say. He should be elated, he thought. He had killed a traitor. He had been part of saving two men's lives. He had stared death in the face and he had become death, all within minutes. He should be swaggering. But it had all seemed trivial at the same time as it had shocked his entire system. He felt neither bad about it, nor good. He knew nothing had really changed in him, yet he wanted to have been changed.

The soldier posted at her door unlocked it. Inside the suite was luxurious. The inlays on the baroque secretary formed a Medusa. The gilded picture frames had cupids at the corners. Marko recognized the sitting room, but could not remember when he had been in it. Old Bronkovich had preferred the Excelsior Hotel, but perhaps he had once met with someone here. Marko would have fetched their coffee and baklava, lit their cigars, and handed the legal documents back and forth. He was a long way from that now, he thought. Bronkovich had treated Marko as if he'd owned him. Now Marko would have the power, not to make vulgar commodity deals but to reshape the nation, bring it into the modern era. I have killed, he thought. No one can own me.

He barely noticed the blonde maid who had come through the door behind him. "As ordered, madam, I began drawing your bath as soon as you entered the hotel."

"Leave it," said Annaliese. "Give instructions that I am not to be disturbed, not even by the colonel. I—we have had a shocking day."

"Yes, madam." The door clunked behind her.

Annaliese crossed to an armoire inlaid with hunting hounds leaping at a stag. "You need a drink, lieutenant."

"I am quite fine."

She was already pouring. "Don't be polite. You cannot pretend with me. You need slivovitz, but there is nothing but wine, chartreuse, cognac, and schnapps." She twisted her nose in disgust. "Schnapps is for August. I hate to have it in my rooms."

"He does not stay with you?"

"He comes when I permit him. This was long ago agreed. He amuses me on occasion." She handed Marko a goblet half full.

He sipped it. "Cognac," he said quietly. "The nectar of the gods."

"Cognac is overrated. If it weren't for Napoleon, it would be a regional curiosity, like your rakia." She looked him full in the face. "My first taste—well, I was certain the rakia was just that, a regional oddity with no subtlety. But the second"—she swallowed, tossed her head as if shaking a crick out of her neck, then ran her fingers down her throat—"was less like fire and more like coals. Do you know what I mean?"

"You have the soul of a poet."

He could see, for some reason, the remark put her off slightly—too conventional, too much like embassy flattery. He took a quick swallow.

"Cognac will do." She sipped, closed her eyes, and lifted her chin as if basking. "There. We both feel it. Like anger burning from the belly downward." She opened her violet eyes and looked straight into his. He swallowed another mouthful.

It was not something he saw. He knew that. He had heard men say that you could see it in the eyes. He had even heard that on some primal level, it was merely chemistry; if a man were truly receptive, a woman, like an animal, emitted subtle odors. But in a world of perfume, cigarettes, gelignite, and the dust of bombed cities, how could one be sensitive enough to that? And what is it that one could take in through the eyes that signaled desire?

Were Annaliese's eyes any different from the eyes of the woman he had just killed? Could he have seen desire for the bullet in her eyes? Whatever occurred in man might have been more like the ancient Greeks' explanation of seeing: our eyes project a beam outward and it bounces back. I cast my want upon her, he thought, and it reflects, blinding me to whatever she truly feels. She, like the future, like the world, is ultimately unknowable. He stepped forward and took her glass. She did not move. When his fingers brushed hers, she audibly gasped. He thought she was going to turn away, but her relentless eyes locked upon his as he lowered the glasses to the wide settee arm.

He placed his hands upon her hips and pulled. The sharp bones pressed through her dress and his tunic. She winced as if startled by the edge of a chipped goblet, then leaned back, amused, her arms limp. Their noses nearly touched. He could smell the cognac as their breaths mingled. Sweat tickled in his groin as he pressed her hips against him again, sharply, his fingers probing the flesh of her buttocks, his thumbs stroking the curve of her hip bones.

She dropped her head and chuckled seductively. Their foreheads touched. She brushed his nose with hers, ran her fingertips over the scars on his cheek, then turned her head and kissed him. She was expertly coy at first, merely playing about his mustache and chin, but when he drew back, her lips would chase his, nipping at his closed mouth as if it could be caught and forced open. Inhaling sharply, she brought her entire body against his, clutching his head in both hands, grasping his mouth against hers, her tongue circling and exploring under his lips as he madly sparred with it, caressing its undersurface, slipping past it to touch her teeth and gums and the warmness of her mouth.

Caught in the tides, they bobbed, almost staggered and fell. She backed away and took him by the hand. "Over here," she said unsteadily, and sat upon the settee. He knelt, paused to peer at her, then reached for the button at her throat. The top of it was pearly and hemispherical. It slipped away from him twice, just awkwardly enough to make him think of where he was. It would have been dangerous enough to touch a daughter of SS-Colonel Dorst, but his wife? As the third button finally slipped through the narrow buttonhole, he glanced at the door wondering if it were locked, but she seized his head and jerked him against her breastbone. Under the hard shell of her rib cage he could feel her heart racing. The perfume was overpowering. When he bit, trying to catch her tight skin in his mouth, a tang like benzine filled his mouth. He pushed downward, exploring until he found the fleshier top of her breasts, but by then he was no longer interested in a bite of skin. He pressed his nose under the lacy edge of her camisole, strained his tongue out until his throat ached trying to touch her nipple.

She began to whisper rapidly in German, as if she were practicing a patter song from a Viennese cabaret, directing it over Marko's head at someone standing behind him. Her long legs had wrapped around his hip, her heels bumping at the small of his back when he reached up and exposed her breast by tugging down the camisole. "No!" she said, evidently meaning that he should not damage her underclothes, for her breathing grew heavier and her sputter of smeared words resumed, louder though no clearer than before. As he took the nipple

[156]

into his mouth, tormenting it with the circular motion of his tongue, he clung to her waist desperately, the pleasure mixing with an intoxicating sense of fear: his mind on the rubbery tip, on the unlocked door, on the stream of incomprehensible syllables pouring out of her.

He lifted his head, studied the redness of the breast awkwardly sticking out of her clothes. Her throat and the tight skin over her collarbones were similarly flushed. She half opened her eyes and clenched him tighter with her legs, grimacing, white teeth flashing like razors. She is finished, he thought, but no, she twisted her head, yearning, her fingers grasping his shoulder straps as if they were handles. "She nearly hit you," she said breathlessly, turning his head to look at the tear where the bullet had passed. A little to his left it would have ripped into his throat; ten inches lower, into his heart.

He unbottoned his tunic and pulled the ornately sheathed dagger from his waistband. Annaliese looked at it with a sexual delight that surprised him. "You are an assassin," she said. It might have been a question or a statement, he couldn't tell, but he could be shot instantly for carrying the dagger. And Annaliese might report him, if it amused her.

The explosion of the woman's jaw flashed across his mind. He placed the dagger on the seat beside Annaliese and dropped his hands to his fly buttons. She picked up the dagger, gave one quick flick of her tongue to its hilt and unsheathed it. She placed the point against the side of his neck and with the other hand yanked him firmly down, loosening the clasp of her legs and sliding her hips out to meet him. Lifting her skirt, he saw the clasp of her garter, the white flesh above, the surprising sky blue silk of her underwear. He slipped a finger under the garter strap, caressed the smooth skin upward under the hem of the pants almost to her groin, then pulled it away. She exhaled with an "Ah!" then began babbling again. He thought she said "My body, my flesh, my life without end . . ." but he wasn't certain.

When she jerked his torn epaulet again, however, he was forced lower and the dagger thudded into the carpet. Directed by her hands, he kissed her knee, then slid upward across the fabric and onto the infinitely soft thigh. He was brushing it with his lips, breathing in the sea-air smell of her crotch, when she grabbed him by the ear, pulling his face against her panties, rubbing his nose and chin against the damp fabric. The intensity was unbearable. The vortex was spinning faster and drawing him into its chaos. He angrily tore himself away. He would not lap at her like some dog. He would not let her take her pleasure this way. Annaliese was here for his pleasure. He felt strong, gigantic, capable of anything, willing to murder Colonel Dorst, to finish the act even if the entire SS came through the door.

He ripped out the seam of her panties with both hands, but with her vulva exposed, the violence of his own act startled him, as if he had caught himself tumbling into madness. His mood abruptly reversed into sadness, powerlessness, and the feeling he had rent not just the silk, but the moment. She, however, had twisted her head back with a whimper, stretched her body, and arched her hips upward. He stared at the torn flap of cloth lying below on the settee. She clawed at his shoulders and he hypnotically dropped toward her. Hands shaking, he placed his thumbs on the soft lips and spread them gently, fearfully, as if he were opening a rose that might fall apart before its secret beauty were revealed.

The German she now spoke was clear. "Yes, there, yes, precisely . . ." He ticked the glassy moistness with his tongue. She hissed through her teeth and he plunged against her, tasting salt and bitterness, wine and brass. He squirmed against her and she clutched his head, as if she were trying to squeeze it inside her body, to take him into her womb. He held his breath until he nearly passed out, then turned to one side to take a quick gasp. The turn began the waves of contraction in her body. She gasped and thrashed, biting her lower lip and murmuring unintelligibly again. He wiped his mouth against the inside of her thigh and flipped open the buttons of his trousers just as she settled downward, slowly panting. He moved forward, smiling and staring into her face pale as death. His erection brushed her knee and the touch was a spark, but before he could place it within her, she closed her legs against his side, wrapping her hand around it.

"No children," she whispered. The contact of her hand was too much. He felt the massage of her fingers for only a few seconds. The warmth spread from his loins like melting wax, and when it flooded his entire body from fingertips to scalp, he spurted so hard that it made a noise. The vortex drew him down and for a timeless moment, everything was darkness.

"Oh God!" said Annaliese, but her voice expressed no pleasure. She was dabbing with a handkerchief at a shoulder-high stain on the settee back. "How will we get this out? Someone will see it."

"That is me?"

"Of course," she said. "I held you too tight."

"It was incredible," he said, reaching for her.

She pulled away, eyes restored to their former coolness. "You did well."

"It was incredible. I have never *kissed* that before."

Annaliese stood and buttoned herself. She smoothed her skirt and dabbed at the stain again. "What will I say this is?" she asked. "What will I say this is? The settee is ruined." She used the cognac as a cleaning fluid. Why was it so important to her? She could order the manager to discard the entire settee if she wished. They ruled here. He walked away from her, buttoning his fly, replacing his father's dagger in the hiding place under his tunic.

Only a few moments later, when the maid returned to ask about dinner, Marko pretended to be studying a painting at the opposite end of the room. His ears, he knew, were red. She spoke to the maid as if Marko were not there. "I am so careless, Greta. Do you think this cognac will dry without a spot?"

"I do not know, Frau Colonel Dorst."

"My husband will be furious if he sees it. He hates stained upholstery."

"Such a little thing will not trouble him, madam."

"He can be so cranky sometimes."

"Frau Colonel, I am sure you fret too much. He knows your background and merely wishes all your things to be perfect for you."

"I am certain you are right. The lieutenant will be leaving now. Tell the Colonel I will join him for dinner in ninety minutes. Prepare my bath!" With that, she flung herself upon a chair and lit a cigarette. "You may go now," she said without looking at him.

Marko swept aside the brocaded curtain and saw the fog marshalling itself into an evanescent layer growing sunset orange just above the trees in the park. Who was it who had killed the woman in the park? He. And was he different for it? He didn't know. He glanced back at Annaliese. The Serbian woman's gold tooth had fallen from Annaliese's sleeve to the floor and she was picking it up. By all rights it should have been his, he thought, but he said nothing. He clicked his heels and left. He felt cold and sticky, as if he were the stain on the settee, and the cognac were evaporating off his skin.

Jelena Filipovich, the Bride

◆

(Krushka, June 10–11, 1928)

Marko's awkward shoes were wet. They had rubbed his heels raw, and the narrow road winding into the hills seemed even more unfamiliar when the moon finally slipped from behind the clouds. He could not be lost—there was only one cart road between the railway station and Krushka—but the trees, the rocks, the now-visible roll of the Shumadian hills were as alien to him as the high Alps. It is true, he thought. When you decide to kill a man, everything changes.

He reeled to one side from the uneven pitch of the road. The eerie moonlight made the earth seem fluid, so he shuffled to an egg-shaped boulder under a tree. Dropping his carpetbag beside him, he inhaled and wiped the sweat from the tip of his nose with the back of his hand. Maybe I am ill, he thought. Once, when he was ten, he had run the entire sixteen kilometers from the station to the village, barefoot, without stopping, just for the fun of it. Now, seven years later, his feet stung, sweat soaked his shirt, and the fingers of his right hand were numb from carrying the three shirts, three socks, razor, brush, soap, and comb in the bag. This was another thing he owed old Bronkovich: his softness. Trains, hotels, streetcars, pastries, French wines, Cuban cigars, cream cakes, Austrian beer, long nights calculating shipping costs, long nights in the brothels of Prague and Vienna and Budapest—all these things had weakened Marko. Old Bronkovich took him for granted because he was weak: "Fetch me an aquavit," "Make certain to bathe before breakfast," "Hire a taxi for Count von Limner," "Check these figures for errors, boy." Marko ground his teeth. "Boy," always "boy." He would show him how much of a "boy" he was. The old bastard would beg. Marko would see the fear in his eyes as the "boy" told him he was going to slit his papery throat and take Jelena. He would laugh as the old man died. Bronkovich would never get his stained fingers on Jelena's white body. Never.

Both of Marko's hands were shaking. Not from fear, he told himself. It could not be fear. He would not let it be fear. He had picked up some illness in the city. Or he was hungry. He'd barely eaten for two weeks, not since he had heard that Bronkovich had finally arranged for his fourth wife and that her name was Jelena Filipovich. He had immediately gone pale, but Bronkovich, who could usually fathom a man's eyes as well as he could the return on an investment, took no notice—Marko was beneath notice. The old man raised his hands in the air and did a small pirouette in the lobby of the Savoy-Carlton in Bratislava, waving the letter from Father Constantine like a small flag. A group of minor nobles and Moravian politicians gathered about him. "First, a man marries for love," he shouted. "Second, he marries for money. Third, he marries for children."

"And the fourth time?" chirped the Mayor of Bratislava. "Aren't you running out of reasons?"

"Fresh peaches," said Joseph Hurban, waving his monocle.

"Of course!" old Bronkovich shouted. When the laughter subsided, he added, "Gentlemen, he marries a girl from home—someone like his mama when she was young. He plows the earth from whence he came." He had bowed and his cronies applauded and laughed. Hurban then dragged Bronkovich out of the hotel for a night "plowing" the girls at Madame Czestchowa's, leaving the nauseated Marko to wander along the Danube. He slept fitfully and worked poorly over the following ten days. On their trip to Prague, Bronkovich had roared into the second class car still wearing the napkin from the dining car. He slapped at Marko, shouting, spitting and threatening to throw him from the train with breath that reeked of fish and tobacco. The reckonings for the invoices were wrong. "Where is your head at, boy? Idiot!" Then, like a summer thunderstorm, he was suddenly gone. The passengers grinned and Marko went to the platform. It was there, the fog and engine exhaust swirling about him, that he had decided what he would do. The wedding was to be in twelve days; he would be ready by then, he had thought.

He squinted up the path to his village and clasped his hands together. They must not shake. If he allowed them to shake, he might appear frightened. He must not let anyone think that. He took off his suit jacket, rolled it up inside the bag, then set off. His stomach growled. He should have eaten in the station at Belgrade. I am not weak, he told himself. I am not ill. I am not afraid. I am merely hungry. Fat living had made him too used to hotel beds and easy food. In the village you could not afford to get used to easy food. Sometimes there was no food, not even for gold, but you learned to survive, like a man. He would regain this in one bloody act. When he reached Krushka, his mother would scramble to feed him with whatever she had: rabbit pie, a chunk of hardened cheese, watery soup. It would make him invincible. She could heat it on the new iron stove he had sent her money to buy, and he would be ready to kill. With just a mouthful of food in him, his hands would be steady as he slit the old man's throat.

A breeze rose and the moonlight dimmed. Rain? His shirt felt cold, though sweat still burned in his eyes. He stepped into a greasy puddle, cursed, shaking his foot, then went on. A few minutes later, he heard the rushing of a stream and the landscape became suddenly clearer. It had been two and a half years since he had last heard that stream. He stopped, walked three more steps, then stopped again. He saw the dark opening of the ravine in which he had watched the beautiful Jelena wading, her white feet gingerly caressing the bottom. Her pink lower lip had been moving, but what she had sung had been swallowed by the noise of the water. She had felt him watching. He was now certain of that. And she had loved him. He was also certain of that. He remembered the curve of her ears, the whisper of her shallow breathing.

He lowered his eyes to the cart path and walked much faster, soon cresting the rise above Krushka. His home was at the other end, the dirtier end, but unless he wanted to scramble through the rocky pastures, he would have to walk through the middle. He did not wish to be seen, though there was little chance of it after dark. Night was for evil spirits, for the Devil, for Gypsies. The dogs behind the thick doors might bark, and the men might instinctively reach for their ancient guns, but they would not come out unless their livestock sounded threatened.

"I am home," he thought, but the recognition wasn't pleasant or sentimental or affectionate. His throat tightened around a lump as large as a plum. The houses lay on each side of a dirt track, scattered in the Shumadian way, but closer than in many villages because of the terrain. There was very little change. He had forgotten who he had been here, and now that he was forced to remember, he felt separate from it, as if his childhood had been a stranger's. Images of his father came back: the sharp face with intense eyes as he nightly smoked his long pipe by the glow of their open hearth. The staring eyes of his crusted, smallpox-eaten face. The priest had held a large napkin soaked in disinfectant over his own beard as he anointed the discolored body with red wine and olive oil. The women must have chanted—they always chanted at funerals—but Marko could not remember it. He had been only eleven when the smallpox struck. It had left only his mother and him, and the villagers' certainty that Svetozar Renovich had brought the disease on them by letting his goat interrupt Easter Mass. And was it not proven by Svetozar's quick death? And was it not proven by the deaths soon after of those who could not help laughing when the goat had brayed? And was it not proven by the near extinction of the Renovich clan? God had spared Radojka, his mother, because she was not born a Renovich. Marko had survived, but had been scarred to serve as a walking reminder of the Lord's wrath.

"Superstitious pigs!" He spun around as if someone had tapped him on the shoulder. A cat loped across a fence. Marko scurried, nearly running. He passed the prosperous wattle-and-daub cottages of the Andrich clan. The smoke from their chimneys was drooping low into the road and stung his eyes. The Raichich cottages looked as ill cared for as always, and someone, old Radosav probably, had left his hat on the gate post. His fat son Vojin would still be living in the next cottage with its flaking stucco. The Andrichs always had complained about the wasteful Raichich family being between them and the church, so near to the center of the village, but no one had ever done anything about it.

The road veered right, opening into the area used for village gatherings. In 1804 "Black George" himself had gathered the patriarchs of the families there to raise them, with refugee Montenegrins who had hidden in the woods, against the Sultan. One of Marko's distant grandfathers, Draga Renovich, had been there and later beheaded ten Janissaries in Belgrade. In recognition for its service, the village was given the small church at the end of the dusty square, with its first foundation stone the rock upon which "Black George" had stood. Marko paused to stare at the building. When the other boys had taunted him, he had pointed to this poor structure and said it was a gift from King Milosh to Draga Renovich, never mind what the stone plaque said. One day, when the boys laughed, he attacked them with a barrel stave, and they beat him mercilessly until Father Peter finally pulled them apart, only to drag the bloody Marko home to his mother, whom he abusively lectured about her "barbarous" boy. Marko's ears burned from the memory of it, his humiliation increased by the commonness of the yellow brick building. He had seen the churches of Vienna, Prague, Bratislava, and Venice. Even the synagogues of Prague made his boasts about the church seem ludicrous. The heads of ten Janissaries should have bought something better for Draga Renovich; but these others, these simple-headed villagers, deserved even less.

He stared at the uneven steps and considered killing Bronkovich here, in front of the entire village, just as the old man emerged from the wedding ceremony. He grinned. Marko could stand upon the top step, blood still dripping from his knife, and claim the church in his grandfather's name. He would shout his love for Jelena and spit on old Bronkovich's body. The dogs would lap the old man's blood off the steps. The village would see the strength of a Renovich then. He smiled.

He passed Father Constantine's small house and heard the chickens stirring in their coop. He passed the Filipovich clan's houses, some of which were old enough to have log walls. A new house had been built where old Filipovich, long dead, had penned his hogs. The path then wound left past the cemetery.

He considered going into it to stop at his father's, brothers', and sisters' graves, but it was too quiet, the light making the grass roll like a sea. Beyond the cemetery, a wide gravel path went over a rise. At the end of it, in his cement and brick house, Bronkovich was snoring, dreaming of Jelena's white body. Marko squeezed the handle of his carpetbag until his hand throbbed. There remained only the final cluster of cottages—his—the cursed and shabby huts of the Renovich clan.

He was surprised by how well-kept they looked. There were few weeds. The thatch on two of them was new. The churned earth revealed that cattle had been corralled next to it. For a second he thought his mother had exaggerated her poverty, that, all things considered, she had done wonders with the money he had been sending. Then he recognized that it was impossible. No woman alone could maintain all this, and he certainly wasn't sending her enough to hire workers. He instantly knew she had let others move into the houses. The Renovich houses—his!—were full of strangers. He blinked at them, turned from what had been his older brother's home, to his uncle's home, to his grandfather's home. The cottages blurred. He dropped his carpetbag and covered his face. "God!" he muttered. "God!" His fingernails dug deep into his heavy eyebrows. They were right, he thought, God had cursed Svetozar Renovich and his line. And because of a goat. All because of a goat. What kind of peasant God would do that?

He stood in the road for some time. His breathing grated against the stillness. He turned as if he expected the sound to awaken the strangers in his family cottages, then sheepishly set out for the half log, half wattle-and-daub structure in which he had been born. He rapped on the door, timidly at first, glancing over his shoulder to see if he had roused anyone nearby, but when there was no response, he inhaled and pounded three times with his fist. The sound faded into the emptiness of the house, and, for a moment, he thought perhaps his mother had died and he was the only Renovich left. The priest would have written, though, wouldn't he? Wouldn't he?

"Who is there?" The voice was muffled. He wasn't certain it was his mother and he felt yet another moment of panic as he thought she had moved into one of the animal sheds.

"Marko," he said.

"Who?"

"Marko!" he said loudly. *"Marko!"*

There was a frantic unbarring of the door, a clawing at the latch, and strong hands jerked his head against wet lips and a shoulder that smelled of smoke and cheese and goats. He dropped his bag and flung his arms around her stocky body. Her heavy breasts pressed his chest and belly.

"My son," she choked. "You are here. I knew you would come. I knew. Marko." She began to sniffle and pulled his forehead down and kissed it until it was wet.

"Mama," he murmured over and over. "Mama," as if he were small and had awakened from a nightmare. They wept on each other's shoulders, and he felt as if he would sink into her, as if she were a featherbed that could absorb all his anger and frustration and exhaustion. She pushed him away. "My son," she said in wonder. "My Marko. It *is* you." She hugged him again quickly and held him away again to try to see his face. The dimness, however, made it difficult, and she caressed his cheek gently with her thick fingers.

She pulled him inside and closed the door. "Come. You must be hungry." She let him go. He barely made out the faint glow of the coals behind the vent of the iron stove. The room was humid and smoky. It would be stifling when the fresh air from the door dissolved in it. He heard her moving comfortably through the dark, fumbling for sticks and breaking them. She became just visible when she blew on the remaining embers and he saw that he had been mistaken. There was no stove. Just the open hearth he had grown up with.

"Where is the stove?" he said. "I sent you money for an iron stove. Where is it?"

"I don't need an iron stove," she said calmly. "Besides, bread tastes strange cooked in those things."

The twigs she had placed on the coals flared up. He could see the vague lines of the dark rafters, a chunk of bacon hanging high above the fire, and a scrawny chicken tied beside it. "But I sent you the money!"

"Sit down. Here." She shoved a three-legged stool at him. "Warm yourself. It is a cool night. I will go to Gila's for some lamb."

He grabbed her arm. "No. Stay here. Whatever is here will do. Don't go waking half the village."

"I told Gila to save me a nice piece because I knew you would not miss Milan Bronkovich's wedding. She is a good person. She will not mind."

"I will mind. And who is Gila?"

"She lives in your grandfather's cottage."

"So it is true, then? You have sold my property to strangers."

"They are not strangers. They came starving to my door, dressed worse than Gypsies. They had four children. Sretan, her husband, has a brother in the monastery at Mt. Athos."

"So why didn't they go to him? Is this all the Renovich land is good for? Charity?"

"Sit down," she said curtly. "You speak as if they were heathen. He worked for the railroad. Now there is nothing for them. They were lost, confused with hunger. I did as any Christian. The buildings were empty. They would soon fall apart. And do you tell me you could have taken care of them? I used my good sense."

He sank to the stool and stared into the fire. He hadn't expected to argue with his mother. "You should have asked me. I am the man of this family now. This is my property you are giving to strangers. And what of the stove? I sent you money. I wrote you to save it for a stove. Did that priest tell you I wrote that?"

"Of course *that priest* did. He is Father Constantine to you! And man or no, you will not speak of him in that tone!"

"Then why are you still squatting over this hearth? You'll get arthritis."

"I told you. I don't need an iron stove. Who needs all your heat flying up a stovepipe? That's how you get pneumonia. Peasant women are healthy as mares until they started with all these modern conveniences."

He started to say they lived as long as mares, but didn't. "And what happened to the money?"

"I have saved most of it. And I had a good gravestone made for your father."

"While you breathe all this smoke, father now has a new stone?"

"With his picture," she said proudly.

"My God," he sighed.

"In porcelain. Beautiful, pearl-like. It will not fade for centuries, they say. Only Bronkovich and King Alexander could do better." She was looking upward as if she were speaking of heaven.

He peered at her, trying to calculate how long he had worked to gather the money. "I should have shipped you the stove."

"I would have sold it and done the same."

He shook his head. "I should never have left."

She touched his knee. "It is terrible to have to live in the city among strangers."

"And what is it that you do, now that there are strangers in our houses?"

She withdrew her hand. "I will fetch the lamb."

"No. Give me what you have. Bread? Cheese?"

"Just *pasulj*," she said. "Let me get the lamb."

"And did you eat lamb today? No. I will have the bean soup. There is no simple food in the city. Bronkovich doesn't care. City food weakens you. I need to be strong."

"You have never looked stronger. You look fine in your suit. Milan treats you well."

"He treats me like a servant."

"He is very rich. This is his reward for going among strangers, like Joseph in Egypt. You will be rewarded, too." She hung a pot on the hook above the fire and stirred it.

Marko crossed his arms and squinted into the dark corners. "I will get you a kerosene lamp. You should not stumble about in the dark. *And* a stove."

"Pah," she said. "I don't trust them. They stink. Night is for sleeping."

"Mama, we are thirty years into the twentieth century. People are throwing away their kerosene lamps for electrical ones, like in the train station."

"I have seen city people," she protested. "Those lights affect their skin. They are all jaundiced. Probably from staying awake all the time."

"And you said I looked better than ever."

"And you said you needed good peasant food." She threw

back her head and laughed. He only grew more surly. "You are as moody as your father," she said.

"I don't know that he was moody. All I remember is that he couldn't keep his goat penned, and then he beat Vojin because it got out. And then they all died: father, Vojin, Ilinka, Father Peter. . . . Two wars couldn't kill papa, so we are to believe a goat brought down God on him." Marko shook his head. "Why did he even have a goat? My God." He knew the answer. Goats were poor man's animals. His eyes felt sandy. He pressed them with his fingers. He didn't want her to say why Svetozar Renovich had owned goats, but she did. Of course. She had always repeated it, exactly the same. It was a litany.

"Goats are as good as sheep. Someday perhaps we would have had a thousand cattle, but goats were fine in the meantime.

"I know, I know," he said impatiently.

"You will soon not worry about goats. You are luckier than your father. When God took him—," she paused, "—and all the rest, he left you. You are the lucky one. You will have success like Milan Bronkovich."

"He won't be so lucky soon."

She leaned over the pot to see how warm it was. "How do you mean? He will have a young bride soon. He'll have a big family. What do you mean?"

"Nothing."

"I think the *pasulj* is ready."

"Then let's have it," he barked. "Old man, young bride. It disgusts me. In the civilized world she would have some say in it. She cannot want an old man smelling of rot."

His mother spoke quietly, soothingly, in the way she had spoken to Marko's father and grandfather when they were in a foul mood. "It is the best thing that could happen to Jelena. She will live like a queen. And if she becomes a widow, she will marry whom she pleases. Her life is set."

He briefly thought of killing Bronkovich in his marriage bed. Jelena would then be his widow and inherit all his wealth. But that was not the point. The old man must never possess her in any way, not as her husband, not for even a minute. It would be like using St. Mark's in Venice for a barn.

His mother began talking of the arrangements for the wedding. Bronkovich had hired not just one *kuvar* to cook the feast, but two, who had immediately begun a ferocious competition over who was the best cook. They had gotten into a bidding war which nearly came to blows over Andrich's youngest pigs, but Andrich fetched twice what he would have gotten otherwise. When Bronkovich's brother Dragan had gone through the village inviting everyone, he had said that there would be no common bowl at the lower end of the table, as was ordinary for the less important guests at a wedding. Everyone would eat off china. Everyone would have linen, even the newcomers in the Renovich cottages. Bronkovich had shipped two crates of silverware from Belgrade, so heavy they made the cart scream with agony.

Marko swallowed a wooden spoonful of the *pasulj*. It was bitter. He stared into the bowl, but the light was so dim he could not see. His mother had always scorched the beans on the bottom of the pot. He sat the bowl down. "I hope the silver is stolen."

"Stolen?" Who would steal it? Maybe Milorad Filipovich— he has a thief's eyes but why do you say this? Is the *pasulj* bad? Let me get some lamb from Gila."

"No! Sit down. Old Bronkovich is just showing off. That's what I mean. He's been married before. Why should he marry a young girl? Why should Jelena's family want him? She can't want him, that's impossible."

"He is a rich man. He has no right to enjoy it? And he has done a great deal for you. I don't understand this at all, little Marko. The outside world has affected your mind."

"I'm not your 'little Marko' anymore." He shifted, avoiding her eyes. She would see how much of a boy he was when he slit the old man's throat! He quickly picked up the *pasulj* and shoveled the food into his mouth so that she would stop fidgeting to get the lamb.

"You must understand that he must use one of his brothers for the best man, Marko. Even if you are his secretary."

His spoon hung in mid air. "Is that what you think? I wouldn't be his best man for all of his money! God help me! What he is doing is a crime. He buys girls in Bratislava and Prague, then he buys a wife at home. It makes me sick!"

She stared at him. He could feel her eyes, though they were shadowed from the light. He spooned up more of the soup and swallowed it greedily. "I'm so hungry and tired," he said to distract her from trying to understand his anger. It worked. Soon she was talking about the *ruvo*, the procession of Jelena's hope chest to Bronkovich's house. All the women had inspected Jelena's handiwork on the napkins and agreed it was very fine. When Radojka Andrich died Jelena would be the finest embroiderer in Krushka. Her delicate hands were a blessing from God. . . .

As his mother went on, the smoke from the open hearth made his eyes water. The *pasulj* filled his belly. The anger's edge blurred and he dozed, picturing the blood streaming peacefully from Bronkovich's neck, soaking into the church stones, flowing like the Sava and the Danube and the stream into which he had once seen Jelena wade.

He woke thinking of his mother's cabbage knife. It was long, curved, as frightening as a scimitar, and sharp enough to cut a neck like cheese. Where was it? He squinted through the shaft of light dividing the cottage. The knife lay on the simple table by the open hearth, exactly where it had always lain when he was a child. He got off his straw pallet and crossed to it. Like everything—hearth, room, village, mother—it seemed smaller than it once had, smaller and cruder. There was a nick in the cutting edge. He would buy her a knife, he thought. She had suffered enough. She deserved a shiny knife with a mother-of-pearl handle. And he would make her buy an iron stove. If necessary he would have it shipped from wherever he fled with Jelena. Then his mother couldn't do anything but have it hooked up.

He suddenly recognized he hadn't thought of what he would do afterwards. He would take Jelena with him, but where? Well, west, of course. Perhaps they should go to Vienna or Berlin. He could take her across the top of Italy, or across Czechoslovakia. Perhaps they should go to America. France or England would be civilized, but America would be even more free of peasants and primitiveness.

"Ah, sleepyhead! The dawn has passed you by! You are looking for something to eat?"

He put down the knife. "No, mama. It will be a big feast, you say."

"Incredible, they say."

"Unforgettable," he muttered. "I promise you."

She was dressed in her holiday costume, and it was amazing how all that embroidery remained so bright despite the circumstances she lived in. The whites almost glowed in the dim cottage. She took his arm and pulled him through the low door into her bedroom. She bent over the old trunk and unlocked it with the skeleton key she always kept on a string under her apron.

"Look," she said, raising a layer of tissue paper. "Your father's outfit. I was told to burn it after he died, but I hid it. It is a special day. You are now head of the Renovich clan." She lifted a vest with shiny coins worked into the embroidery. "Isn't it beautiful?"

"It could have been contaminated," he said.

"It has been years. Am I dead?"

"You should throw it away."

She was stunned. "Throw it away?"

"Burn it, whatever."

"But, look!" she said. "The shirt, the pantaloons, even his fez. No one wears the fez anymore. But look at it. The quality!"

"I am no longer some rube from a village. I have a suit and three celluloid collars. Why should I wear this?" He turned to leave.

"And you reject your father like this? Look"—she clawed at his sleeve—"here is the dagger which Draga Renovich plunged into a dozen Janissaries before Belgrade. Are you too good for your blood anymore?"

Marko paused. "Is it sharp?"

"Sharp? I don't know. Your father brought it back from the war with the Austrians and—what do you care if it is sharp? It is your destiny, your history. What has the city done to you?"

He reached down and took the dagger. He unsheathed it. He remembered his father wearing it whenever he went to church, along with that ridiculous fez. The blade was no longer as shiny as it had once been, but the edge felt keen. "You are right, mother," he said curtly. "If it is my history, how can I refuse to wear it? The dagger, and the belt, but nothing else."

[173]

She was angered and would continue arguing, he knew, so he snatched them up and left the room. She said something behind him, but he ignored it, plucking the whetstone from the nail above her cooking table. Outside in the sunlight, he leaned against the gate, carefully drawing the blade across the stone. This was working out even better than he imagined. This knife, Draga Renovich's knife, his father's knife in the Great War. It was going to be as if his father had come back as a ghost to pay back these superstitious clods for heaping curses on his family. This was too good to be true. Destiny was with him.

The blade was shiny as ice when his mother came out, bearing a basket with a gift for the bride. She was still miffed, however. She said nothing but "The procession will begin soon."

"Quick," he said. "We must go."

He began by walking, but soon the excitement overtook him and he ran. It was as if his feet knew each heave in the hardened path and led him. The clouds had cleared away and Mt. Rudnik was visible to the west. For a moment he was a child again, before the Balkan Wars, before the Great War, before the smallpox had scarred his face, and running was effortless. Papa would be returning from market with sweets; Vojin would be helping Old Filipovich shear his sheep.

He stumbled on gravel and landed on his belly. The dagger rammed hard into his groin. He rolled over and sat up, stunned. He felt warm moisture in his trousers. He lifted his belt and stretched his fingers. Blood. A chill came over him, but when he withdrew his hand, he saw only the clear glistening of sweat on his fingers. He sniffed them. The sheath had protected him. He stood, erupting with anger and kicked the gravel into a clattering spray. "Stupid!" he shouted. "Stupid!" It was loud enough to echo off Mt. Rudnik. He dusted his jacket and trousers. He was at the end of the gravel roadway leading to Bronkovich's house. He could hear shouting and singing. The carriages were already assembled for the procession to the bride's house. He clutched the grip of the dagger and slid the blade out, then back in. Suddenly he remembered one of the wedding customs. He spun and ran into a pasture, twisting the sheathed blade up with one hand, so that he could not fall on it again.

There was a shortcut he had often used as a child. Across the corner of the pasture, through a small copse, and then up behind the Filipovich houses. He reached the back of their dairy shed and leaned against it to catch his breath. He peered around the corner. The main house looked different than he remembered. There had been an addition and the whitewash looked fresh. A stout woman came out of the side door and flung a bowl of wash water onto the bare ground. It took a moment for him to recognize her: Ruzha, Jelena's sister. Marriage to Vojin Raichich had fattened and aged her more than anyone had predicted. When she went inside he eased up to the well. The dog, sleeping in the shade of the chicken coop, lifted his head, looked at Marko, and went back to sleep. Marko scurried to the main house and put his back against the wall, sliding along it to the small open window at the end.

He listened, heard nothing, and glanced in. An empty bedroom. He slid along to the next. A narrow storeroom. Laughter cackled out of the next window. He peeked with one eye over the edge. They were just finished dressing her. Her grandmother was telling a story about her wedding night while Jelena's mother was fastening the necklace of gold coins around Jelena's neck, her flushed and perfect neck with its soft and almost invisible hairs. Someone laughed, startling him, and he dropped below the sill. "Go on," he thought. "Go on. Arrange the tables, damn you!"

The dog stood up, yawned, and stretched. It sniffed in Marko's direction and slowly approached him. It stopped, lifted his head high and blinked. "Go away!" whispered Marko. "Good dog. Good dog." The woman laughed. The dog went back to his nap.

Marko looked again. The room was empty. Damn! Then the coins on the necklace clinked. She was sitting with her back to the wall, to his extreme left. He could see only her profile. She was chewing her thick lower lip, head dropped, contemplating her hands resting on her knees. She was unhappy. He could see that instantly. She didn't want to marry Milan Bronkovich. That old man was no groom for her. She loved Marko. It was obvious.

He pulled himself up and stuck his head in the small window. "Jelena!" he whispered.

"Marko!" She glanced at the closed door. "What are you doing here?"

"I'm here to rescue you. We'll run away."

"What?"

"We'll run away. I'll take you to Berlin and London. To civilized places."

"Suppose someone hears you? I'm supposed to be alone. This is my wedding day!"

"No, Bronkovich will never have you. We love each other."

She suddenly paled, then raised both hands as if she were trying to get control. "Please," she begged, "you mustn't tell anyone that. My father—my mother—"

"Don't worry about them. This village is no place for you. Bronkovich just wants someone to spawn children and clean his houses while he buys whores in Hungary and makes deals. He is no husband for you. You don't love him."

"But it is all arranged, Marko. Please . . . my father would kill me. My mother—"

"Are you deaf? You don't have to marry this old man. You're not a cow that can be auctioned off. You have something to say about this!" He twisted his arm in to take her hand, but she stepped back.

"Go away, Marko. It is too late. I told you to forget about me years ago. I told you. This is my wedding day. Please. Do not ruin it."

"It isn't too late—"

There was a tapping at the door. "Jelena?"

Marko froze. Jelena pushed at him. He gripped her wrist.

"Jelena?"

She couldn't get loose. "Yes, mama?"

"Did you say something?"

"I am praying, mama!"

Her mother *aahhed* with great approval. They could hear the muffled sound of her bragging about it to the others, then silence as the women moved outside to set the tables and wait for the groom's party.

Jelena struggled to pull free, then jerked her arm loose.

[176]

"You hurt me," she whispered. She covered her face. She was weeping.

He didn't know what to say. "I love you," he pleaded. "I wouldn't hurt you." He felt sick to his stomach.

"But you have!" She was silent for several seconds, then wiped her eyes with both hands.

"We'll run away. You will be my queen."

"The only thing you can do for me is go away. I can't turn my back on my family. How could I do that?"

"And what is your family? The Obrenovichs? The Romanovs? The Hapsburgs?"

The rumble of the carriages and singing had gotten steadily louder. The groom's party was out front and the leader of the procession would be trying to retrieve the ceremonial gourd before entering the Filipovich property. There was loud laughter, as if he had fallen. The wedding jester shouted an insult and there was more laughter.

"They are my *family*. You can't replace that. Just go away if you love me. The past is past. I will be living in Bronkovich's house tomorrow."

He spoke so loudly she jumped. "But you belong to me!"

She slumped to the floor. "It will kill me if you tell. Kill me. I am going to Bronkovich as his virgin bride. Do not ruin this day. If you love me, do not make a scene."

There was a cheerful roar out front, then the women began singing the traditional songs mocking the groom.

He did not know what to say. His arm, stretched out in front of him, wavered. The tiny window was closing in, like a hangman's noose. He closed his eyes and pulled himself out. His hand reached for his father's dagger and he thought of how it might feel to drive it into his own heart. Eyes still closed, he raised both hands and placed his forehead against the sill.

He felt her hand upon his head. "Try to be happy for me," she said. "A wedding day should be a happy day. 'The weeping mother, the father's pride, The well-dressed groom, the virgin bride . . .'"

He slowly reached up to take her hand, but a shot startled her and she jerked away. "They are coming," she said, and closed the window. He once more glanced inside, but the door to the room was closing. The dog lifted his head once more and looked at him. He staggered back across the yard and into the pasture. He couldn't bear to watch her kissing her in-laws' hands, standing at the end of the table with that old man while all their relatives ate. He sat upon a stone at the edge of the copse and took out the dagger, staring at his own reflection in the blade.

He could hear the blood pounding in his temples. He wanted to die. He could go to the feast, slit his own throat, and die staring at her. No. If he couldn't have her, no one would. She had betrayed him in allowing this wedding. He would kill her—one stab in the heart—then himself. He would fall on her body and their bloods would mingle and—. He choked up, then clasped his hands together around the dagger grip as if trying to squeeze juice out of it. He wouldn't cry. No, he wouldn't cry. That would let the energy out; it might wash away the feeling. He had to hold on to it. It was his power. He would die like a hero, without showing the slightest fear. He stood, put the dagger back in his sheath, concentrated on looking calm, and walked toward the main road.

The Filipovichs were prosperous by village standards, but could not afford to feed the entire village, as Bronkovich intended. Nonetheless, when Marko wandered back a large crowd of onlookers had gathered in the road just outside the Filipovich fences, and some of the bride's relatives were handing sweets, cheeses, and hunks of pickled pork across the fence for others to taste. As he pushed his way toward the fence a gourd was thrust into his hands. "Try this!" said Chedomir Raichich, pointing at the tables. "They aren't drinking any better than we!" Marko pushed it back, but Raichich, red-faced and grinning, said "Drink! Drink! It's a happy day." Marko saw the top of Jelena's headdress just over his mother's shoulder and brought the gourd to his mouth. It was *ljuta rakija*, strong as benzine. Marko coughed, his eyes blinded with tears.

Raichich laughed. "Nothing like that in the city, eh, boy? More! It gets better."

Someone moved and Marko now saw Jelena's face. The memory of a hog screaming when old Filipovich slaughtered it shrieked through his head and he drank again, deep, to keep up the courage to kill her—killing himself would be easy. The rakia went straight to his brain, it seemed, and the earth reeled. He closed his eyes for a second to regain his equilibrium.

"Nectar from heaven!" Raichich laughed. "Theirs is no better!"

"Theirs is no better," said Marko, thrusting the gourd back into Raichich's dirty hands.

"Isn't she a lovely bride?" Marko's mother was saying. "I just told Derinka—"

"Marko! Marko Renovich! Since when are you back?" said a woman. "I used to hold this young man in my lap when he was just this tiny and now look at him!"

He did not recognize her, but both she and his mother were beaming.

"Come, Derinka! Look how Radojka's son has grown! Soon he will be as rich as Bronkovich."

He was confused; they were blocking his way. He raised his arm to push her aside when she suddenly jumped, slapping at the wedding jester who had prodded her with a carving fork.

"I think she's about finished," said the jester. "Ready for carving."

"I'll carve you!" said the woman. The wedding guests laughed.

"Not if I tell your husband about this young man you are flirting with, eh, grandma?"

"Well, I hope you go where he is to tell him: to hell!"

Jelena's brother laughed so hard he pounded the table with both hands.

"Oh," said the jester bowing deeply, his necklace of garlic and red peppers nearly touching the ground, "I am very, very sorry, madam, for your loss. I cannot say how sorry."

"You are forgiven."

He turned to the tables and mock-whispered, "Of course. A widow. It only proves how ready she is!" The brother pounded the table again.

"Why, he could be my son. I was just saying I held him in my lap, when he—"

"Excuse me? Your lap?" The jester spread his arms and spoke at the top of his voice. "Well, what could be better? He already knows the planting ground!"

The woman charged after him and whacked at him with

her empty basket, nearly dislodging his flaxen wig. Everyone was laughing, cheering her on.

Except Jelena. She stood at the end of the table, Bronkovich beside her, staring at Marko. She was pale as milk, her lower lip thrust out, as if she were going to cry. His hand brushed the dagger, but the touch startled him. He couldn't kill her. She was too frightened. He couldn't let her die that way. The ruckus died down.

"Ah, my protegé!" said Bronkovich. "Where have you been?" He spoke to the tables. "Marko is such a hard worker. He insists on getting everything right. Too much work, too serious this boy! He will be my partner some day. Come, Marko, we're soon to the church! Sit among my family."

Marko thought of the way Bronkovich had spat on him and abused him on the train. The old bastard was always the benefactor in public, the slave driver in private. He had treated his first wife that way and would treat Jelena the same. The anger rose in his throat, and he closed his hand on the dagger. Bronkovich looked startled by his expression.

"And does your protegé take care of things when you are away on business?" asked the jester in a high-pitched voice. "Do you trust a young man with *everything*? Yow!"

The jester was between them. It confused Marko. Everyone was laughing. Bronkovich was kicking at the jester, who hopped the fence and quickly sang a risqué rhyme. Whatever anger Bronkovich had felt turned into laughter as he threatened the jester with a fist. Someone stuck a glass of wine in Marko's hand. Jelena was watching the antics, trying to preserve her modesty by not laughing. Marko drank the wine in one gulp and pushed toward the fence gate. The best man, however, stretched out his hands and said, "Father Constantine will be waiting! Bring up the carriages!" Bronkovich and Jelena were surrounded. The guests were pressing Marko back. "To the church! The church!"

There, then. On the steps of his grandfather's church. Just as he had imagined. Raichich staggered into him. Marko took the rakia again and drank deeply. A round-faced oaf suddenly rushed up to Marko and embraced him.

"Hey, hey, home, little brother! How is the city boy?"

Alexander Andrich had tormented Marko worse than anyone in the village when they were children, but somehow in Alexander's mind all of that had turned into a kind of affection. Marko handed him the gourd and said, "Have some."

Alexander swallowed, puffed out his cheeks, and exploded a burst of air as if the rakia had punched him in the stomach. "Whew! The best! Raichich makes it best, doesn't he? How is life treating you, little brother? I sometimes think of going to Belgrade myself. This farming—," he shook his head, "—pah!"

An older Andrich interrupted. "A good life isn't good enough for Alexander the Great!"

"I would be appreciated there! Not treated like an ox!"

The rebuttal sounded like something Alexander had said dozens of times.

The older man spoke to no one in particular. "A week and he would beg to come back. Off to the city like an orphan!"

People had begun to drift toward the church, leaving a wide pathway so that the carriages could pass.

"In the city," said Alexander, "I would not have to put up with 'Do this, Alexander! Do that, Alexander!' "

"The city is no paradise," said Marko. He wasn't certain why he bothered to say it. He had no reason to want to please these people.

"At least it doesn't have my father!" whispered Alexander.

"You'll never go," said Marko. "You are as much a windbag as ever."

"What? You will see, Renovich. You will see."

The bridal carriage passed with Jelena sitting next to the best man in his white sash. It happened so suddenly Marko saw only the back of her headdress and the clink of the gold coins in her necklace. He stopped and stared stupidly at the rear of the carriage. On the church steps, he thought. Before they go in. He would leap at Bronkovich, slit his throat, and take Jelena off in the bridal carriage. He imagined it as if in a steel engraving: Bronkovich reeling back, the astonishment on his evil face . . .

"Hey, little brother, what is that?"

Before he could react, Marko felt the dagger plucked from his belt.

"Very nice!" said Alexander.

"Give me that back!" said Marko.

Alexander showed it to his friends. "Look at the embroidery on the sheath."

"Give it back!"

"Ho, ho, our little brother's angry." The clod was grinning. It was the same grin he had always had when he had ripped things from the hands of Marko and other smaller boys.

Marko glanced at the wedding party. They were climbing out by the church front. "Give me that! Now!"

Alexander took a step back, graceful for such a big man. "Look, he is hardly polite."

"Please," said Marko. "It was my grandfather's. Give it back."

"Oh, yes, the great hero. And now you have inherited the throne and the dagger. The heir to the throne!" Alexander's face was pink when he laughed. He was the same bully he had always been. And the others stood around laughing with him, just as they always had.

"King Marko! Marko Kraljevich!" shouted Raichich. "Drink, Marko! Drink!"

Marko stepped forward, brushing Raichich and his gourd aside. "Give me my father's dagger," he said. His voice was so sharp that everyone stopped laughing. Alexander glanced at his friends.

He grinned, shrugged, grinned again. "Yow, Marko, we were just having fun. You are too—."

"The dagger."

"Well, if that's the way you feel about it. No hard feelings, eh?" He held out the dagger sheepishly. Marko snatched it off his fat hands. "No hard feelings, eh?" He reached out to put a hand on Marko's shoulder.

Marko jerked away. The wedding party had moved into the church. "You are still a child. A stupid, bullying child!" He examined the sheath and rubbed at a dark spot that had come from Alexander's hands.

"Oh, now," said Raichich, "don't be that way. My rakia has gone to your head."

An old woman frail as a dried weed said, "You boys ought to be ashamed, squabbling on a solemn day!"

"It is a happy day, too," said someone.

"The jester is too filthy and you are squabbling. These things would not have happened in my day!"

"In your day—let's see . . . the fourteenth century? You are right, King Dushan would never have permitted it," said Alexander's father. They all laughed.

Marko, suddenly touched with a fit of sadness, touched the old woman on the shoulder. "You are right, dear lady, this is all tasteless and barbaric, and a woman like Jelena deserves better." He was dizzy. He shook his head to clear the cobwebs, then headed for the front of the church.

"Bless you," said the old woman.

"Marko is now too good for us," said Alexander's father angrily. "Not like Milan Bronkovich!"

The jester was sitting on a bench smoking a cigarette half a dozen meters from the church steps. There was a glass bottle of wine next to him. He looked up at Marko. His eyes were puffy. "Sit down," he said. "It won't take long."

Marko could hear the ceremony through the open door. Soon Father Constantine would be placing the silver crowns on Bronkovich's and Jelena's heads and they would begin circling the altar.

"Rest while you can," said the jester. "There's never enough." He lifted the wine and patted the seat next to him. He swigged it and offered it to Marko.

Marko took a large swallow. It was good wine, not local at all. He handed the bottle back and looked at the dagger cradled in his lap. "You're not clowning."

"You're not paying. Besides, it's disrespectful during the ceremony."

"You are disrespectful anyway. That old woman there was—"

"The old hag says it at every wedding in the area. She says it for attention."

"Your songs and your jokes are . . ." he had trouble getting out the last word, "filthy."

He pointed at the people around Alexander. "That's what they like."

"You are still filthy-mouthed."

"And you, my friend, are drunk."

"And who are you to say so?" He turned up the wine

nearly emptying it. "My name is Marko, like Kraljevich Marko. He could drink gallons and still cut a Turk in two. They were so afraid of him, the Sultan himself would drink wine with Marko in Ramadan." He brandished the sheathed knife. "I could cut you or anyone in two, from the head to the navel. You know who Kraljevich Marko was?"

"Of course. A big lout who served the Turks. Our national hero, a drunken traitor. And people accuse me of being foolish!"

"From the belly to the chops!"

"Yes, well," said the jester, turning the covered point away from him, "I think he unwrapped his blade first." He crushed the tip of his cigarette between his fingers and put the butt in his pocket.

Drunk! He had accused Marko of being drunk! Marko closed his eyes. He felt like he was bobbing on a gondola in the Grand Canal. Bronkovich and he had gone there to hire a cargo boat to ship—what was it? Beans? Corn? It was raining and the waves rose and the gondola pitched. He opened his eyes. That godawful *ljuta rakija*. If he could vomit it up, he could do what—What? Kill Bronkovich. Kill him. Of course. And Jelena. If she did not understand their love, she deserved to die. He'd better hurry. He paused to get his footing then lurched past the plaque celebrating Black George's rebellion. Holding one of the buttresses, he leaned over, plucking up a long weed to gag himself, but the jester's shouting interrupted him. The jester was singing another lewd rhyme. The wedding guests were gathering to dance when the couple emerged.

Marko plucked the knife from the scabbard. He concentrated on holding it steady. His arm bobbed like a stick in a stream. There was blood on the edge. He squinted in wonderment. He had already killed Bronkovich! He twisted to see the body. And where was Jelena? Blood dripped on the ground. His other hand was throbbing. When he lifted it, he stared at the bright slash in the skin between his thumb and index finger. It took him several seconds to know that he had done it when he pulled out the knife. He turned and leaned against the buttress, then slid down until he was sitting. He pinched the cut together with his fingers. He leaned back against the wall.

He couldn't do it like this. He would have to wait. The

feast would go on for hours. He would get them at the feast. He hated himself for getting drunk. He hated himself for hesitating at the bridal meal. He hated himself for not holding his liquor as well as one of the stupid peasants. But he would get them later. Just as soon as some of the rakia wore off. While she was still pure. Just before the old bastard put his shrivelled penis in her. Just a while. Not long.

He closed his eyes.

Someone was calling, "Marko! Marko!" Then the voice faded into muttering. His neck was stiff from leaning against the cold church wall. He stretched to loosen it and saw the stars dully glowing behind a wispy fog. A *kolo* played loudly. Dancing? An explosion of laughter. The wedding feast! "I was going to kill," he said numbly, then started, as if the church had moved behind him. His trousers were damp from sitting on the ground. He began to walk, every few steps pinching the cloth away from his buttocks.

He stumbled in the road, barely keeping his balance, moving steadily toward the light at Bronkovich's house. He heard a woman's giggling inside one of the Andrich sheds, and a man growling like a lion. The widow Andrich was still at it, he thought, then remembered she had died in the smallpox epidemic. He touched the scars on his cheeks. His face was numb.

He passed many people on Bronkovich's gravel walkway. No one much noticed him. He saw Alexander snoring under a tree, a dog lapping at his mouth. Three older men holding each others' shoulders for dear life nearly collided with him, then went on singing a sad song, tears pouring from their eyes. The kerosene torches were bright, and the stained table cloths receded in rows into the shadows. Under the trees, a professional *guslar* with a broad, white, handlebar mustache was singing one of the epics of Tzar Lazar. The children around him were entranced by the dancing of the bow on the single-stringed *gusle*. Empty bottles lay everywhere. The ruins of roast pigs were scattered from table to table. One woman was sneaking pig's hocks into her apron. There were more people here than lived in Krushka. Bronkovich in his vanity wanted the whole world to see the young girl he had bought. It would be a fine killing, thought Marko, a fine killing.

He smelled Turkish coffee being boiled. A good coffee would shake off all the fuzz, steady his hand, steel his anger. He looked at the head table. Bronkovich and Jelena were gone. They had already gone to the bedroom. It was as if he were drunk again. His stomach spun. Bronkovich had defiled her. Now they must all die. First the old man, then her, then himself.

He moved toward the front door, sickened, nearly weeping. The jester, arguing with Dragan Bronkovich and two others, blocked Marko's way. Dragan was pushing a bundle of straw into the jester's hands.

"No," said the jester, "it is one thing to go up on the roof of an ordinary house, but I could kill myself up there. I didn't agree to this."

"But this is tradition," said Dragan. "You are being paid well, too well. What did you expect?"

"And if I fall, will that make it a happy wedding? The roof is too high I tell you! It is breezy tonight. You can't ask me—"

"Where is Bronkovich?" interrupted Marko.

"Where do you think?" winked Dragan.

"Let me pass."

Dragan shoved him. "Don't be silly. What is the problem?"

The jester shoved the straw back at Dragan, who pushed it back. "My brother wants a traditional wedding, he will have a traditional wedding," Dragan said sharply, "and the jester will dance on the roof with the burning straw, or he will get the beating he deserves!"

"Let me pass," repeated Marko.

"How much?" said a third man.

"No," said Dragan, "he has been paid."

"I will pay," said the man. "A gift from me. How much?"

"We have already—"

"Twenty," said the jester.

"Twenty! You thief!" said Dragan.

"I'll give you ten," said the man.

"Fifteen, but only because of my respect for Milan Bronkovich and the handsome way I have been treated."

"Thief!" said Dragan. "You already—"

[186]

"It is my life! I could—"

"Done!" said the third man. "Here is your money. Go to the bedroom on the right and out the back balcony—"

"Let me pass!" said Marko, trying to shove his way in.

A shout froze them, then a scream.

"He has broken her now!" said Dragan, amused. "We'll soon toast the bloody sheet!" No one laughed. Something hit the bedroom shutters hard. Glass tinkled to the courtyard. Struggling shadows moved across the window.

"Jelena!" shouted Marko.

The music stopped. The villagers looked at one another and drifted closer to the house, trying to make out the shouting and screaming. The shutters flew open, striking the wall and bouncing back. Window glass tumbled to the ground.

Bronkovich stood in the window, silhouetted against the yellow light. He was wearing his long underwear, his belly straining the buttons. He was sweaty, his white hair sticking up from the struggle. Jelena was half dressed, holding one hand across her bosom, holding up the other, beseeching, touching the hand that grasped her hair and jerked her head from side to side.

"So, this is your daughter, Filipovich!" shouted Bronkovich. "This pure bride!" he sneered. "Do you think I'm a fool? Do you think I, Milan Bronkovich, don't know used goods? You bastards!"

He threw something downward with all his fury. A tiny pursed bag struck one of the banquet tables and exploded in red. "Sheep's blood! Sheep's blood! Did you think I would fall for that?" He was so angry he was spitting. He slapped Jelena hard across the face. She wailed.

"Please! Please! It wasn't a man. I was riding a donkey when I was a girl, I—"

He slapped her again and dragged her head close to the window as if he were going to throw her out.

"My child!" screamed her mother.

Jelena's father shoved his wife aside. "Please, sir, we had no idea. This is no fault of ours. We have watched her carefully."

"And the girl learned her little trick from the clouds? To disgrace me like this!" He slapped her once, twice. Blood trickled from her nose, then he shoved her head backwards like a rotten cabbage. "The slut! The whore!"

The villagers murmured, then a woman shouted, "The whore!"

"Let us have her!" shouted a man.

"Whore!"

Filipovich looked at his wife. It was clear who he thought had given his daughter the purse of blood to fake her deflowering. Unable to control himself he slapped at her, then shoved her into the crowd.

Marko was stunned. The twisted, savage faces around him were like the carnival masks he had seen in Venice. The villagers were almost all drunk, and those who weren't were vicious. They would beat her to death and there was no one to stop them. She would simply disappear. No one would mention her again. If she survived the beating, scarred and tainted, no one would ever marry her; her life was over, either way.

For some reason he looked at the jester, who shrugged and lifted off his red pepper and garlic necklace. "It's not like she's the first who tried it," he said. "Sometimes the groom helps." He turned and slipped away.

"We'll teach her a lesson!" shouted Dragan.

"Yes! Drag the slut out! Drag her out!"

Marko no longer cared that she had betrayed him. He jumped at Dragan, shoved him aside, and slipped through the door. He slammed it shut and brought down the bar. He took the stair two at a time and ran into Bronkovich.

"Marko, kill her for me!" he said pathetically. "Kill her!"

Marko seized the chest of his long underwear. "Still giving orders?!" He jerked him forward. Bronkovich tumbled and rolled to the bottom. Marko reached for his dagger and took two steps down. Bronkovich raised his knees almost to his head, which he held in both hands, and began to sob.

The door thudded. They were hitting it with a table. Marko charged for the bedroom. He kicked back the door. The kerosene flame sputtered out from the sudden gust. The only light came through the gently swinging shutters.

"Jelena?" he said. "I'll protect you, Jelena. We'll go away. Did he get inside you?" It made him sick to think of it. "I don't care!" His own words startled him, but he loved her, loved her. He would be her hero; he would protect her from these animals.

The noise downstairs increased. They had broken in. Almost simultaneously the shutter opened enough to let him see he had been talking to a clump of bedclothes. He saw a second door opening onto a narrow staircase. He quickly moved a chair against the bedroom door and scrambled down the stairs, coming out in a corridor to the kitchen. At the end of it was another door to the outside. Through it he saw Jelena disappearing into the dark trees.

He ran after her, churning the soil of the kitchen garden. "Jelena! Jelena!" He stumbled and fell. He ran, limping. "We'll go away! Together!" He crashed into the underbrush, glancing off trees, spinning, collapsing to his knees in the dank leaves, and charging on. Like a pack of hunting dogs the villagers were howling behind him, barking directions at one another. Torches flickered. At one time he thought they were all around him. At another, falling behind. Someone fired a rifle in the air, the flash lighting the gray branches. Marko skittered down the side of a ravine, crashed through the tiny stream, and up the other side. He collapsed against a slimy log, lowered his head and tried to recognize where he was.

The darkness. The distant shouts. They had caught her. No. How could he hope to find her out here more quickly than men like Raiko Raichich, who often hunted these woods at night? She was fleeing aimlessly into the dark, perhaps intent on killing herself. She couldn't do that, he told himself, not without him there. They would have to die together. So where would she go? To the place where she had waded in the stream. Where he had surprised her that day and they had first spoken of love. Yes, she still loved him, and that was where she would want to die.

How could he get there? He hefted himself up and stumbled on. The woods were north of the road to the railroad station, so he went across and down. He couldn't see anything except the dark outline of the distant hills against the clearing sky and the black trees that cut off his view, but he hurried on, the branches clawing at his face and arms.

It seemed to take hours to get to the road and he did not recognize where he came out. He followed it in one direction for a while, then reversed when he recognized a particular switchback, much farther than he thought he had run through the woods. The partial moon now came out and he found the hill overlooking the stream bed where he expected to find Jelena, though he could see nothing below.

He paused to listen to the water rushing with a low roar. It had been a rainy summer. Would she have drowned herself? Drowning was supposed to be the easiest, least painful of deaths. He clambered down, moved along the stream edge, looking for the flat stone they had once sat on. "Jelena?" he whispered. Only the water answered. "Jelena?" She would be here. He hunched up with his back against the outcropping and wrapped his arms around his knees.

As the night progressed, his shivering kept him awake. Once he thought he heard her crying. Another time he thought he saw the glimmer of the wedding necklace, but it was only the reflection of the moonlight on a wet boulder. She had betrayed him. She had forgotten. He had gone to the city and she had agreed to marry old Bronkovich. He peered up at the stars and swore by all that was holy he would never love another woman. Never! He choked out the words as he said them and the flood of tears washed his pain into numbness.

He waited until past noon the next day, then climbed back to the road, where he was startled by six villagers with dogs who assumed he was searching, too. They were certain they would find her body, eventually. The oldest man scratched his hound between the ears and said, "What my Zhivi cannot find, is not there." They then speculated briefly about bears and wolves, though none had been seen for years in that area. They spoke casually, as if being ripped apart by animals would be an appropriate ending for her, then seemed astonished that their dogs could trace no scent. They spoke of going back for another shoe, one that perhaps she had worn longer than the wedding shoe.

Marko said virtually nothing to the men. Jelena had evaporated like the moonlight. Marko, too numb to think, knew only that the train for Belgrade and the world beyond would pass the station in two hours and that he would be on it, his father's dagger in his belt, trying to dismiss his life in Krushka as a bad dream.

Jelena Filipovich, The *Vila*

◆

The air was heavy by midafternoon, hot and dense as the smoke from a green wood fire. The stationmaster had talked of thunderstorms: "This will not last long. It becomes impossible to breathe, then the sky cracks open." But there was no smell of distant rain, no faint rumbling. Each slap of Marko's shoe sole on the dirt road raised a fine cloud of dust. The leaves on the trees drooped. The flies and gnats seemed to be hiding in the shade. Mt. Rudnik was blurry, as if melting. Everything was hazed. All edges had smoothed; everything was melting.

Marko wiped the stinging sweat from his eyes and sat on a boulder shaded by a lightning-scarred ash. He placed his wet cap upside down to dry on the hot stone and leaned back, thinking that his mother would be angry. She had promised the Andrichs he would help them repair their chicken coops, but he would have been lucky afterwards if Mrs. Andrich had given him a tiny crock of jam for his labor. Milan Bronkovich hadn't given him much more than that—a few silver coins— for helping him put his trunks on the dawn train, but it had given Marko the chance to once again ask Bronkovich about working for him. Bronkovich had snorted and said, "If you want to make your fortune, boy, you should simply leave. What do you need me for? I needed no one when I left." But as Bronkovich pressed the coins into Marko's hand he had cocked one gray eyebrow and said, "A factotum—well, I'll think about it, boy, I'll think about it."

Marko lay back and closed his eyes. He didn't know what a "factotum" was, but probably Bronkovich had started that way. To be a refined man of substance, to walk into Krushka with everyone admiring his clothes, his watch, the smell of his pomade: that would be sweet. He would have a new house built, just as Bronkovich had, and would tell the cook to leave the kitchen window open, so that the smell of his roasts would carry to every house in the village as they sat down with their beans and *kajmak*. They would come wanting to be his friend, forgetting about the "curse" of his father's goat, ignoring the smallpox scars on his cheeks, and he would, like Bronkovich, check his gold watch and politely send them on their way. They would bow their heads, caps in hand, and thank him for his time. He smiled.

It was too hot to move, too hot to nap. The ash leaves rustled. A fat bee buzzed near his head. He plucked up his cap and strolled on. He dawdled up the rise until the path swung left, then paused. He listened for the sound of the stream at the bottom of the ravine, but the water must have been low. Glancing up the road to the village as if afraid someone would see him, he told himself that the Andrichs wouldn't be working on their coop in this heat anyway. He could help them later—if he felt like it.

He pushed aside the brush and scrambled down the slope, sliding on the leaves, holding the branches of young trees to keep from falling. He landed on his rear twice, but gradually the water grew louder. The air became denser with the odor of vegetation decaying on the banks, and soon he was crossing a beach chalky with dried mud. He recognized the place. Usually the whole area was under water. He got down on all fours and dipped his head into the cool water. It tugged at his hair as he blew bubbles into it. He raised his head and spat a long stream of water at a school of tiny fish darting in a pool to his left. He drank again, then began picking his way downstream, over the limbs and clumps of dead vegetation.

He thought he heard someone's high-pitched laugh just before he got to the outcropping. Above the bank a slab of mottled white stone overhung a circular rock platform. He had discovered it long ago with his brother Vojin. They had called it "the secret castle of Tzar Lazar" and told no one about it.

Since Vojin died, Marko had often spent whole days under its shelter, watching for animals who came to drink at the large pool below. He thought the laugh meant someone else had discovered the secret castle and it angered him, but when he got to it, it was empty except for the bits of charcoal left from his last fire, and he decided the sound of the laughter had carried from above. He crawled into the castle and settled back against the cool stone. If he could just think hard enough, he might be able to find a way to get rich in the city. His mother and he would be treated with respect. They would own cattle and an iron stove. He would have an automobile large as a locomotive and three drawers filled with silk cravats. Alexander Andrich would no longer mock him. Chedomir Raichich would no longer joke about the Renovich goats and Father Constantine would humbly kiss the hands of the boy he had so often slapped and threatened.

Bronkovich had always said the key to wealth was to know what people wanted before they wanted it. In Krushka their imaginations were so small that what they wanted was only more of what they had: more food, a bigger harvest, a better gun. There was no fortune in that: There wasn't enough wealth in all of the Shumadia to make him rich. The trick was to do as Bronkovich had done, go among the cities of Austria, Italy, and civilized Europe. The key was to know what those people wanted. But how could he, who had only been as far as Kragujevac, know what people in Vienna wanted? He had to get there, even if he had to run away to do it. While Bronkovich was thinking about his "factotum," Marko could be looking for his opportunities in Vienna or Budapest. He could send money to his mother, he could—

The laughter was louder. Girls. They were too close to be on their way to the railway station. They were somewhere to his left, above the outcropping. He crept forward and heard them giggling, then fragments of their conversation.

"No, that is not what I said, Budimir is—"

Murmuring. More laughing.

"But this—"

"How can you be such a goose?"

"I'll tell your father and he will beat you until you cannot walk!"

"You will not, or—"

More murmuring, then silence. Something else was shouted, more distantly. He settled back into his niche. Budimir? Budimir Filipovich? He wished he had heard them. It might have been a secret and he owed Budimir, the big mouth. Secrets were precious in the village; everyone's nose was always in everyone else's business. Only Bronkovich was rich enough to have privacy. Well, who was Budimir, anyway? He'd be begging for Marko's favors soon, too, just like the Filipovichs fawned over Bronkovich.

A white movement startled him. A girl was making her way across the log at the end of the pool. He held his arms tight around his knees and remained absolutely still. She delicately crossed, holding her ankle-length skirt with one hand, then hopped off onto the opposite shore. She was humming. He recognized her soft profile.

He moved to speak, then slowly settled back. Jelena Filipovich had not seen him. She picked several tiny white flowers growing on a low bush, then put the petals of one of them in her mouth. The taste pleased her. Her face was flushed and glistening with sweat. He told himself that he had not spoken because it would have revealed Tzar Lazar's castle, but he knew this wasn't true. Of all those in the village, he would least have been bothered by Jelena's knowing. She was quiet and kind. She had never mocked him or mentioned his father's goat. She wasn't like the others at all.

But he was transfixed by watching her, seeing her act without knowing she was observed. It was hard enough in the village to be alone, and never had he seen a girl alone. He remembered a time he had brought his father's rifle to shoot a doe who regularly came to drink at the pool. When the creature lowered her head, Marko had aimed at her heart but had not fired. He had merely watched her drink and leave. Pity? No. This pond was magical and the doe was a spirit of the place. To kill here would destroy the peace forever. Jelena was more than Jelena here. She was a *vila*, a beautiful wood sprite who would disappear if she knew he was there.

Jelena stuck a bouquet of flowers in the top of her embroidered vest and sat on the yellow sand with her arms around her knees. She rocked for a moment, humming a spinning song, then brushed an insect away from her face. A strand of hair had fallen across her eyes. She blew it away twice with short puffs then tucked it back against the braid pinned on the side of her head. Still squatting, she crawled forward and dipped her hand in the water, wiping her face with it. Impulsively, then, she began unfastening the straps of her boot and tugged at the heel and curved toe until it came off. When both were off, she reached under her skirt and peeled off her black stockings, wiggling her white toes in the air. She rubbed at some dirt between her toes, then squeezed them with a little groan of pleasure. Marko lowered his eyes.

He heard water splash. She was wading in, her skirts lifted to her thighs, the light reflecting off the water and dancing on her face. Her calves were strong, but their paleness made them as delicate as milk-glass. She gently felt her away across the slippery stream bed, swaying her torso to keep her balance, making sharp squeals as she slipped, raising her skirt higher when the ripples dampened it. She stopped in the middle and bent over to watch a stick float by. She craned her neck staring at something under the rippling surface of the water, then she straightened up, peered at the canopy of trees above, blinking at the sun.

She must have been daydreaming, for she leaned too far back and lost her balance. She let go of her skirt, clawing the air. She lurched forward, then back. The flow caught the fabric and pulled her legs out from under her. She tumbled backwards, flailing like a wounded pigeon. With a whump! the water closed over her, shooting up a spume of glittering droplets.

The spell was broken. Marko laughed, banging his head on the stone behind him. He rubbed it, knocking off his cap, then lay back laughing harder. The water was shallow, only as deep as her knees, and he expected her to come out of the water sputtering and shaking like a wet dog.

But she did not come up.

He raised himself on his elbow, listening. There was only the sound of the water from higher up emptying into the pool.

"Jelena?" he asked. Only the water answered.

He jumped off the stone ledge and charged across the beach into the stream, his thighs spraying water in his eyes. He glimpsed the red of her vest and the motionless glitter of its embroidery. He slipped and fell forward, catching her sleeve. Resting his knees on the bottom he wrapped his arms around her chest and lifted her. There was blood on her ear. She was pale and bluish. She was dead. "Jelena!" he said. "Jelena!" He tried to lift her higher and turned her face against him to pour the water from her nose and mouth. She sputtered. Her eyes flickered. She coughed. He stood, his arms clasped around her limp torso and dragged her to shore. When he reached the stones he lowered her gently and sat gasping beside her. She moaned and sat up, holding her ear. Spittle drooled from her lower lip.

She made a soft, painful sound. "Oh no," she murmured, "Oh no."

"Are you all right?" he panted.

The braid on the side of her head had come loose. She lifted its dripping end and stared at it. Her lips came out further, then she choked up. "I'm all wet," she wailed. "And muddy!"

"My God," he begged, "don't cry. Please. Don't cry."

She covered her face with her hands and wept silently.

"Please!" He moved his head from side to side, then stood, agitated, shifting from one unsteady foot to the other. "You could be dead!"

She touched her ear and dissolved into tears.

"I thought you were dead! My God!" He turned away as she wept, then he edged closer to see the side of her head. Her ear had turned purple, but the skin did not seem to be broken. "If you had struck a bit further forward, you would have cracked your skull. Don't cry. You are lucky."

She caught the idea of her own death like a slap. She instantly stopped crying and stared at the stream. She faced Marko and shakily touched her ear. "Where are my sisters?"

"I don't know," he said. "They went away."

"To the high meadow," she said. "We had an argument."

"Do you want me to get them? Which meadow?"

"No."

"I can run back to the village for your mother. It will only take me twenty minutes or so. I know, I'll get your father's cart—"

"No," she said. Her face scrunched up as she helplessly brushed the water off her vest. "My mother will beat me."

"It was an accident." He took her arm. He felt protective and wanted to carry her. "I will carry you up to the ledge, there. The stone is dry and clean."

"I can walk," she said. "Look how filthy I am."

"You'd better let me carry you. You may be dizzy."

"It was just a knock on the head."

"You were cold as a trout."

"I can walk."

"Walk, then!" he said in exasperation. He spun and crossed to Tzar Lazar's castle, jumped up and sat on the edge of the ledge, watching her timidly walk across the stones and mud in her bare feet. It took her three tries to heft herself up beside him. He didn't help her.

"What are you so angry about? I am the one who got hurt."

He said nothing. She waited a few seconds then brushed at the mud on her skirt. He could smell the dampness of her clothes.

"I wanted to help you. When you did not come up, I—I don't know. I wanted to help you."

He could feel her looking at the back of his head. He turned to her. She was fidgeting with the end of her loose braid. She lowered her eyes.

"You should have left me to drown. Now my mother will kill me."

"She will not."

"Then my father will beat me."

Marko had once seen the welts on Jelena's brother's back. "If he does, I will kill him!"

Their eyes met. Her pink lower lip was full and moist. She shivered.

"Are you cold?"

"The clothes are damp."

"Sometimes I have had a fire. But I did not think I would need it today. This is my secret place." He thought to tell her that it was Tzar Lazar's castle, but that seemed childish. "You must promise you will not tell anyone about it."

"Why not?"

"Because it is my secret place. This place has magic. It is sacred to something."

"What?"

"I don't know. I simply know it is sacred."

"I have been here before," she said with a shrug.

"You are lying."

"No! Your brother brought me here."

"Vojin wouldn't have done that."

"He did. About a month before he died."

"I don't believe you."

"He told me it was Tzar Lazar's castle."

Vojin *had* brought her here. She could not have known otherwise. He angrily pulled his knees close to him.

"He tried to kiss me," she said matter of factly.

He picked a leaf off his knee.

"He did. And I let him. I was just a girl."

Marko nodded as if he already knew or as if he were worldly and did not care, but mostly because he did not know what to say. "Then this place is to be a secret between you and me."

"You will not tell how I fell in?"

"By God, I swear. If you swear, too."

"And not about Vojin kissing me?"

"If you swear."

"I do."

"By God."

She crossed herself. "By God. There are many things that are no one's business."

"Good," said Marko. He was looking into her eyes again. They were deep and brown. There was a lump in his throat. He turned away.

She shivered, then began unbuttoning her vest. She took it off and held it out in front of her. "The embroidery may be ruined. I did it all myself, you know."

"Everyone says you have a talent for it and will make a good wife in a couple of years."

"It can't be too soon. I will like being a wife. They treat me like a baby, a baby who is big enough to work like a horse." Her linen shirt clung to her small breasts.

He took the vest from her and draped it over a nearby

branch. "There," he said. He stood awkwardly by it for a moment. He could not look at her. "If you rinsed off your clothes and hung them like this, they would soon dry." It did not sound like his own voice.

"You would look at me."

"I wouldn't. I have seen many women before."

"Someone might come along. My sisters might come back."

"No one comes down here. Back under the stone you can't be seen."

"I am cold," she said. "Will you promise not to look? Can I trust you not to tell?"

"By God," he swore. "I will sit with my back to you." He came up to the castle. "Here. Like this." He put his forearms on his knees, his round back to her.

"But you will tell."

"Who would I tell? Why?"

"Because boys brag. You would tell my brothers or Alexander Andrich."

"I hate them. Do you think they are great friends of mine? You have seen how they talk about my father, my dead brothers—" He ground his teeth. "I hate them."

"My father would kill me, as well as you, if he ever knew."

"He won't. I will not look. I will not tell. Trust me or not: that is entirely up to you. Die of pneumonia if you like."

She thought for several seconds, then gave a short laugh. She pushed his shoulder. "There, then. And do not turn for any reason. Exactly like that. We can talk as I dry."

"I will not look," he said.

He heard the rustle of her wet garments coming off. He saw a flash of white as she spread it on the stone, but he turned further away. He heard the sound of her buttocks touch the stone behind him. She was close enough he could smell the water in her hair. He could hear her breathing.

"Are you shivering?" she asked.

"No." He put his tongue between his teeth. He was, but he didn't want her to know it. "Maybe I should take off my shirt."

She did not respond.

"Would you mind?"

"I won't look," she said, then chirped another short laugh.

"I have seen boys. I have brothers, you know. I saw them swimming once. Men are nothing special. I don't know what all the bother is. If you think they would dry faster, spread out all of your clothes, too. I'll pretend you're not even here."

He took off his boots and spread his shirt on a tangled bush, but as he untied his baggy pants, he felt as if he were being watched. He looked at her. Jelena's white back was still to him. She had released the braid on the other side of her head, too, and both now fell over her shoulder blades. She moved and he quickly turned to avoid her seeing him look. He quickly took off his pants and was dizzy from the breathless sensation of being alone with her. He backed up carefully and sat with his back to hers. He felt a tickling on his back and he imagined it was the end of her braided hair, though he thought they were too far apart for that. He was breathing fast. Could she hear it? He tried to think of something to say, but couldn't.

"Do you think winter will come early this year?" she suddenly asked.

"Why do you ask?"

"My father says it will. He has made a wager with old Andrich."

"Oh."

He heard her shift slightly and the stone seemed to be cutting into the bone in his buttocks. He moved backward into a slight basin. Their shoulders touched. He held his breath and turned. She had done the same. She bit her pink lower lip. His mouth felt dry, but he was falling into her brown eyes, spinning. He roughly reached out and pressed his lips hard against hers. She twisted away, "No! No!" Her forearms were pushing against his collar bones. He glimpsed her breasts, the curved line where hips met thigh. He pulled away and averted his eyes, but when he had the courage to look again, she was biting her lower lip, smiling weakly. Slowly, gently, their lips came together again and they pressed tightly against each other, timelessly, without breathing. His quivering arms reached around her and they clumsily reeled sideways until they were lying flat.

He was drawn into the feeling, spinning in it, lost in it, a vortex of sensation he had only felt in dreams. The older boys had taunted him, urged him to gather up the dinars and travel

[200]

with them to the gray brick house in Kragujevac, where a widow had a taste for young men. But he had not. He had listened to them, disgusted at their bragging, swearing he could never be an animal like they were. And now he knew he could never be like them. As strange and frightened as he felt in kissing Jelena, he had transcended all that was animal and filth and had become a lover, a true lover, an angel rising into a cloud.

She was on her back, his mouth still over hers, and they were breathing each other's breath. He was embarrassed by his penis when it brushed her thigh. It seemed to have grown to become half his body. He frantically moved atop her. She scratched his shoulders and pushed at him, twisting her head. She murmured, "No." Her thighs squeezed tight together, but he forced them open with his knee. The down of her pubic hair crushed against his scrotum and he used his hand to search for the opening. He pushed, she resisted by struggling and saying "No" much louder. He remembered seeing a woman roughly pressed against an alley wall in Kragujevac, her skirt hiked, smiling as a drunken man pawed her. He was a tom clamping a howling female by the throat and stabbing into her. He was a boar mounting a sow. This was how you had a woman: you fought her and you took her, and that was love.

He clutched her squirming shoulders in his hands and fiercely kissed her silent. He felt her body yield, then fight again. She screamed and he was inside her, a moist fire spreading out from his groin to his head and toes. When it reached the ends of his body, he shuddered, pushing, pushing, whirling and dropping like a white eagle from the sky.

She had turned away, her face in pain. He felt suddenly detached, as if what had happened had been merely another dream. "Did you like it?" he asked. She did not answer. He kissed her collarbone. He pulled away and saw the blood on his penis and on her thighs. She slapped him, hard.

"You promised," she cried. "You've killed me." She sat up, sobbing into her hands.

"Please," he said. "This makes us lovers. We will be married. Please. This makes us lovers, Jelena. You are mine."

"You *hurt* me!" She shoved him away and climbed after her clothes.

"It always hurts the first time," he said. "It means you are mine. Our love is pure. I have saved myself for you and you for me. Now we will be lovers and—" He tried to caress her but she pulled away.

She was already half-dressed. The wet clothes stuck to her skin. "I didn't want to do this. You have ruined me. My family—" She broke down again, crumpling to the ground.

"We are lovers!" he said angrily. "What has your family to do with it? *I* own you now. I'm going to be richer than Bronkovich. I'll take you with me to the city! You are mine now."

She jumped up and charged across the stream after her boots and stockings. She plucked them up, then ran along the opposite side and into the trees.

"Wait! You can't leave me! You are mine!"

He took two steps toward her, twisting his ankle on a stone. He scurried back to his clothes, frantically slipping on his boots, his pants. He left his shirt and cap and ran into the stream. "Jelena!" he cried out. "Jelena!"

His voice faded up the ravine. He swayed gently in the middle of the pool. He could neither see nor hear her. She had vanished like a *vila*. She had not understood the sacredness of what had happened. He was changed; she was changed. All of creation had changed, but she had not understood. When she got back to the village, she would tell her father. The man would come with his brothers, his dogs, and his rifle. Marko wouldn't live long after that. He would wait for them. He didn't care. He would die here, in this sacred and magical place. He would let his own blood drip into the stain of Jelena's blood in Tzar Lazar's castle.

"Jelena!" he shouted. "I love you! Please!"

His voice faded into the sky. The trees rustled.

He squatted in the water and saw a bleeding scrape on his elbow. "Please," he repeated, "Please," as if the water could hear him whisper.

Then he watched his tears drop into the stream and flow on, changing the colors of the pool and the Morava and the Danube and the sea. Ultimately, he knew, they would evaporate and also change the color of the sky.

Ruzha Filipovich, the Lamb

♦

(Krushka, June 25, 1915)

Perhaps it had never really happened; the memory was like something he had read about or seen in a film, not like something remembered. And yet it was vivid, more vivid than anything that had happened since. The colors were too sharp, awkward, unnatural, as if done by a talentless photograph tinter. The sun was a bone china plate and the mud was molten chocolate. The ammonia rising from the mire of old Filipovich's hog pen stung in his nose and mouth. He buried his face in his mother's smoky skirts and her thick hand clamped his head against her hip. The women, girls, and old men were wailing, praying. Some had dropped to their knees in the shit and were begging mercy with clenched hands. The Austro-Hungarian soldiers marched past, bored as only combat soldiers can be, eyes glazed, their mess kits rattling. They stepped aside to let a field cannon drawn by horses rumble past, then continued wearily.

Where was his father? Where was his grandfather? Mama said they were gathering against the enemy in Kossovo. They were going to unite the Montenegrins and the Shipetars and beat back the invaders. Marko didn't understand. Why didn't everyone go to where the men were? The villagers had risen at dawn to flee, bundled their few possessions and had been gathering in the square to leave when the airplane rumbled low over the forest, then circled over the main square. The pilot was low enough that Marko could see his blue scarf. His greenish leather helmet and his shiny goggles made him look like a grasshopper and the villagers had all stood in the open watching him circle and rattle their doors. It had been marvelous, like seeing Elijah's chariot, and when the pilot had flung his long-handled grenade into the Andrich barn, no one had screamed or run. A baby had cried at the explosion and then suddenly the Austrians had been leaping over fences, running into the empty huts. There had been a shriek and a shot and then somehow he was here in the hog pen, face buried in his mother's skirts, someone else's knee bumping his back.

He wiped his nose on the coarse cloth and looked up at his mother. "Are we going to see papa soon?"

"Shush."

"Are we going to Kossovo?"

"Shush."

"Our country is over," whispered someone. "They have broken us. We are in for another five hundred years of slavery."

"Perhaps the Turks will drive them out. They will be sorry to dance with the Turks!"

"And you think the Sultan will be better than the Austrians? You *are* a fool!"

"*We* beat the Turks only a few years ago, now the Austrians beat us, and you expect the Turks to save us from the Austrians!"

"Shut up!" The villagers separated somewhat and Marko could see their guard. The brutality in his voice made Marko's mother clutch the boy's shoulder until it hurt. The prayers grew louder. "Oink, oink, oink!" he said. "Look! These pigs don't even know how to cross themselves. It disgusts me. We will have to bring up Father Otto from the regiment to teach them how to pray. Even pigs we allow a chance to redeem themselves." He poked with his bayonet. A girl screamed and they all huddled closer. He laughed. "We prefer our pigs to be Christians"—he twisted his bayonet—"before we hang them up to cure." The soldier laughed again and made a gesture to his companion. He put his rifle in the crook of his arm and began rolling himself a cigarette.

Old Filipovich removed his fez and eased forward. "Sir?" he said. "Sir?" The soldier licked his cigarette paper and looked at him with narrow eyes. "You speak our language."

The man spit, then picked at a flake of tobacco on his fat tongue. "No, you speak some pig's language. Oink, oink, oink. What do you make cheese with?

Filipovich blinked. "What?"

"Answer me." The soldier pointed toward Marko. "You, boy, what do you make cheese with?"

"Milk," said Marko. His mother held him tighter.

"What?"

"Milk!"

"You see?" said the soldier. "Oink, oink, oink." He pulled a lucifer from a tin box and lit his cigarette. The paper flared up at first, as if he had not rolled it tightly enough, then the flame settled down.

The old man rotated his fez in his hands. "But, sir, this is merely the difference between your country and ours. You understand us is what I am saying. You might convey our words to your superiors. As to me, I say, let the Croatians say 'milk' as they please. We mean them no harm."

Filipovich's daughter pulled his sleeve. "Don't beg him. We have no reason to beg him."

"We will see about that," said the soldier. He whispered something to the other soldier with him.

Filipovich pulled his sleeve away and pushed his daughter back angrily. "You see us. We are simple folk. Just women and children and old men like me. We have never harmed you. For centuries we have worked this land for whoever ruled it. There is no reason you should not want us to go on doing so. In my home there is rakia as fine as anywhere. Let me fetch it for you. There is no reason to keep us in this sty. Let the women cook for you—"

"Never!" said his daughter. "As God is my witness!"

"Who said that?" said the soldier. "She takes the Lord's name in vain. Do you hope God will witness for someone who can't even cross herself correctly? The devil's pigs stay where they belong: in a pen. Later we may have some slops for you, but only if you are good pigs. Maybe we'll even let your women cook our big sausages for us!" He and his companion cackled. "So behave. And pray to the Devil no weapons are found in your houses or you shall all be learning how to cross yourselves in hell."

Marko could now see the second soldier. He was grinning, face shiny with sweat. Marko heard the shrieking of hogs being slaughtered behind the far huts. Marko had many times seen swine killed, but their so many shrieks seemed higher pitched this time, coming one on top of the other, penetrating to the bone. It was if they knew their killers were invaders. There was a break in the line of soldiers, then about a dozen cavalry pulling another field cannon. The two guards sat on buckets about half way to the road. The day turned hot. The air was dense with dust, smoke, and the animal odor of all the villagers. It sometimes seemed as if there was no air at all and some of the older women panted, gape-eyed, their wide mouths expelling even more fetidness.

Later, when their guards were brought chunks of roast pork, they taunted the villagers and ate it with exaggerated expressions of delight. Filipovich recognized one of his rakia bottles and shouted that he hoped they enjoyed it. The second soldier clutched at his own throat and bugged out his eyes as if he were poisoned by it, then laughed. It was funny. Marko and some of the other children laughed with him.

They heard a strange clicking and roaring. Two pairs of mounted soldiers were leading an automobile down the hill. The villagers pointed and stared. At first they thought it was some peculiarily noisy wagon, but then they saw that the horses were not pulling it. They knew about the horseless carriage. Young Dragan and Milan Bronkovich had seen them in their trip to Belgrade and described them in great detail on their return. Later some Gypsy tinkers had left magazines with pictures of them. But this was the first real one most of them had seen. It was long and shiny, so brilliant that the trees were reflected in its doors. Its red spoked wheels bobbed over the lumpy road, and the two officers sitting in the open back rocked from side to side, the plumes on their hats flicking back and forth. The guards tucked the rakia under the buckets and saluted. A girl began to cry. Like the pilot they had seen in the morning, the officers and their driver were wearing goggles and their canvas overcoats and cheeks were caked with dust. The younger officer brushed his handlebar mustache with the back of his gloved hand and tipped his hat at the villagers entranced at yet another version of Elijah's chariot.

The car went past and down to the square, stopping just in front of the church.

Noon dragged into afternoon. It grew hotter. The guards sang Croatian songs with each other and were joined by two others. A fifth strolled up, chatted and drifted away. Some others came up and eyed the prisoners. More of the villagers tried to settle onto the ground, but no place was clean. Filipovich's swine had churned up the entire area. Marko and his mother continued to stand. His brother, Vojin and his sister, Ilinka chattered about the automobile with some of the old folks. She then spread her apron on the ground and shared the tiny square with Vojin, who whispered how their father would be back to kill every one of the Austro-Hungarians and to cut out the tongues of the Roman Catholics.

By now the guards' uniforms were stained with sweat. Their eyes were red and their language more coarse. Four others had joined them, then two more. They clustered in a circle and told jokes until a soldier on horseback, dressed finer than they, came by and barked at them in German. They saluted him and he rode off. They muttered about him for some time, then the guard who had "oinked" at the villagers approached the fence.

"Ah, friends, we shall be leaving you soon. Our officers—excuse me—our Austrian officers are intent upon us settling on the ridge." He leered.

"You are welcome to our homes, sir," fawned old Filipovich. "Would you not prefer to sleep indoors?"

"Do you expect your lice to give us more trouble than your Royal Serbian army? I agree with you. They would! I wouldn't touch your beds." He spat. Filipovich lowered his eyes.

"Our army gave Franz Josef more than he bargained for," said someone. The voice was that of an older woman.

"Who said that?" said the guard. He sneered. "Doesn't matter." He looked back at his companions. "You see," he said loudly, "the Austrians have a custom. They like to prove to their subjects who is the master."

Again the voice: "We are King Peter's subjects."

The Croatian laughed. "Perhaps you shall all die as King Peter's subjects. The choice is yours. This is what I am here to say. The Austrians have a custom. You give us a woman for the Count's bed and, if she pleases him, he will spare your lives. If she is uncooperative, or if you refuse, you will all die."

"Are they going to kill us, mama?" asked Marko's sister, Ilinka.

"Shush."

The villagers had risen from their seats in the filth. They were silent. Old Filipovich licked his lips. They looked at each other, then, almost uniformly, they turned their heads and eased back. A path opened to a broad-faced woman squatting alone at the rear. The widow Andrich. "Why are you looking at me? Don't look at me." She reached out to her white-haired uncle. "Bogdan, tell them. I would rather die!"

Bogdan averted his eyes. He said nothing. She grasped his sleeve and he jerked it away. "What's another?" he muttered, turning his back.

"Yes," said one woman. "What's another to you?"

"We will owe you our lives," said old Filipovich.

"You old coward!" she spat on the ground. "My son gave all he had—his life. I will give the Austrians nothing."

"We beg you!" Ilija Filipovich pushed her daughters Jelena and Ruzha forward. "Think of my girls. I will give you anything. I will bless you every day. Save our lives."

The widow Andrich sneered. "And what have you ever done for me that I should believe you? And what do you think this would mean to the memory of my son Dragan, who died before Belgrade? And my husband, who died killing Bulgarians in 1913?" She blinked. Her eyes filled with tears.

"Please," whispered Ilija, squeezing her daughter's arms.

"Please," said others. The begging merged to a clamor. Marko saw that Bogdan Filipovich had lowered his white head onto one of the fence posts.

"Don't be absurd!" The soldier's loud laugh silenced them. "Do you think I could offer this old baggage to *my* officer? He is a Count!" He glanced back at his companions and wryly smiled. "Austrian men are rather like Serbian men. They aren't particular what they poke: whores, sheep, Serbs, even their disgusting wives. They have no pride, they aren't the stallions we are." He sighed. "But have some sympathy. We"—he gestured at the men behind him—"have to warm their bitches up for them. We could never settle for worn out goods like her."

"Stallions!" said the widow Andrich. "I wouldn't have known when you were in."

The silence was absolute until the insult registered in the soldier's brain. His eyes widened. He leveled his bayoneted rifle at the widow and threw the bolt. The villagers cowered on each side of the pen, but the widow simply stared. Her look was so powerful it was as if it were material, a rod of ice connecting her head to his. Marko felt his mother's hands trying to twist his face away, but he did not turn. Between the fingers wrapped over his face he saw the widow staring, staring straight up the barrel of the rifle, her eyes weary. A bullet could do nothing to her that had not already been done by the death of her husband, the death of her son, by the insults of the villagers and the condescending charity of her uncle Bogdan.

It was the soldier who blinked first. The rifle quivered, then was lowered. He blinked again. He turned back to the other men. "You see," he finally said. "I've had enough of killing Serbs. But don't provoke me. I think no more of it than squashing ants. But the stink bothers me." He swung the rifle around. "It is her we want."

Old Filipovich stepped into the line of fire. "Not my daughter. She is a good woman, a fine mother."

"Mother? We don't want the mother. We want the daughter."

Ilija Filipovich did not seem to understand. No one did. "Ruzha?" she said. "She is only twelve."

"What makes you hags think we want you? Fresh fish are better fish. We won't have to hold our noses."

"My God, sir," said old Filipovich, "I beg you. You will spoil her for marriage. And she is a good child, a saint."

"Good. There is less chance of disease. She is ours or you all die. All."

"No!" Old Filipovich blundered forward. The soldier swung his long rifle and swatted him across the face with the barrel. The old man fell back, holding his cheekbone. He sat in the pig mire staring wide-eyed, terrified he was going to die.

"Don't hurt my father!" shouted Ilija. The bolts of all the

soldiers' rifles clicked and the villagers froze. Bogdan Filipovich crossed himself. The soldiers stared down their bayonets.

"The girl," said the soldier. "The pretty, pretty girl. Don't worry. We will train her well."

Jelena turned her face into Ilija's skirts. The other villagers had all begun to drift back from Ruzha. Her eyes widened. Her voice was as quiet as a night breeze. "Mama . . . ?" Ilija looked into the soldier's eyes. She glanced down at Marko, then toward her terrified father. She touched her daughter's head. "Pray to God, Ruzha. God will protect you. It won't be so bad . . ." she said, and gently, entranced by her own soothing words, she began to twist Ruzha's outstretched arms away from her.

"Mama! Mama!" Jelena cried. "No! No!" Ruzha was pale and silent.

"Come over here, girlie," said the soldier. "Come on. You'll like it."

Her mother was pushing her. The soldier was opening the gate. They were giving her over, thought Marko. He didn't know what they were going to do to her, exactly, but he knew she was afraid and he couldn't stand to see her that way, nor could he look away. One of the other women had begun to help Ilija push her stunned, panting daughter towards the opened gate.

"Ruzha!" screamed Jelena. "Ruzha!"

Marko tore loose from his mother and leapt at the soldier. He was pummeling the soldier's side with fist after fist. The soldier was stunned at first. "What the—!" He swung his rifle around trying to whack Marko like he had old Filipovich, but it passed over his head. He swatted at the boy with one hand and clipped him on the ear. The fury of Marko's assault, however, made him stumble and fall back. Marko heard his mother screaming. "Don't kill him! He's just a baby! Don't kill him! My God!" He smelled the guard's sweat and his drunken breath. The soldier recovered his balance and brought the butt of his rifle around to hit the boy, but Marko was so close, it only skinned his cheek. Marko was kicking at the guard's boots when he felt the wet hand cover his face and shove him back. He landed so hard he was stunned. When he lifted his eyes, he saw the bayonet gleaming, pointed directly at him. The soldier's eyes were glowing slits.

A voice cut through the noise. *"Gott im himmel! Halt! HALT!"* The other soldiers snapped to attention so sharply that their boots cracked. The bayonet leveled at Marko wavered, then rose. The guard turned to his officer and slowly straightened the rifle by his side.

The officer was wearing a plumed helmet. His handlebar mustache was shiny and black. His boots were clean, his eyes bright as a mountain waterfall. He leaned his face into the guard's and spoke rapidly, ferociously. The guard answered with a sneer. The officer, almost beside himself, flicked the gloves out of his belt and slapped the guard. The guard flexed his cheek muscles. His stare was pure hate but he did not move. He said something grimly but quietly. The officer called over one of the companions. Questions were fired. The guard responded. The officer snapped his head at the other soldiers who said *"Ja wohl,"* several times. The officer slapped the guard again.

The guard turned to the villagers and said through clenched teeth, "I have been told to apologize, but he does not know the language, so I tell you all, quite gently, that I will kill every one of you, personally, as soon as I get rid of this jackass."

The officer prodded one of the other Croatians on the shoulder. More words were exchanged, then the officer pulled his pistol. He cracked it hard across the guard's face. The man crumpled to his knee, touched his face, and stupidly looked at the blood on his palm. The officer approached the pig sty and spoke, the second Croatian translating at his side.

"He greets you as new subjects of the Emperor Franz Josef. He says he apologizes for your having been penned. This was not an order. He apologizes for any unnecessary abuse you may have taken. In his army he maintains discipline and innocent civilians will never be threatened by his soldiers, unless they threaten first." The officer pointed at Marko. "This boy should not have attacked a soldier of the Emperor under any provocation. And this should be a capital offense."

Marko's mother rushed forward, hands clasped, and fell on her knees, "No, please, sir, no—"

"Silence!" The officer covered her clasped hands with his one hand and continued through his translator. "He says, however, that he understands. He says you are blessed with a brave boy who will someday make a fine soldier for the emperor. Fear not." The officer nodded and smiled.

"Oh, thank you, thank you."

The officer then came to Marko and bent over him. The Croatian followed. "You are a brave boy. He asks your name."

Marko looked into the man's pale eyes. "Marko."

The officer smiled and spoke gently.

"He says you have the courage of Kraljevich Marko, then, as well as his name. Did you know that the poet Goethe once learned your language just so that he could read the epic of Kraljevich Marko?"

Marko had never heard of Goethe, but he nodded nonetheless. "Marko fought our enemies," said the boy.

"Yes, he says, but you are too young to know who your enemies are. He says he would never wish to be your enemy. Alone of these people you stood for the right. It could have cost you your life. He says he wished all his men were as brave as you."

The officer winked. Marko stared at his clean face. He smelled of rosewater and pomade. Marko smiled. The officer bent over and picked him up. *"Komm, komm, Kraljevich Marko."*

"He wants you to come with him. He wants to have dinner with the bravest man in this village that—that is not worthy of him." The officer reached into his tunic pocket and held out a square wrapped in pink-striped paper. It was marzipan. Marko ate it as he watched more soldiers lead the villagers out of the pen. Most except his mother and Jelena seemed embarrassed to look in his direction. Ruzha blubbered into her hands and pulled away whenever her mother tried to touch her. The widow Andrich came out last and stared at him eating his candy. He was not certain what her stare meant, but it chilled him. Jelena then smiled at him and he scurried over to give her the corner of the marzipan that was still left.

The officer laughed and took him to their mess. No one bothered to translate for him. The other two officers kept pushing food at him, as if he were a stray kitten. One wiped his chin solicitously when the pork grease dribbled down. Later, the oldest one held him on his lap and tried to teach him simple German songs. He leaned back against the fine texture of his tunic. He inhaled the officers' clean smell and the strong odor of their pipes. The one with a gold tooth let him try his monocle and the one who had saved him laughed when the boy curiously touched his waxy mustache, producing a locket with a photograph of a small boy. Marko fell asleep in the old officer's lap while they were singing old songs. The last thing he remembered of that night was tears in the officer's bloodshot eyes. The old man looked down at him and gently smiled, finishing the last words.

Marko woke the next morning on the floor next to the hearth. He was wrapped in a soft woolen blanket his mother would use for years. He rushed outside and saw only the villagers, dirty and scratching, straggling in from their night sleeping in the fields. His mother called out to him, but he did not want to live among them, they who had been so willing to give over Ruzha. When his mother embraced him, he stared over her shoulder, down the empty road where the Austrian army had gone.